The Top of Her Game

The ache of wanting Zach had literally hurt. He had held her too tightly; he'd trapped her. And Julia hadn't wanted it to stop. She'd loved it. She lay beneath him as if a hurricane had blown her over. What the hell was wrong with her? She'd behaved like a submissive with a fetish for constraint instead of the dominatrix she was.

She looked at his big, beautiful body. She'd left scratches on his back – long, bloody rakes. Not on purpose, either. She hadn't even realised she'd done it, she'd been enjoying herself so much. Of course this was a one-off, wasn't it? Accept it and move on, she thought. But she had a feeling it wasn't going to be that easy.

The Top of Her Game

EMMA HOLLY

BLACK
lace

Black Lace novels are sexual fantasies.
In real life, make sure you practise safe sex.

First published in 1999 by
Black Lace
Thames Wharf Studios
Rainville Road, London W6 9HA

Reprinted 2000

Copyright © Emma Holly 1998

The right of Emma Holly to be identified as the Author
of this Work has been asserted by her in accordance
with the Copyright, Designs and Patents Act 1988.

Typeset by SetSystems Ltd, Saffron Walden, Essex
Printed and bound by Mackays of Chatham PLC

ISBN 0 352 33337 5

To the Four Seasons Club, for stories by the fire.
Yippee-ki-ay, ladies. You're the best!

Chapter One

*A*ll her life Julia Mueller had been searching for a man she couldn't master. It seemed she wouldn't find one tonight.

The open gift box sat on her lap, tissue paper blossoming over its edges like a fallen angel's wings. A custom-made riding crop nestled inside. Julia lifted it out, her mouth pursed in admiration for its workmanship. She'd say one thing for Durbin: he had exquisite taste in toys. The handle was thicker than the whip and dotted with small brass studs that pressed cool and smooth against her palm. She ran the flexible length under her nose, inhaling the scent of resin. Her pleasure centres fired. She shifted in the deep green chair. Silk rasped silk as her thighs brushed together. They were strong thighs. A sense of health and power filled her awareness. Her heart rate slowed. Her sex warmed.

A knob swelled from the base of the whip like the

1

head of a good-sized penis. Julia pressed her thumbnail into the bulge and smiled. If Durbin had been watching her, instead of being stuck in a meeting, he would have shuddered at that smile, shuddered and hardened with delight. Durbin loved a threat almost as much as he loved the execution of a threat.

She opened the accompanying gilt-edged card. 'I think it's time we moved to the next level,' it said. 'I adore you. D.'

Julia stood so abruptly that the box spilt from her lap. The next level. Beyond play-acting and spanking, beyond a harsh voice and a velvet blindfold. She paced to the balcony window, her heels clacking on the marble floor, the whip swinging beside her impeccably tailored skirt. The lights of Manhattan twinkled in the off-black dark. Like blood through a stiffened cock, the city's energy thrummed through the walls. She flattened her fingers against the glass as if it were a too-tight skin she needed to escape.

But there was no escape, not even when she closed her eyes. She was there again, frozen at the door to the general's office, her face stained with tears from some forgotten school-playground trauma. The door was open only a crack. They didn't see her. The general was bent over his government-issue desk, his uniform trousers shoved to his knees. Beneath the hair of his thighs muscles tensed, some thick, some narrow. Julia's mother stood behind him. She'd unbuttoned her jacket and she held something in her hand, something long and dark. Julia watched her arm rise; heard the breath she took to gather her strength, the huff as it rushed back out. The doubled belt descended with an eerie whistle. When it struck the general's ass, he bit his wrist to muffle his cry.

Even at fifteen Julia interpreted it as a cry of

pleasure. Her instincts did not mislead her. The shadow of his cock jerked beneath his khaki shirt-tails. Its head was large, the proverbial baby's fist. She recalled the plop, plop, plop of his pre-come hitting the brown carpet. Back then she thought the drops were sweat, but the sound was no less enthralling. The belt fell again, and again. The dripping silhouette jerked higher, vibrating with the force of pleasure-pain. Julia clutched the door, her body humming with a strange excitement. The general's legs stiffened. His chest swelled. The belt cracked once more and he came in milky, twisting spurts. They rolled down the army-green drawer. The general sighed. 'I adore you,' he said.

Then the strangest thing of all happened. Her mother bent down and licked the sweat from the back of the general's neck: her mother, that model of Swiss propriety, who buttoned every blouse to its neck and never slept without a nightgown, who said, 'Rule yourself, Julia, and you rule the world.'

The whip rolled now beneath Julia's palm, trapped between her hand and the glass. Her mother hadn't ruled herself. The game had seduced her, just as – two years ago – Julia had been seduced by the chance to play dominatrix to her boss. He was the up-and-coming director of Durbin-Moore Investments. She was his executive assistant, his whipping girl until the day she'd thrown his espresso in his face and told him to get his own damned lemon peel. He'd stared at her, coffee dripping on to his starched white collar. A current sprang to life between them, shockingly new to him, old as sin to her. She'd locked this tiger in its cage too long. Now it was too strong to resist. Energy prickled her skin like static; tweaked the flesh between her legs. As one, their eyes fell to his cock. It rose

3

swiftly behind his trousers, a thick, unruly bulk. She didn't stop to think. She touched his hand. He clutched her wrist. One wild and desperate kiss later they were both lost.

She bent him over the desk and spanked him until her wrist ached. He shot a river of come, then dropped to the floor and kissed her shoes. It had been so long since she'd played the game. Once a year she allowed herself to; no more. His slavish kiss sent a spasm through her sex. When he lifted her skirt and mouthed her there, she came in seconds.

She promised herself she'd only take a taste. She wouldn't succumb to the spell the way her mother had. But even now, when she caught herself falling into the old seductive pattern, hot, thick moisture seeped from her core. She wanted to go to the next level. She wanted to go as far as Durbin could bear. Farther. She wanted to annihilate him.

She rolled her forehead against the glass and moaned. Like mother, like daughter, she thought. Except that her mother had loved the general. What she felt for Durbin was nothing like love.

Her reflection mocked her from the window. She was tall and strong and elegant; Grace Kelly with muscle. Her cheekbones were high and wide, her skin smooth as ivory. No hint of emotion shadowed her grey-green eyes. Her carriage was regal, her composure flawless. No one could fault her manners, but a woman would be no happier to find Julia Mueller seated next to her husband than to meet her in a dark alley. Nor would the husbands care to confront her there. She was a formidable creature. Looking at her, no one would guess she had any vulnerabilities at all.

But she did. She longed to fall in love. She was thirty-two years old and she had never come close. She

4

wanted the freedom to be tender as well as cruel, not
as part of a game but in truth. She was never going to
find that with Richard Durbin. She was going to have
to break it off with him. Soon. Before it was too late.
Maybe tonight.

The outer door thudded against the hallway wall.
Her heart leapt. Durbin had arrived.

'Julia,' he roared, not yet shed of his public persona.
'Julia, where the fuck are you?'

She did not answer. She turned from the window
and composed herself. He would see her as he saw her
in the office, cool and competent in her dove-grey
business suit.

He rounded the corner of the spacious living room.
With an air of satisfaction, his gaze traversed the
lacquered green walls, the recessed lighting, the elegant glass and steel. He stopped when he saw her. His
respiration increased. His face coloured. He was a big
man, six foot four inches to her six foot, and at least
fifteen years older than she was. He ran his own
company, was responsible for more than a billion
dollars in assets, and she still had the power to halt
him in his tracks.

Her cunt tightened with pleasure, but she did not
lose her presence of mind. She saw that his tie was
askew, his iron-grey hair ruffled from running his
fingers through it. Something must have happened
after she left the office. Normally he was as meticulous
in his dress as she was. He tossed his overcoat on to
the leather sofa, then his six-hundred-dollar suit jacket.
His crotch bulged impressively. The ride up the lift
could do that to him, or sometimes just the sight of this
building from a distance. Neither of them lived here.
This astronomically expensive art-deco penthouse was
their playroom. They fucked here when Durbin could

5

escape his wife and family; when Julia decided he had earnt an escape. Two weeks had passed since their last visit and the flush that coloured his broad, brutal face declared his impatience to end the wait. They stood on opposite sides of the room, an expanse of black marble shining like the sea between them.

'Jesus,' he said, aroused by her icy silence. 'I could fuck you where you stand, Jules.'

She tapped the whip against the side of her leg. 'You know better than to call me that.'

'Right. Ms Mueller. Sorry.' He ran his hand through his mussed hair, then retrieved a spiral-bound folder that had fallen on to the sofa. 'But you won't believe this, Jules. We lost the Go-Tech account to Capital Edge. That bastard Santorini underbid our fees by one quarter per cent. One quarter! And you know what they were pushing? A mix of conservative growth and A-rated bonds. In the same fucking proportions as our proposal.' He pointed the rolled-up papers. 'It can't be a coincidence. Somebody leaked our strategy. DMI has a traitor.'

Just saying the word proved too much for him. He slammed the folder down and turned to the well-stocked bar. Ice cubes rattled as he threw them into a glass. 'It's either that *shvartzer* Isaacs or Prentiss. Frigid bitch.' He poured a generous slug of bourbon over the ice. 'She's been shitting bricks ever since I made Marty a senior VP.' He snorted. 'As though she deserves a promotion.'

He lifted the tumbler towards his mouth. Julia stopped him with a quiet cough.

'Oh, God,' he said. He strode across the room and offered the drink to her. 'Please forgive me, Ms Mueller.'

She should have made him kneel, but that would

wait. She brought the heavy glass to her lips. The liquor burnt her throat until that passage was as hot as the one between her legs. She filled her mouth again, grabbed the back of his neck and kissed him. He choked as she pushed the alcohol into his mouth, then swallowed and moaned, opening himself to her invasion. The change was on him, the spine-tingling transformation from her boss to her slave. Julia loved this moment more than any other. He was passive under her kiss, his neck limp, his hands fisting and unfisting at his sides.

But he had to misbehave. That was part of the game, too. He sidled closer, brushing her hip with the ridge of his swollen cock. She pushed him away.

'Down,' she said, a low, soft order.

He knelt so swiftly his knees cracked on the hard black floor. At once he began removing his clothes. He knew what she wanted. Always they began like this, a ritual. His hands fumbled with his shirt buttons, shaking with arousal and apprehension. From the first she'd inspired this cocktail of emotion in him. She watched impassively but inside she was drinking it in. He had to have her, would die to have her, but – oh – to suffer first was best. Eyes flickering from her face to her hands, he ripped off his shirt, then undid his trousers and shoved them down. He wore no underwear. She did not allow it. His cock was hard and red, its glans shining with eager juices. She was glad she'd made him wait a full two weeks. He was like a teenager now, thrusting thick and potent from the jungle of grey hair at his groin. He was a hairy man. When he got excited, sweat ran down his body in streams. He was sweating now.

He sat back to remove his trousers and shoes, then crawled to her feet. 'I'm sorry, Ms Mueller.' He kissed the toe of her three-inch grey heel. 'I shouldn't have been discussing business. It was very wrong of me.'

'Yes, it was.' She ran the tip of the riding crop down his naked spine. He was strong and firm, much firmer than when they'd met. She'd ordered him to use the company gym every weekday; told him that if he did a good workout he could masturbate afterwards and think of her. No one but she understood why he'd immediately installed doors in the men's showers. Smiling to herself, she stroked the leather over his hairy buttocks. He quivered.

'Does my mistress like her present?' he dared to whisper.

Rather than answer, she swung the whip sharply across his bottom. He jumped at the stinging blow, but made no protest. A line of pink appeared on his flesh. The whip had a good reach; she barely had to bend. She gave the weal a mate, then another and another, then judged she'd better stop. This crop was fiercer than anything she'd used on him before. Durbin had not cried out, but his back was bathed in sweat and a small puddle of pre-come had formed on the marble beneath his belly. Worse than hurting him would be allowing him to come too soon. He could do that, she had discovered, without her ever touching his cock; domination affected him that strongly.

'Turn around,' she ordered, then prodded him on hands and knees towards the bar. To speed him along, she pressed her shoe between his thighs. His scrotum was heavy, pendulous. It warmed the top of her foot as she separated his balls with her shoe. The toe was sharp. She dug it in just hard enough to suggest a threat.

He whimpered through tightly closed lips. Without waiting to be told, he opened the bar's bottom cabinet, then shifted aside for her. Julia knelt. His shoulder brushed her hip, hot and damp, but she didn't scold. She had enough in store for him. Reaching towards the back of the shelf, she extracted a jar of lubricant.

Durbin winced and looked away. Anal play made him nervous. He was no homo, not Durbin. But only an idiot would imagine he'd be using that blatantly phallic whip-handle on her! Whether he cared to admit it or not, by giving her the whip he had invited this very torment.

'Now, now.' She stroked his head before forcing his face around again. 'Do you want to move to the next level or not?'

'Yes,' he whispered. His eyes caught on the whip-handle, the same cold brown eyes that made his employees – and most of his competitors – quail. He licked thin, dry lips. Julia suppressed a shiver of delight. Yes, indeed, she thought. The mighty had fallen.

'Kiss it,' she said and thrust the whip in his face. He complied with a shudder. 'Now put the lube on it, slave. Nice and thick. We want it to go in easy, don't we?'

While he did as she asked, she pushed lubricant into his ass herself. The ring of muscle puckered, then gaped with a greed he would have denied if he could. She adored his panicked squirms, his heat, his deep-seated fear of the pleasure she was giving him. She rubbed the lube in slowly, gently, working dollop after dollop into his smooth dark passage. By the time she finished he was gasping for breath and whimpering with excitement. She took the whip from him, then hiked up her skirts. He watched her position the whip between her stockinged thighs, knob end out. It wagged there like a phallus.

'It won't fit,' he gasped, eyes riveted on the thick, shining pole.

The words sent a thrill through her sex. He might have been the virginal heroine from a novel. She flicked her hand across his cheek, a light, admonitory smack. 'Turn your head, slave. And grab the edge of the bar.' She kneed his thighs wider; big, hairy thighs, heavy with muscle but powerless to resist her will. 'Prepare yourself,' she growled. Using her hand to guide the whip, she pressed the handle past his sphincter.

He moaned and pushed, instinctively trying to expel the intrusion, but that made it slide in all the easier. Lube gushed out and ran down his legs like a woman's cream. Julia tightened her thighs. His passage was so slippery she could pull the whip back and forth with the strength of her leg muscles. She could fuck him, fuck him like a man.

She had to bite her lower lip to contain her moan.

The end of the handle pressed hard against her panties, easing between the soft, juicy split of her sex. Each time she thrust, the leather-covered wood mashed her clit. Delicious. She draped herself over him, still clothed in her prim grey suit, still completely in control.

'Do you know who I am?' she asked. 'Do you know who's fucking you?'

He shook his head and gulped for air. His knuckles whitened on the edge of the bar.

'I'm Marty, Richard. I'm Marty and I'm fucking you the way you always wanted me to.' She had a gift for mimicry. It was easy to infuse her voice with the senior VP's distinctive Bronx drawl.

'No,' he protested, head wagging. 'Don't.'

She laughed. 'Go on, Richie-boy, you know it's me. I'm fucking you, mister, and I ain't gonna stop till we both blow our wads to Kingdom Come.' He should have laughed but he couldn't. To him the thought was horrible: his protégé, his golfing buddy, taking him in the ass. Marty Fine was the office stud; always had a female co-worker loitering at the door to his office. He had a full head of curly black hair and a five o'clock shadow that started at two. If Durbin weren't attracted to him, at the very least he'd been jealous. And now she was forcing him to consider whether there might be something more.

Pushed to his limit, Durbin tried to pull away. Julia manacled his wrists in an iron grip. For all his hours at the gym, she knew more about overpowering people than he did. She'd wrestled with army grunts, after all. She could take Durbin down in a minute. She brought her mouth to his ear. 'Come on, buddy. You know you want it. You've watched my cock, haven't you? Seen me shake it dry. You know it's a big one. I bet you've wondered if I know what to do with it. I know you've wondered how it would feel, in your mouth, up your ass. You can't lie to me, buddy. You want it so bad you're dripping on the floor.'

She shifted her angle, catching his prostate on the handle's bulge. He moaned with anguished pleasure. The muscles of his back were rigid, bathed in sweat. She pulled back and stopped. He hesitated, but then his hips tilted towards her, mutely begging. He wanted what she was giving him. He wanted more. Yes, she thought, tightening her thighs and sliding in again.

'Cold,' he gasped, and she knew he meant the little brass rivets that studded the leather.

'Cold as ice,' she agreed, taking up a rhythm now. 'Cold as fucking ice, Richie-boy.' In and out she went, not hard but steady, knowing the effect of her thrusts was cumulative. His body stiffened beneath her,

11

tensing for orgasm even as he tried to resist it. She could hear his teeth grinding. 'Oh, yeah,' she said. 'It's coming. I'm gonna shoot you full of spunk, Richie. You better get ready to take my load.'

'No,' he said, head shaking, spine arching.

She knew he was going through the roof.

He spasmed in climax just as hers began to rise. The air hissed from his lungs. His seed hit the marble floor, four splashes, five. He groaned at the sixth and shivered like a wet dog. Julia pushed back from him and stood. She pulled her skirt down. The whip handle was still embedded in his body. The lash end shook with his tremors.

She drew a slow breath to still her own shakes. She hadn't come. She should have been furious, or pretended to be. Instead, she eased out the whip and offered her hand to help Durbin to his feet. He dragged on it heavily, then staggered to the leather sofa and collapsed. He threw one arm over his eyes and released a languid sigh. Once upon a time they would have snuggled together in the aftermath. Once upon a time he would have wanted her to. But he'd got what he wanted tonight, all he ever wanted these days.

'You should move in here,' he said as if unaware of the distance, both literal and figurative, between them. 'No point paying for your place when this is here.'

A bitter heat turned in her belly. How dare he treat her like some tart to be housed at his convenience, available at his demand, especially when she was inches from leaving him flat!

'I don't think so,' she said. The ice in her voice made him sit up. He blinked at her, wary.

She began unbuttoning her fitted jacket, then her blouse. She slipped both from her shoulders and stalked towards him, her breasts bouncing in their cage

12

of fine white lace. Her steel-tipped heels clacked an unspoken threat. She didn't often let him see her naked, but not from insecurity. She knew her body was a dream most men had forgotten they had. No rake-thin model, hers was a body of firm, generous curves, of melting soft skin that smelled of baby powder and lust. The muscles beneath provided the necessary hint of danger. She was stronger than her lovers. She could enforce her will with more than feminine wiles. Not that she scorned feminine wiles. She didn't scorn anything that gave a woman power.

She undid her bra and tossed it on to a chair. Her nipples were peaked with arousal and as pink as a fresh spring rose. She ran one finger around each swollen areola. The pink deepened. The centres lengthened. Entranced by the display, Durbin's recently sated cock twitched and began a wavering ascent. She planted her shoe on the couch.

'Do you honestly think I would allow a lowly slave the privilege of paying my expenses?'

'No, of course not. I just –'

She backhanded his cheek. 'I am not moving in here. In fact, little man, you and I will soon be parting ways.'

He gasped. His penis leapt under the shock of her words, as if this were a new and better form of play-acting. He slid off the couch and fell to his knees.

'No,' he pleaded, kissing the smooth, bare skin of her belly. 'Anything but that.'

She gripped his ears and shoved him back. 'I'm serious. I'm leaving you, Richard.'

'Of course you are,' he said, but she knew he didn't believe her. His hands slid around to the back of her skirt. He lowered her zip. His movements were tentative, respectful, as if he feared being stopped and desperately hoped he wouldn't be.

'I didn't give you permission to do that,' she said, but the protest was weak. Ignoring it, he dragged her skirt down. Within moments she stood before him in stockings and heels and a short double strand of South Sea pearls. His eyes slid shut at the picture she made. For a moment her eyes drifted, too. His expression . . . His hunger . . . Her blood felt thick, drugged with her own power.

'I'm such a bad slave,' he soothed. 'But I'd die without you, Ms Mueller. You must let me make it up to you.' He dragged his face, open-mouthed, across her belly, over her golden thatch. His lips slid lower, finding her unappeased clit. She couldn't stifle a tiny cry as he caught it on the tip of his tongue. 'I came without you, didn't I? That was wrong of me. So wrong.'

His mouth was clever and warm and avid. His subservient murmurs rose like smoke from a hookah, dizzying silver-blue spirals. She swayed. He eased her from her shoes and tipped her on to the couch. He burrowed between her legs amidst the dark, skin-soft leather.

'I adore you,' he said.

Memory jarred her. The general. Her mother. The sticky-sweet trap that had caught them both. She gripped the cushion, torn between desire and anger. Had she forgotten everything she meant to do? She took Durbin's arms in a bruising grip, meaning to shove him away for good. He lifted his head. His breath panted hot across her sex. His face was flushed, his eyes glassy with need. Truly, he was her creature, her slave. Her pussy squeezed itself in longing.

The ache was unbearable. One more time, she thought. Just one more.

'Turn around,' she said with a sternness that made

him quiver. 'I want to watch your cock while you worship me.'

He repositioned himself so that his cock and balls swung above her face. He was good with his mouth. Twice she almost came, but she held off by relaxing her muscles and controlling her breath. His jaw would be aching but that was for the best. He needed to suffer, loved to suffer. His cock was so hard now it defied its own weight, angling towards his belly. She ran her hands up his trembling thighs and on to his buttocks. She found the heated stripes that her new riding crop had left. She pinched one between forefinger and thumb. His small, pained cry vibrated through her pussy. He would come soon if she kept this up. He'd never had her discipline.

Rule yourself and you rule the world, her mother had said. It was so true.

But now she had earnt a reward. She rocked into his mouth, imposing her own rhythm. The tight, hard heat curled inside her, an aching coil of pleasure preparing to burst. He didn't deserve it but she would bring him with her. His pleasure intensified hers. It was proof of her mastery. She gave his balls a quick, threatening squeeze, then slid her fingers up his swollen shaft. She bent it downwards until she could see the deep red slit. His mouth paused, slack with enjoyment, then redoubled its efforts. She gave in to her urge to purr. His veins throbbed beneath her fingertips. She wouldn't stroke him, though; that wouldn't inspire the kind of explosion she craved. Instead, she set all ten of her nails into his glans and let them bite.

He cried out and jerked from her hold, his body obeying a reflex he could not control. A second later, he jerked straight back.

'Oh, yes,' he cried as she pricked him again. 'More, please, more.'

He returned to his duties, lapping and suckling with the knowledge that he bought his pleasure with hers. Again she pricked him and again he moaned, his flesh whitening and reddening beneath her nails. The coil of climax heated between her legs. She tugged his hips lower until she could catch his heavy scrotum with her teeth.

'Yes,' he hissed, his words muffled by her flesh. 'Bite it.'

She licked him, twice. Crisp silver hair tickled her tongue. He growled. This was too gentle for him. She gave him a taste of the edge, a tiny bite, a delicate tease of pain. His cock struggled against her grip, fighting to rise higher. Moisture welled from its tortured cap.

'Not yet,' she ordered. 'Not fucking yet.'

He groaned, the sound reverberating through her cunt. He slid his thumbs into her slit, pumping her, desperate to bring her off before he lost control. His efforts were not in vain. Her tension rose, the sweet almost, almost there. Her thighs tightened around his ears. The signal of her coming climax put him over the edge. His cock jerked, spewing in her hands, and then she lost her sense of him. The belt fell, a flashing image on the screen of her mind. The general bit his wrist to muffle his cry and her orgasm broke in a surging red wave, rolling through her sex, through her limbs, blood and pleasure, anger and satisfaction and then a great, empty peace.

Afterwards, they lay together on the leather couch. Julia was bone-weary, her head so heavy she wasn't sure she could lift it from his shoulder. Durbin stroked her fallen hair, absently, territorially, with no more sentiment than a man stroking his tie.

16

'I am leaving you,' she said, though she didn't usually repeat herself.

His hand stopped moving. His fingers tightened on her skull. 'Where would you go, Jules? There aren't many bosses who'd pay their secretaries what I pay you.'

Her weariness increased. Two years together and he still didn't understand her. Concern for her financial future was the last thing on her mind. He had indeed paid her generously. Given Durbin's spending habits, her liquid assets were many times his own. But even if money had been a concern, it wouldn't have swayed her from her course. She would never permit herself to become a slave to a job or a person or, she vowed, to a way of life that no longer fulfilled her.

Tonight's events forced her to admit she was as much of an addict as Durbin. She had meant to resist, but she hadn't. She'd sucked up the power high and then she'd crashed. If she had loved him, she might not have regretted the obsession, but she never had and she no longer respected him, either. They had worked too closely for too long. She'd had too many opportunities to see how selfish he was, how short-sighted and how petty. Even his ambition, once so admired, was revealed as no more than ego. He didn't care about Durbin-Moore Investments, only about how its success reflected on him.

She shifted on to her back, her head cradled on his upper arm, her gaze on the geometric ceiling frieze.

How could she persuade him to let her go? The crueler she was, the more he liked it. If she left him, he would hound her, would convince himself it was part of the game. There would be scenes. He did not realise he had lost his ability to behave in a rational manner. He knew only that the pleasure she brought him was

17

more intense than any he'd known and he did not want to lose it. She doubted he could do her any lasting harm, but he might do himself a great deal. If he did, she would share the responsibility. She had set him on this road. She might not like him, but she wouldn't let him crash and burn if she could help it.

Overcome with frustration, she sat up, swung her legs to the side and leant over her knees. Any other man would have asked what was wrong. Durbin merely spread his hand across the small of her back. He stroked his thumb over her skin.

'I'm sending Ben and Carolyn on a retreat with Marty this weekend. I told them they can't return until they come up with ten good ideas for increasing business. I want you to go with them.'

Julia looked at him over her shoulder. 'Why?'

His eyes followed the motion of his hand. 'I want you to watch them. I want you to unmask the traitor. That bastard Santorini will rue the day he crossed swords with me.'

Julia fought a sigh. She hardly wanted to spend the weekend babysitting three squabbling portfolio managers. In her opinion, Durbin's fast-talking golf buddy Marty was the likeliest candidate, not that he wanted to hear that.

'You'll like it,' he said. 'It's a dude ranch in Montana. Gorgeous country. It'll warm even your cold heart. Bob Kingsley over at Alliance takes all his big clients there. Fishing, hunting, steaks the size of dinner plates. The owner is about to go private. You'll be his last paying guests.'

'An honour, I'm sure.'

Durbin seemed oblivious to her sarcasm. 'I need to know who slipped Santorini our proposal. If anyone can find out, it's you.'

Julia squeezed her knees in annoyance. But maybe she should go. Maybe a weekend far from New York, far from Durbin, was just what she needed. She could walk in the mountains and clear her head, set her priorities, devise a plan of action. Revealing the culprit's identity could be her parting gift, the dominatrix's version of a diamond kiss-off. The thought of treating Durbin like a discarded mistress brought a tiny smile to her lips. She stretched her back until it cracked, then got to her feet.

'Where are you going?' he asked with a hint of injury. 'I don't have to be home for another hour.'

She reached for her discarded skirt. 'I need to pack,' she said. Her smile was still in place.

She headed for her exercise room as soon as she reached her apartment. Forty minutes split between her weights and her rowing machine worked off most of her disgust with herself.

Still sweating, she mopped her face with a towel and reached for her cordless phone. Montana was two hours behind New York. It wasn't too late to reserve another room at the ranch. At least, she didn't think it was. But the phone rang twelve times without rolling over to an answering machine. She draped the towel around her neck. Perhaps, out there in cow country, they didn't believe in such newfangled contraptions. Finally, on the thirteenth ring, a male voice responded.

'Taylor,' said a husky baritone.

After waiting so long, the answer caught her by surprise. 'Oh,' she said, uncustomarily flustered. 'This is Julia Mueller. I work at Durbin-Moore Investments. I need to reserve an additional room for this weekend's retreat.'

'Hm,' said the man called Taylor. 'I've been meaning to call you folks about that. I think you'd better cancel.'

Julia swiped the towel across her sweaty chin. 'Cancel?'

'Yep,' he said. 'Snow's a-comin'.'

Snow's a-comin'? Who taught this character to talk? 'Nonsense,' she said. 'I was watching CNN weather at lunch today. There's no precipitation anywhere near the Rockies.'

'Still,' he said, the way other people said 'nonetheless'. She expected more, but that single word was all he had to offer: 'still', as if he knew more than a million-dollar satellite.

She found it surprisingly hard to argue with a man who spoke in monosyllables.

'The arrangements are made,' she said in a slow, clear voice. 'Do you have accommodation for an additional guest or not?'

'Yep,' he said. 'But you'd better plan on staying more than a weekend.'

Then he rang off. Julia stared at the phone in disbelief. Snow or no snow, this retreat was shaping up to be a long one.

Chapter Two

*D*MI's private jet bumped gently over the turbulent air. Julia sat in solitary splendour at the front of the cabin, soothed by the hum of the engines and her sense of escape. A wide stretch of country lay between her and temptation. She intended to burn some bridges while she was here, to which end she had a trunkful of toys guaranteed to light the match.

But it was time to take stock of her suspects. They sat at the rear, safely out of hearing range, or so they must have thought. Allowing herself the faintest smile, Julia folded her hands over her seat belt and closed her eyes. She had learnt to exploit the deceptions of appearance from a drill sergeant at Fort Benning. Old Hothead Hopkins had used her to embarrass new recruits. See what this girl can do, he'd say. Turn your back on her and she'll whup your mangy butt. He taught her to fight dirty and he taught her to fight smart. Then he taught her a few tricks he'd picked up on a tour of Asia.

21

She clocked her breathing just as he'd trained her: four seconds to inhale, eight seconds to hold, four seconds to exhale, eight to hold again. Her pulse slowed to sixty beats a minute, fifty-five, fifty. Her senses sharpened. She could smell the solution that the flight crew used to clean the carpets, a stick of gum the pilot was chewing, the cigarette Prentiss had sucked back five hours earlier. Glass ticked in the window at a slight change in temperature. She pictured a white-gold funnel leading from the three portfolio managers to her ear.

'I don't know why he sent her,' Carolyn Prentiss was saying. 'Except it's obvious he doesn't trust us. Shit, it's like big sister is watching. Her face would crack if she had to smile.'

A seat creaked as someone pushed it back and stretched. 'Look at it this way,' Marty Fine said. 'Now we've got someone to take notes and make coffee.'

'Like hell. The Ice Queen only makes coffee for senior VPs.'

'Jealous, Prentiss?'

'Fuck you, Fine.' Her necklaces jingled as she changed position. 'Christ, I need a smoke. How long till we –'

Julia started as a hand settled on her shoulder. She'd been concentrating so hard she hadn't heard Ben Isaacs come up the aisle. She looked up at him and experienced a familiar twinge of awe, the same she felt on seeing a Rodin or a Michelangelo. He had to be one of the most beautiful men she'd ever met. He was a light-skinned African American of mixed descent, part Jamaican, part white and part Asian, she suspected, from the slant of his clear green eyes. Everything about him was elegant, from the shape of the skull beneath his close-cropped hair to the simplest gesture of his hands. He smiled at her now, a shy smile, though there was pride in it: the defensive pride of an outsider. Few African Americans held management positions in the hallowed halls of high finance.

'Do you mind if I sit with you?' He cocked his head towards Marty and Carolyn. 'Those two are at it again.' Rather than point out the existence of ten other empty rows, she lifted the unread copy of *Forbes* from the seat beside her. He settled in with another quick smile, flashing his teeth this time. 'Thanks,' he said. 'I've had all the "did so, did not" I can stand.'

'I can imagine.' Her tone was pleasant but not encouraging. She flipped open the magazine. Unfortunately, attempting any more eavesdropping was pointless. Ben's presence was too distracting. Hell, his cologne was too distracting. Whatever it was, it had formed an intoxicating bond with his natural body chemistry. The tissues of Julia's sex began to swell.

After a moment of silence, he turned in the seat. 'Do you mind if I ask you something?'

'Be my guest,' she said.

'Why are you here?'

She shrugged. 'To take notes and make coffee.'

'Bullshit.'

She was startled into revealing her smile. 'I'm sorry that isn't the answer you wanted.'

'It doesn't matter.' He shook the fall of his trousers down long, slim legs. She realised he was nervous. The timbre of his voice had deepened. 'I'm glad you're here.' His head turned and he pinned her with his exquisite green eyes. 'I've been meaning to get to know you better. I have a feeling you're not at all the way you seem.'

She blinked once, taken completely by surprise. Before she could respond he laid his hand over her wrist where it rested on the magazine. His palm was warm and dry, his skin strangely smooth. His eyes showed his awareness of the barriers he was crossing, between co-workers, between races, never mind the barriers he was crossing unawares. He probably knew she slept with their boss, but she sincerely doubted he guessed what they did together. Their games would have shocked him. He had too much simplicity of character for it to be otherwise.

She turned her hand under his, meaning to pull away, but he immediately wove their fingers together. He was making sure she could not mistake his touch for a simple, friendly gesture. Arousal fluttered through her groin, hot and soft. She swallowed. 'I'm not in a position to get to know anyone better right now.'

'Are you sure?' His voice was warm oil with a hint of island music. His thumb stroked her palm, sending another fountain of sensation through her sex. 'If Durbin is stopping you . . .'

'No.' She eased free, perilously close to laughing, or crying. Did this quiet, decent man think she needed rescuing from Durbin? If only he knew! 'No, it's not that.'

'I see,' he said, though she hadn't given him any answer at all. He stared at the wall that separated them from the cockpit, probably wishing he could sink through the floor of the plane. Embarrassment prevented him from speaking, pride from leaving, and Julia couldn't think of a single thing to say that wouldn't have made him feel worse. He shook his trousers straight again and she noticed they were tented at his groin. Their brief touch had aroused him as fiercely as it had her.

24

Hell, she thought, sweat prickling beneath her arms. This trip was getting more complicated by the minute.

Julia's breath caught as she descended the stairs to the tarmac. Mountains surrounded the little airport, huge craggy green mountains capped with creamy white. The sky was so deeply blue it seemed more a night sky than day. Incredible. The colour beat through her eyes, through her body, as though it had the power to root her to the ground. She turned in a slow circle to take it in. Fluffy clouds swam through the ocean of blue, like sheep wandering among the peaks. Tears pricked her eyes. She'd travelled this country from coast to coast, and never in her life had she seen anything so breathtaking.

But there was not, she saw, a speck of snow on the ground.

'Welcome to Big Sky,' said a husky masculine voice.

She turned, still transported, and looked into a lean, smiling face half-shadowed by a dusty cowboy hat. A light brown moustache curled upward with the smile. The man was tall, taller than her, and solidly built but not fat. He shoved the brim of his hat back and his eyes twinkled at her. Before she could respond to his greeting, Carolyn Prentiss clattered down the stairs.

'Good Lord, what a view!' she exclaimed. Carolyn was a rail-thin, foul-mouthed, born victim who honestly thought she was a ball-buster. When it came to relationships she never walked if she could run. The ladies lounge at DMI had witnessed many of her Monday-morning crying jags. Men are bastards, she liked to say, never seeing the KICK ME sign that drew the worst of the lot like magnets. Now she fluffed her gamin-short hair and tugged her ski jacket over her tiny waist.

The stranger crossed to her and shook her hand. 'Welcome to Big Sky,' he said.

Her eyes gave him a quick once-over before she flashed a brilliant smile. 'Well, thank you, sir. I appreciate a warm welcome.'

The stranger retrieved his hand and tipped his off-white hat, shyly, as if he wasn't used to such effusion. 'Zach Taylor, ma'am.' He nodded at Marty and Ben, now blinking in the bright sunlight. 'Zach Taylor,' he said again. 'Glad you all made it. Hope you don't mind about the snow.' He waved towards the belly of the plane. 'I'll just get your luggage and we'll be off.'

'Well, yippee-ki-ay,' Marty muttered, sidling up to Julia. 'You ever hear such a drawl in your life? "I'll jist git yer luggij."'

Julia tried not to laugh but it was a struggle. She realised this must be Mr Snow's a-Comin'. He didn't look as stupid as she'd expected; the eyes under the brim of that stetson had been sharp. But he was a bit much. His shearling coat was so worn it might have been unearthed from an archaeological dig. And his boots had flames shooting up their sides! She turned to get another look just as he reached into the luggage compartment to pull out the first bag. His coat rode up. The view improved. Well, well, she thought, admiring the fit of his jeans. Apparently, everything people said about cowboy butts was true. His glutes were rounded and firm, a true sight for sore eyes.

She went to help him retrieve her steamer trunk.

The cowboy seemed surprised to find himself shoulder to shoulder with a woman. 'Big girl, ain't you?'

'Yes, I am,' she said, and hefted the trunk out herself. Idiot, she thought, watching him scratch his head over that. She forced herself not to let her arms drag. Luck-

26

ily, there was only one place the trunk could be stowed and it wasn't far. A dusty red sports utility vehicle sat by the edge of the tarmac with its back door popped open. Julia heaved her luggage inside and slapped her hands together.

Marty and Ben followed, each having grabbed their own bags.

'Jeez, Mueller,' said Marty, catching sight of the trunk. 'You planning on moving in?'

Julia didn't deign to answer and in a moment there was no need because Carolyn came tripping over with the cowboy, already hanging on his arm.

'I just love four-wheel drives,' she gushed. 'You can roll the windows down, hang your head out in the breeze. You don't mind if I sit up front, do you, Zach? I don't want to miss an inch of this gorgeous scenery.'

I'll bet, thought Julia, climbing into the back between her two male co-workers. She had a pretty good idea what scenery had caught the female VP's eye.

'Oh, dear.' Carolyn batted her lashes at the cowboy. 'I can't seem to fasten this seat belt. Do you think you could –?'

'Sure thing, ma'am,' he said, and leant across her to do it.

'That's funny,' said Marty. 'You didn't have any trouble with the belt in my truck.'

'Oh, stow it,' Carolyn snapped.

Julia saw the cowboy's moustache twitch before he ducked his head to start the ignition. Amused or not, he did nothing to shake off his new friend. He chuckled when Carolyn draped her arm along the back of his seat. Julia suppressed an urge to grind her teeth.

He swung them on to a narrow mountain road, explaining that they were heading north towards Glacier National Park. That seemed to exhaust his conversational repertoire. Unfazed, Carolyn played with the hair at the nape of his neck. The cowboy patted her hand. Resigned to watching this love-fest all weekend, Julia craned past her seat-mates to catch the scenery. To the left of the road, a scarp of lichen-splashed rock towered over their heads. To the right, the land fell sharply to rolling grassland. A river rib-boned through it, its placid surface reflecting both the sapphire sky and a copse of trees in full autumn dress. She leant closer to the window, causing Marty to grunt and steady her shoulder. Brown humps were moving amidst the glowing foliage, like small, shaggy tanks.

'Bison,' said the cowboy, who must have been watching her in the rear-view mirror. 'A few of the ranchers hereabouts raise them for meat.'

'They're adorable,' Carolyn said before Julia could respond. With a too-sharp laugh, the VP removed the man's hat and plopped it on to her own head. He took that liberty with equanimity.

'Looks good on you,' he said. 'We'll have to pick one up for you in Taylorsville.'

Julia's mouth softened in amusement. Apparently the cowboy drew the line at giving up his hat. Not that Carolyn noticed. She simpered with pleasure.

'Taylorsville?' she said. 'Any relation to you?'

'Great grandaddy,' said the cowboy and scratched his unsheltered hair. A nice honey-brown, it was receding at his temples. It was clipped short, though, so he wasn't trying to hide its retreat. 'We'll be stopping there before we head up to the ranch. I need to get some feed.'

Marty pressed one hand over his grin.

'For the horses,' Zach clarified. 'In case it's a big snow.'

28

Marty whispered in her ear. 'Why does he keep talking about snow?'

Julia was struggling so hard not to laugh she couldn't answer. If she got through this ride without busting, it would be a miracle.

Zachary Taylor thought of himself as a simple man. Whether he was or not was another matter, but he had his own notions about himself and this was one of them. He loved horses and cow dogs. He loved to stand in a snowfall at midnight. He loved to kiss. He loved to fuck. He loved the sound of a woman's laugh. He loved being naked. He loved the smell of leather and hay, and just-washed babies, though he wasn't entirely sure he wanted any of his own. Of all those things, he probably loved fucking the best, though cantering Starlight across a field of wildflowers came close.

Thing was, he needed to fuck: every day if he could get it, all day if he couldn't. He'd started early, barely old enough to shave, and his body had been greedy from the first. He'd never had the knack of coming quickly. His body clung to its pleasure, and clung and clung, until he sometimes thought he'd sell his soul for an orgasm.

He was popular with the ladies. This was a good thing because, as his mother put it, Zach was a shy 'un. Not just a little shy, either; Zach had the sort of shyness that stuns a man to silence. It wore on him hard. Seemed to him the whole world knew how to talk; just opened their mouths and let whatever was in their heads fall out. Sometimes he had things to say, but he'd look around and think: there isn't a soul in this room who'd understand a word. Even in the bosom of his family he'd think that. So he'd keep his mouth shut.

In all the world there were two places he felt completely at home: in the saddle and between a woman's legs.

Today he'd caught sight of a pair of legs that had his six-shooter bucking in his jeans. They were long legs, wrap-around-your-neck long legs, and the woman they were attached to . . . she was something all right. She had skin like cream dusted in rose. Her eyes were real steady, as if she'd ridden some rough trails in this life. She didn't talk much, which might pose a problem, given his own lack in that area, but her voice was as smooth and cool as a dish of vanilla ice cream. That voice had given him a hard-on the first time he heard it. Now that he saw her, he had an itch that wouldn't quit. He couldn't imagine when he might be allowed to scratch it, either.

For all that, he was happy to have her sitting in the back of his vehicle, within spitting distance, as it were. He hummed under his breath, an old Bonnie Raitt tune about not being the only one, the lonely one. He liked that Bonnie Raitt. She was all right.

He pulled into the newly paved lot of the Taylorsville Coffee Stop. The genuine gold-leaf lettering in the window looked nice. That artist fellow from Butte had done a good job. Zach didn't mind spending money, but he liked to see it well spent.

'Stay and have a cup,' he said, when his passengers climbed out from the truck. 'I got to see a man about some oats.'

Flo poked her head out of the door as he was crossing Main Street's second lane. 'Hey, Sev,' she called. 'Stop in when you're done. I've got a rent cheque for you.'

He touched two fingers to his hat brim. Flo would see to his guests. Flo knew how to be friendly. When he hit the pavement in front of the feed shop he couldn't resist turning for another look at the blonde; Julia, she called herself. Flo had seated the easterners by the window. Julia had the profile of a queen and, despite the brisk mountain breeze, her hair was barely mussed. If a cock could have moaned, Zach's would have. It was pressed up tight against his zip, aching to be freed. He let his breath out in a sigh and thanked God for the length of his coat.

The cowboy was staring at her. Julia could feel it clear through the window. Annoyed and unsettled, she left her seat and moved to the counter instead.

The café was surprisingly attractive, 1950s vintage but not too kitsch. Miniature juke-boxes sat on the tables. Two songs for a quarter. The waitress-owner had 'Flo' stitched across the pocket of her uniform. She was a nice-looking older woman, soft around the middle and worn at the edges, but pretty. Her bouffant hair was an improbable shade of red.

'Howdy,' she said, as Julia slid on to a stool. 'You look like a double-espresso type to me.'

Julia confessed that she was. Flo winked and tipped a scoop of fresh grounds into the machine. 'Bet you're surprised you can get fancy coffee in a little place like this, but we're up to the minute here. Sev sees to that.' She nodded sagely. 'All sorts of rich folks are moving to Montana these days: Californians, Hollywood types. Got to have someplace to spend their money. Our galleries are every bit as good as Whitefish and, if I say so myself, our coffee puts what they pour in Missoula to shame.'

As good as that, thought Julia. But all she said was, 'Sev?'

Flo laughed and slid a small, steaming cup across the counter. '"Sev" is what the women round these parts call Zach Taylor, on account of his limit.'

Julia dipped a spoon in her cup and made what she hoped was a disinterested noise. She did not want to know the cowboy's life history. Flo, however, was not to be discouraged. She propped her forearms on the counter and lowered her voice. 'Never sleeps with a woman more than seven times. Want to know why?'

'I'm sure it's none of my business.'

Flo pushed back from the counter and chuckled. 'Because by the seventh time they all want to marry him! It's true,' she said, though Julia had made no protest. She crossed her arms and nodded. 'Wanted to myself.'

Which was far more than Julia needed to know. 'I'll just take this back to the table,' she said. 'Thanks for the chat.'

The table wasn't much better, though, because Carolyn was full of budding romance jitters, jiggling her knee and playing with her assortment of silver chains until Julia wanted to rip them from her neck. Every five minutes she looked around as if expecting Zach to appear. Julia wondered if it would do any good to send her to Flo for the low-down on her prospective beau. She doubted it. Carolyn didn't have the self-protective instincts God gave a flea.

Finally, the hyperactive VP popped up from her chair and muttered something about checking the view from the back. Wanted to light up, more likely. Carolyn knew better than to smoke in front of a new man before she'd discovered where he stood on the issue.

Her perfume hadn't faded before Marty peered at

the juke-box. 'Say, Mueller, you got a quarter? I see a song here for Prentiss.' He grinned from Ben to Julia, both of whom stared at him blankly. 'Right here, see: "Working on My Next Broken Heart".'

Julia shuddered. Country and Western. Her favourite. She decided it was time to retreat to the ladies'.

Zach dumped the feed in the rig and returned to the Coffee Stop by the back way. Flo had a view of the Swan Range that was pure poetry. High black mountains rose from a grassy plain, their shadows stark and purple, their peaks dusted with white, as if the earth were baring her spine to mortal eyes. He breathed in the sight for a long moment. Behind him, from the west, he could smell the coming storm, a strange, pale scent, a mixture of mothballs and fragile alpine flowers. The smell was stronger than yesterday. Yesterday he'd been annoyed at the thought of being snowed in with his last batch of paying guests. Today he was happy.

He wondered if he might be in love. The idea was pretty crazy but, in truth, he'd never met a woman like Julia before. It didn't matter that he didn't know a thing about her; he could feel her, smell her, like the coming snow. She was mysterious and powerful, but real, a thing of the earth. His body yearned to join up with her until his very marrow echoed the aching beat. Fuck her, said the bone-shaking pulse. Fuck her, fuck her, fuck her.

He shoved his hands into his back pockets and thrust his erection towards the mountains, as if the rocks would see his need and answer it. A hand touched his shoulder. The moment seemed so magical, he thought it must be her, but when he turned he found the other woman, the bird-like one with the brittle smile. She smelled of expensive perfume and cigarettes.

She slid her hand around his shoulder and up his neck. His jacket was still open from the heat of the feed shop. When she tucked herself against him, her skinny thigh slid between his legs and pressed the swell of his balls. Good news, said his cock. The rest of him wasn't so sure.

'Fresh air make you horny, too?' she said, low and sugared against his neck. Her lips opened. She tongued his racing pulse.

With a sex drive like his, Zach didn't often turn a willing female away. Force of habit made his hands settle on her waist. Lord Almighty, it was small. He could just about span it. She squirmed closer and gave his cock a nice firm rub with her hipbone. Her hands wandered down his shirt and took hold of the metal button that fastened his jeans.

Oh, yeah, said his cock. 'I'm not sure this is a good idea,' said his mouth.

'It's a very good idea.' She raked him through the denim with her nails, drawing circles round his scrotum and up his shaft.

His eyelids started to slide downward about the same time as his zip did. She lifted him free and stroked him lightly from root to crest. She had little hands, little bird bones under baby-soft skin. It felt as if he were being given a hand job by a child, creepy and exciting at the same time. His chest went up and down a little faster. He was so hard his skin hurt.

She wrapped her fingers around his shaft and tugged him. 'Walk back this way,' she said. 'I don't want anyone to see us.'

He wasn't too clear on where she was heading until he heard her back hit the aluminium siding of the building. She dropped to her knees in the grass and rubbed her face across his thighs.

'Want me to suck it?' she asked.

'Oh, yeah,' he said, too lost to think. He grabbed the windowsill to support his weight and eased his cock down to mouth level. He closed his eyes when she took him. Her mouth was as small and tender as her hands. She didn't swallow much, but she played a symphony on the bulging crown, a combination of tickle and rub and suck. She gripped his thighs for balance and he swung his knees to either side of her torso so that he could brace them on the siding. He wanted to thrust in the worst way but he didn't dare. She was like a glass ornament hung from a tree, too delicate to touch.

'Mm, you're so big,' she said, pausing to grab a breath.

He wasn't really, just a bit more than average, but it was something women said and he appreciated the sentiment. Good manners, Grandpa would have said. He looked down and stroked her short, feathery hair, marvelling at the cat-like neatness of her skull.

'Is it good?' she asked, a shy whisper.

He smiled and rubbed the tip of his cock around her little mouth. 'It's great,' he said, and she took him in again, resuming that wonderful-awful teasing suck. He wasn't sure he could come from such soft, slippery torment but he was willing to try. He closed his eyes again, his mind wandering deliciously. He saw Julia descending the metal stairway from the plane; saw her face turn to his in that first moment, her mouth open in wonder, her eyes shining. He'd wanted to kiss her, to lick those incredible Nordic cheekbones.

He'd lay her across the engine of the plane, he thought. The metal skin would be hot from the sun and maybe somebody would fire it up, so it would rumble through her sex while he shoved up her skirt and yanked down her panties. He bet she'd have a nice, meaty bottom. He bet a man could hold it in both hands as he eased himself inside. She'd be warm there, that coolness all for show. God willing, she'd be greedy. God willing, her soft little cunt would suck his penis dry.

His knees began to tremble, and he thought: maybe this little lady can make me come.

'A little harder,' he said, his voice thick and husky. 'Sweetheart, just a little harder.'

The mouth tightened on him and the tongue dug in, tastebuds rasping his slit. His grip on the windowsill tightened. He let his hips swing towards the mouth, just a little, just enough to push the kill spot under the head over that flicking tongue. Pressure spiralled up from his balls, turning, swelling. His neck sagged back. Oh, yeah, he thought. Oh, Julia.

He opened his eyes. He didn't know why. He hadn't heard anything, hadn't smelled anything, but when he did, he met a mocking, grey-green gaze. The window was open and the object of his fantasy was leaning on the sill, cool as you please, her jaw propped in her hand, her index finger bracing her temple. Her bare pink lips curled in a sneer that seemed to say this was no more than she'd expected. The only sign that the show moved her at all was a faint flush across her cheeks.

None of which mattered to his cock. It swelled up fit to burst and his balls nearly crawled into his body. The ache was more than he could stand. Lord, he needed to come.

Carolyn whimpered. He realised the polite roll of his hips had turned to a thrust. Her nails dug into his thighs, holding him off even as she sucked harder.

Julia's mocking grin deepened, but he couldn't look

away from her mouth any more than he could stop pushing. Her lips parted. Her tongue crept out. The wet pink tip touched the little valley between the peaks of her upper lip. That was the last straw. Stars exploded up Zach's spine, as if a mule had kicked his tailbone. He slammed forward, come shooting from him like a train from a tunnel. He groaned and shook, only pulling back when he felt Carolyn's throat spasm around his cock. He finished in the air, in the cold.

Carolyn fell to her hands and coughed, come spilling from her lips in a thin, glistening stream. Their audience started a slow, resonant clap. Carolyn gasped and looked up.

'Very impressive,' Julia said, clearly meaning the opposite. 'But I think you two had better be more careful in the future. I'm betting a town like this has laws against indecent exposure.'

'Fuck you, Mueller,' said the little lady. She swiped her lips with the back of her hand. 'Why don't you get your own man and stop spying on people who have a life.'

Julia's mouth pursed in a wry moue. 'As you wish,' she said.

Despite her mild response, Zach had a feeling Carolyn was going to pay for that crack.

Julia had nothing to say about the glorious technicolour sunset. Nor did anyone else. Only the truck's engine broke the silence, rattling up a mountain whose pine-studded peak was wreathed in red-gold clouds. TAYLOR'S MOUNTAIN, the sign at the start of the gravel switchback had stated. 'Your own mountain!' Carolyn had exclaimed. Zach had grunted. Then Marty tried to needle Carolyn with his rendition of the mournful

Country-and-Western tune. When that failed to provoke a response he, too, fell silent.

Ben was no better. Julia could tell he felt awkward about the pass he'd made on the plane. He kept glancing at her from the corner of his eye. His thigh rested against hers from hip to knee, jiggling in the bumpy ride. He didn't press it closer but he didn't pull it away. Its warmth added to the heat she already carried, a dull but insistent throb at the meeting of her legs. She wedged her shoulder against the door and attempted to push the memory of Zach's climax from her mind. It was impossible. She could picture every detail. His lips had pulled back from his teeth. The lines of his face had deepened. She hadn't been able to look away from his eyes. At the final moment, tears of sheer, primal feeling had glistened in their corners.

Here was a man who put his whole heart and soul into his orgasm. Here was a man who really loved to fuck.

Of course, he didn't have much else to recommend him. Poor Carolyn had nearly gagged when he tried to deep-throat her. Julia's eyes narrowed. Carolyn was going to pay for that crack about finding her own man. Not in the way she expected, though. Julia knew how Carolyn's gears turned. She'd expect Julia to make a play for Zach herself, and clearly believed she'd triumph in a battle of the cunts. To her simple mind, any woman who'd let a dick near her mouth before the hundredth date had to have an advantage over the rest of the female population. Besides, what man in his right mind would choose a size sixteen over a size eight?

Julia smoothed her skirt over her knees. She felt, more than saw, Ben's eyes follow the motion. A muscle in his thigh jumped. He'd folded his coat over his lap.

She knew if she looked beneath it, she'd find him hard. Carolyn, that poor misguided stick, didn't understand the lure of rich flesh and an indomitable will.

But she would when Julia was through with her.

Chapter Three

Zach could tell the ranch wasn't what Julia expected. She stood in the entrance to the great room, hands arrested in the process of removing her long leather coat. He moved to help her as the other woman exclaimed how darling everything was.

'Darling' wasn't the word he'd have chosen. It was a big place, despite being neatly tucked into the landscape. Eight guest rooms filled a wing on the ground floor, the basement housed a gym, and skylights flooded the main rooms with clear mountain light. The conference room could seat twenty at a pinch and the barn had every amenity that a pampered dude horse could desire. In the office that led off the great room, four computers, each with its own modem, awaited the demands of busy executives who'd had their fill of fly fishing. Thanks to his grandmother's business savvy, everything at the Taylor Ranch was first-rate. Zach had always been proud of it.

His chest warmed as Julia's head tipped back to take in the vaulted ceiling. His grandfather had built this place of solid pine, from the polished floors to the slanted cathedral roof. The sun's last rays slanted through the windows, and in that golden light, the peeled log walls glowed like honey from a comb. This ranch had been Zach's sanctuary from an early age, the home he'd wished was his, until one day it was. Soon he'd have it all to himself.

Julia must have shared his pleasure because he caught an appreciative sigh as he eased her coat from her shoulders. The leather was buttery soft, the construction Italian. It must have cost a bundle. Carolyn had made a point of telling him that Julia was 'only a secretary'. Zach sympathised with the impulse behind the put-down; a woman like Julia could inspire insecurity, but clearly there were secretaries and then there were secretaries. In any case, Julia sure seemed like the lead bull of this herd.

Not that she didn't have her soft spots. The hair at the nape of her neck was silky fine. She smelled of baby powder, surprising, but nice. His cock jumped up to take a sniff, worse than Gracie after a bone. He draped her coat over his arm to hide his sudden erection. The whole world didn't need to know what she did to him.

'This is a lovely place,' she said, her face serene.

'My grandfather built it.' He sounded strangled. He cleared his throat. The removal of her coat had revealed a severe grey suit that fit as if it had been sewn on to her body. It skimmed her generous curves, all six feet of them. She was ripe and firm and strong. As she strolled towards the stone hearth, she trailed her hand along the back of the leather couch. He immediately pictured that hand trailing down his spine, one vertebra at a time. She was a sensualist, he decided with a tiny shiver, a creature of touch and taste and smell.

'Where should we hang our coats?' asked one of the men.

Reluctant to turn from this vision, Zach waved behind him. 'There are pegs in the hall.'

Maria must have turned up the heat before she left. The room was warm. Julia began unbuttoning her snug grey suit jacket. A flush prickled across his groin with an intensity he hadn't felt since he was a teenager. The sides of her jacket parted and through her starched white blouse he saw the curve of her breast. His palm itched to weigh the luxuriant flesh, to shape it, to squeeze it. Her bosom rose as she lifted her arm to touch the photograph his grandmother had hung above the mantel.

He shook himself. It was an old rodeo picture. In it he was getting the tar bucked out of him by a bronc called Sunfish, so named for his habit of turning his belly towards the sky. That horse had helped him win the world championship five years ago, his best ride and his last. By the time the pick-up men dragged him off that fool bronc, his wrist had been busted bad enough to require a metal pin. He'd earnt more than a hundred thousand dollars in prizes that year, which he'd used to stake his first real-estate venture. His eyes crinkled at the memory. He'd been proud to add his acquisition to those of his grandparents.

He wondered what Julia thought of his former occupation. Did it dampen her panties, the way it did the rodeo groupies, or did she think he was as loco as that horse?

Before he could interpret her expression, Carolyn grabbed his arm. The two men stood behind her, the tall black man and the shorter, curly-haired one with the funny accent. That one had the devil in his eyes. Even now he was grinning about who knew what. Zach noticed everyone but Julia wore jeans and expensive sweaters. Seemed his Julia could stand to loosen up.

Carolyn tugged on his hand. 'Come on, Zach,' she said. 'Show us around.'

He gave them the grand tour, sort of. It lasted a lot longer when Maria led it. All Zach could think of to say was 'kitchen, bedrooms, exercise room' and 'out back there's the stable'. The curly-haired man, Marty, was amused by the fact that there were windows in every wall, even the walls between the bedrooms.

'This dude ranch must be popular with peeping Toms,' he joked, pretending to peer into the next room.

Zach yanked down the shade. 'My Grandpa Joe liked windows. First time he saw my grandmother she was walking past the window of her father's house. He said he wanted to frame her like that for always.'

Carolyn pressed her hands to her heart. 'That is so romantic.'

'Mm,' said Julia.

Zach turned away, his face heating. That mocking hum told him, clear as day, that she thought his grandfather was an idiot. Well, fuck her, he thought. A second later his mouth lifted in a rueful grin. Fucking her was, of course, exactly what he wanted.

Carolyn sat at the end of the table, playing lady of the house to Zach's gent. Julia watched her look from the platter of meat to the handsome man who held it, her face a picture of dismay. Apparently, the latest Mr Right was teetering on his pedestal.

'Steak?' she said faintly.

Seated to Carolyn's left, Julia hid a smile behind her hand. Someone named Maria had been given the weekend off, due to the much-threatened snow. As a result, the cowboy had prepared their meal. Steak, potatoes and an overcooked vegetable medley were hardly fare to tempt a borderline anorexic like Carolyn. He'd made gravy, too, which Marty was happily ladling over his baked potato.

Taken aback at Carolyn's protest, Zach froze with a huge slab of meat dangling from the serving fork. 'Nobody said there were vegetarians coming.' He sounded as if vegetarians were akin to international terrorists.

Carolyn hastened to assure him she was nothing of the sort. 'I do eat meat, of course. It's just, well, red meat is so unhealthy.'

Zach looked even more horrified. Julia decided it was time to administer the first light tap of the whip. She speared the steak with her fork, plopped it on Carolyn's plate and cut it in half. The meat was beautifully prepared, lightly charred on the outside and blood-rare in the middle. Mouth watering, she slid half the portion on to her own plate.

Carolyn bent towards her. 'I don't want any,' she hissed. 'I'm watching my cholesterol.'

Julia snorted and pitched her voice just as low. 'Try selling that bridge to someone else. If you were concerned about your health, you'd quit smoking and go to the gym once in a while.' Carolyn's mouth opened to deny the charge, but Julia's sword was fully drawn. 'You and I both know you're calorie-counting and, frankly, you're crazy to do it. If you were to take your clothes off now, you'd scare somebody.'

'Oh, really?' she said, but her face was pink with

doubt, and with guilt; on some level she knew she'd taken her weight-consciousness too far.

'Really,' Julia insisted, more kindly this time. She reached under the table and squeezed Carolyn's knee. 'Twenty pounds would do you a world of good. You have no idea how beautiful you could be.'

Confusion deepened the colour of Carolyn's cheeks. The two women had always been antagonistic, more by Carolyn's choice than Julia's. She begrudged the respect Julia got from Durbin, and from her own clients. Plus, with Julia around, her tough-girl act rang false. Julia was the genuine article. Carolyn was at best a wannabe. Naturally, she detested her rival, but she craved her approval, too. Julia could tell she didn't know whether to thank her for the compliment or tell her she must be kidding. Satisfied she'd achieved the effect she wanted, she released her co-worker's knee and took a bite of steak.

'Excellent,' she said to the cowboy, who'd resumed his seat.

He was staring at them with the concern peculiar to the slighted cook. 'My daddy raised this cow,' he said. 'Free-range. No hormones. Good clean forage. I promise you, this cow lived well and died happy.'

Julia burst out laughing before she could stop herself. Her co-workers gaped, but even so little snorts of merriment escaped her control. Lived well and died happy! A claim to hearten diners everywhere. She covered her mouth with her napkin. 'Forgive me, Mr Taylor,' she gasped, 'but you do have a way with words.'

'It's Zach,' he snapped, and he sounded very angry indeed.

Her laughter died as suddenly as it started. She noticed his eyes were very blue, and when he frowned,

45

even his moustache turned down. A funny feeling began in the pit of her stomach. For a moment she couldn't put a name to it. When she did, it intensified. It was shame. She was ashamed of herself for laughing at him.

'I am sorry,' she said, sincerely this time.

The cowboy busied himself with splitting his baked potato. A cloud of steam rose to obscure his face. 'That's all right,' he said gruffly. 'I imagine we seem pretty strange to you city folks.'

Marty glanced from her to Zach, his eyes wide with interest. Julia gave him a quelling look, but he merely shook his head as if to clear it. 'So, Zach, how long have you owned the ranch?'

Zach looked up from his plate. 'Just a year, since my grandma died and left it to me. But I've worked here since I was seventeen. My grandpa and I, we didn't like cows.'

Julia's throat jerked convulsively, but this time she managed to contain her amusement. 'I take it the rest of your family raises cattle.'

'Yep.' His eyes turned warily to hers. 'Got a big outfit down in the valley. My brothers and sisters all help out.'

There seemed to be a story behind this, but Zach wasn't saying any more and, ashamed or not, Julia wasn't sure she wanted to draw him out. After all, he had nothing to do with the purpose behind this weekend; at least, nothing to do with her purpose.

'We should get to work after dinner,' she said. All three portfolio managers groaned. She ignored them. 'We check out at noon on Sunday, so that only leaves you tonight and tomorrow to brainstorm.'

Marty laced his hands behind his head. His grin was

an unabashed challenge. 'I'm too jet-lagged to brain-storm. I say we start in the morning.'

Julia stared down her nose. 'Durbin wasn't happy about the loss of the Go-Tech account. If you three don't generate some good ideas for improving business, he may decide it's time for heads to roll.'

'Roll-schmoll,' said Marty. 'Rich likes to bluster.' He reached out and slapped Ben and Carolyn on the shoulder. 'But he's not going to do anything to break up his best team.'

'He will if he's given cause,' Julia warned, but Marty merely shrugged and returned to his steak.

'Ben would rather start tomorrow, too,' he said.

Ben looked startled at being put on the spot, but he nodded in agreement. 'I have some notes I'd like to go over tonight.'

'It's settled then,' Carolyn crowed. 'We start tomorrow.'

From the way she was twinkling at the cowboy, Julia could guess how she intended to spend the night. This annoyed her more than she cared to examine, but she knew better than to argue with the three of them ranged against her. Apart from calling her authority into question, this battle wasn't important. Moreover, what she failed to win by frontal assault, she would certainly gain by more subtle means. She'd already learnt one important fact: Marty Fine would be a tough nut to crack.

Zach knew he owed her. She was not what he was hankering after, but he owed her. Julia thought so, too. The memory of her smirk as she leant out the window of the Coffee Stop stung his pride. Not only did she consider him a hick but a ham-handed lover as well, which simply wasn't the case. He could prove it, too, if only to himself.

He knocked lightly on the door.

'Just a minute,' said a light feminine voice. A second later Carolyn swung it open.

'I, uh . . .' His words dried up like trail dust when he saw what she was wearing, a light silk robe with a cherry blossom print, and nothing else. Through the sheer cloth, he could see both the colour and shape of her nipples. She had delicate breasts, less than a handful, almost a mouthful. His body reacted predictably and he forgot what he'd meant to say.

'You, uh, what?' she said with a girlish giggle. She shifted her weight and a pale length of thigh appeared between the flaps of her robe.

He scratched his head and stared at this new revelation. 'I, uh, I was going to invite you to my rooms, but I can see you're not dressed for wandering around.'

'No, indeed.' Her eyes tilting with her smile, she caught his hands and set them on her tiny waist. 'I guess you'll have to stay here.' His gaze cut to the little window between her room and her neighbour's. The shade was pulled down on the other side, but not on Carolyn's. She tugged him closer to the bed. 'Don't you worry about the Ice Queen, Zach. She's off pumping iron in your basement.'

The Ice Queen, he thought, then realised she must mean Julia. Was she that cold? She didn't seem so to him. Controlled, yes, but molten, like lava bubbling underground. This was not, however, the moment to argue. Carolyn was shrugging her robe off her narrow shoulders. Her right breast appeared, then her left. Both were pale and round. With a quickening of his pulse, he saw she'd rouged her nipples. Their tips were elongated, and as shiny as if they'd been kissed. The robe fell to the tie that bound it at her waist. He inhaled sharply. Her collar bones stood out with painful prominence. He could count her ribs.

'You're so thin,' he said before he could think better of it.

She blushed from her belly to her brow and turned away. She fumbled for the chain to the bedside lamp. 'I'll put out the light.'

'No,' he said, but the light was out and the damage done. He reached through the dark for her and pulled her against his body. Words couldn't help now. He crossed his arms beneath her breasts. He rubbed the swell of his cock between her silk-clad bottom cheeks, soothing her with his warmth, letting her know he still wanted her. After a minute she relaxed and began to rub back at him.

'That's nice,' she said, and turned in his arms. Her breasts were warm, her nipples hot. When she caught his thigh between her own, her pussy lips spread wetness over his leg. That put one fear to rest. In his experience, skinny women tended to be slow to rouse. Not enough hormones, he reckoned. This one at least was ready to roll.

'Help me with my shirt,' he whispered and shivered as her tiny hands moved over the buttons. He unzipped his jeans and shoved them down before she'd finished, wanting to feel her fragile body against his own, skin to skin, pussy to cock. With admirable skill, she rolled a condom down his shaft. The feel of it sliding on increased his impatience. She laughed when he ripped his arms free of his sleeves. She was a slender shadow in the dark, but his hands moved unerringly to the tie of her robe. The silk fell to the floor with a teasing hiss. Her palms slid up his chest, grazing his nipples before twining behind his neck. She pressed against him full length, her skin wonderfully smooth.

'You're too tall,' she said, laughter in her voice. 'You'll have to lift me up.'

He lifted her. She was so light it shocked him, but she clung with surprising strength, winding her legs around his waist as she searched for his mouth with her own. Her kiss was as wet and open as her pussy. Her juice ran into the crease of her buttocks where it met the upward arch of his cock. He gripped her bottom and shifted her until the tip of his penis met her wet, warm entrance.

'Sh,' he said at her quick intake of breath. 'Don't you worry. I'm a slow goer, sweetheart. You'll get yours this time. I promise.'

'I'm not worried,' she said, but he knew she had been.

He carried her to the bed and laid her gently down, using the descent to slide fully into her. Her easy acceptance pleased him. He'd been afraid she'd be too small. Despite the way she'd taken the lead before, it seemed natural to command her now. She was so pliant, so soft. He stroked her pussy with his cock, a steady thrust and withdrawal intended to comfort as well as arouse. When she began to purr at each insertion, he rolled her on top of him. She tensed.

'It's all right,' he said. 'I'm doing the work tonight. This is for you.' With one arm bracing her spine, he sat up until they were face-to-face. She kissed him and began to rock but he stilled her. 'No, no work for you.'

'But I need to move.'

'Not yet.' He slid his hand down her flat little belly and curled his thumb over the rise of her clit. Her groan was delicious. Her pussy pulled at his shaft. See, he said to Julia in his mind. This is what I can do to a

50

woman. He rubbed firm circles over the seat of her pleasure and nuzzled her breast in search of a nipple. He chuckled when he found it because whatever she'd painted on it tasted of cinnamon. He sucked one peak clean, then the other, then drew nearly the whole of one breast into his mouth. She came with a shuddering moan, her hands clutching his shoulders, her thighs tightening round his hips.

A promising start, he thought, but only a start. Sitting back on his heels, he cradled her head and eased her on to her back. His thighs supported her bottom. The position forced him hard against the front of her vagina. He pushed down on her mons to intensify the pressure on her G-spot. She was laid out before him, barely able to move except to roll her hips a little. The sense that she was entirely at his mercy sent a quiver through his sex. He kneaded her soft lips around the root of his cock

'Oh, yes, that's good,' she said, her head thrashing. 'But aren't you going to come?'

He smiled. 'Why do you ask, sweetheart? Are you sore?'

'Oh, no. I feel lovely, but you – oh, God.' She squirmed again and tightened on him hard. 'I want you to fuck me. Please, Zach, please, fuck me.'

'Not yet,' he said, even softer than before. Though he'd hardened further at her plea, he continued his slow, deep massage at the junction of their bodies. 'I like feeling you come around me. I like the sounds you make. I like the way your pussy creams just before you moan. You can feel how big it makes me, can't you? You can feel how hard it makes me pound.'

'Please,' she panted, but he wouldn't relent. He massaged her until she came again, then began a shallow rocking motion, just as far as tightening his buttocks would take him. She gripped his wrists in an attempt to sit up. Rather than let her, he ran his hands from her hips to her shoulders, holding her down with pleasure. His palms slipped easily over her perspiring skin, long strokes, like a carpenter planing wood. He caught her budded nipples on every pass. She liked that. Her back arched into his touch. She would come again, he knew, and this climax would be the sharpest.

At the sight of her restless movements, the signals that his nerves were sending finally shifted from pleasure to need. He knew his body well. It had reached the pitch of lust where he could come. He ceased his slow massage.

'Stay,' he ordered, fearing she'd try to sit up again. When he saw she'd obey, he slid his left hand beneath her buttocks and gripped the top of her thigh with his right. He could control her movements completely then, pulling and pushing precisely as he wished. What he wished was to give her the greatest pleasure possible. A woman's pleasure always intensified his own. His cock pushed hard against the sensitive pad of tissue behind her pubic bone. It was swollen from her orgasms, juicy and soft. She whimpered as he quickened his thrusts, then groaned when he deepened them. Her hands fisted in the coverlet. Her heels dug into the bed behind his hips.

'Yes, yes, yes,' she cried, the sound rising in pitch and volume as she spasmed around his swollen cock. Unfortunately, the contractions weren't enough to tip him over. He knew she'd be sore if he went on much longer, so he drove as hard as he dared until she collapsed with a final sigh. As soon as she did, he pulled free of her body, ripped off the condom and squeezed his cock. Urgently, hand over hand he pulled it away from his body, hard tight strokes that stretched his shaft and drove the air like fire from his lungs. He tugged until his skin stung, until his balls grew heavy and tight. He closed his eyes and remembered her squirms, her sighs, the way her back arched off the bed.

Come on, he urged his stubborn penis. Come on, you bastard, let go. He squeezed the head of his cock, his palm sliding over a slick of gathered fluid. Julia's cream. No, not Julia's. Not anyone's. But his mind had slipped where it wanted to go.

Please, Julia said in the unruly regions of his imagination. Please fuck me. The sudden pang of longing alarmed him, but not enough to pull back from the fantasy. Her nipple was in his mouth. Her silky blonde hair swept his shoulder. She was wet. She was coming. Julia was twitching around his cock, tight, tighter. Oh, God. He was going to blow. He groaned, a sound like bulls make when they're roped off their feet: animal shock, animal pain. Julia, he thought, and his climax exploded, an aching rush of heat and fluid.

Carolyn murmured in confusion as his seed hit her belly.

On the other side of the wall, Julia turned away. She hadn't seen but she'd heard plenty, as Carolyn had assuredly intended. No wonder she'd chosen the room next to hers. She'd wanted to rub Julia's nose in her triumph.

It should have been an empty triumph. Julia rolled off the bed, cursing her own stupidity. Listen and learn, she'd told herself. And she had. She'd learnt she'd got to Carolyn with her admonition about her weight. She'd learnt Carolyn liked to be controlled. She'd learnt Zach wasn't as bad in bed as she'd expected. Neither was Carolyn, if the cowboy's orgasmic bellow was any indication. She didn't believe she'd ever heard a man make quite that noise before.

None of these revelations would have bothered her if she hadn't also discovered something about herself. She wanted the stupid cowboy. She wanted to call that sound from him. She wanted to feel him striving between her legs. Her cunt was swollen with arousal now, pulsing, twitching, positively running with desire. She dug her nails into her palms, willing the pain to calm her. She couldn't afford this distraction. Her future depended on this weekend proceeding as planned. If she wanted to break free of Durbin, she had to keep her wits about her. She couldn't afford to fuck the help!

The murmur of foreplay resumed in the next room. Julia gritted her teeth. Didn't Carolyn know she was using up her quota with 'Sev'? Two down and five to go. At this rate she'd be history in a single night. The thought pleased her more than it should have. Muttering a curse, she grabbed a robe and left her room.

A dim light drew her through the great room to the kitchen. The tiny bulb above the stove was on. She found Marty seated at the table in his boxer shorts, moaning over a piece of the departed Maria's pecan pie. He liked to eat, that Marty. But he was stocky, not fat, the kind of man who ate what he pleased and burnt up most of it. The only time she'd seen him sit still was in front of a full plate.

'Hey,' he said, grinning through pleasure-slitted eyes, 'that caterwauling keep you up, too?'

'What do you think?' she said, annoyed to have been caught listening but too proud to deny it.

'I think if those two fools can get laid, there's no reason we shouldn't.'

Marty had been propositioning Julia since they'd

met. She'd never deigned to answer him with more than a cold stare. But perhaps this weekend demanded a change of strategy. Perhaps her throbbing sex did, too. She folded her arms and lounged back against the big stainless steel refrigerator. 'What did you have in mind?'

He set his fork down as if his muscles had gone numb. 'I'll be damned. Are you saying what I think you're saying?'

'That depends.'

He swiped his mouth with the back of his arm and approached her, slowly, like a dog stalking a cat. I just want to play, said his dark, laughing eyes. Please don't scratch me. She remained as she was even when he braced both hands beside her head in a classic gesture of dominance. His chest was broad, his arms well muscled. She'd gathered her hair in a simple braid and now he nuzzled the fine strands at her temple. His gold wedding band clinked against the refrigerator. The sound didn't make either of them flinch. As far as Julia was concerned, Marty's marriage was his business. She wasn't his first adulterous affair, and she doubted she'd be his last.

Obviously untroubled by guilt, he tipped his lower body closer and settled into the cradle of her hips. He sighed with pleasure and rolled his cock from side to side. He wasn't fully hard yet, but he was getting there. He bent his arms and nipped her ear. 'What does it depend on, Julia?'

'On what you've got in mind.'

'Honey, I've got so much in mind for you, it would take years to do it all.'

She wove her fingers through his curls and pushed his head back from her ear. 'You'll have to make a choice. This is strictly a one-shot deal.'

'In that case –' he wagged his bushy brows '– I've had my eye on this jar of home-made caramel sauce I saw in the pantry.'

'Perhaps you should get it.'

His eyes widened, then narrowed. Clearly, he thought this was too easy. It was, though he didn't need to know that yet.

'All right,' he said. 'I will.'

He returned with a wide mason jar, a wooden spoon and an impressive erection. Half of it stuck through the placket of his shorts, bouncing merrily with his steps. She found herself thinking of the game she'd played with Durbin, where she'd pretended to be Marty. Durbin must have seen this fat, shiny cock many times: over the urinals, showering at the club. Had he lusted after it the way she did? Did it make Durbin lick his lips?

Screw Durbin, she thought. Tonight was for her. She returned her attention to his grinning protégé.

Marty gestured at her moss-grey velvet robe. 'You'll have to take that off, along with whatever you've got underneath.'

Julia undid the tie and let the robe drop to the floor. She was naked. Marty clutched the mason jar to his chest and pretended to stagger. 'Good Lord, woman, you should warn a man before you do that.'

She couldn't help but smile. Marty was good for a woman's ego, even a healthy woman's ego. She nodded towards his boxers. 'Don't you think you should strip off, too? You wouldn't want to get sticky.'

He wrenched his shorts off with flattering speed, then patted the sturdy kitchen table.

Julia advanced one swaying step at a time, her hand behind her back to hide the tie of her robe. She watched his eyes rove her body; watched his cock bob in admiration at what he saw. His lips were parted for his shallow breaths. His hands clutched the jar of caramel like a lifeline. She hopped on to the table and spread her thighs. The scent of pussy rose between them, musky and rich. His eyes fell to the shining flesh of her sex. He sighed.

'You're blonde,' he said. 'You're really blonde.'

Fighting a laugh, she pulled the jar from his paralysed hand. 'I think you'd better set this down.' She unscrewed the cap and stuck her pinky into the sticky sauce. His eyes followed as she brought it to her mouth and sucked it clean. 'Mm. Very good.'

'Oh, yeah,' he growled and reached out with the wooden spoon.

She let him dip it in the jar. She let him pull it out coated in sauce. She let him hold it above the slope of her breast until the first heavy golden drop began to form . . .

Then she whipped off the table, hooked her foot behind his ankle and downed him. It wasn't easy to trip a grown man without hurting him, but Julia caught his head with one hand and managed to send most of his weight on to his posterior. He gasped a sharp curse, too shocked to yell, too stunned to struggle. In a matter of seconds, she'd lashed his wrists to the table leg.

'What are you doing?' he demanded, trying to lift the table and get free. 'Damn, this thing is heavy.'

Julia allowed her laugh to bubble free. She patted his heaving chest. 'Come on, Marty. I bet you're always in charge. Wouldn't you like a change of pace?'

'Wouldn't you?' he fired back, eyes glittering with fury.

She shook her head. 'No, Marty, I wouldn't.'

'You crazy bitch,' he said, but he was half-laughing himself.

She drew the jar of caramel sauce off the table, and the spoon. He stopped struggling then, curious, his cock beginning to recover from its shock. As it rose, she dribbled a spoonful of sauce over his right nipple.

'It's cold,' he complained, but his toes curled in anticipation.

In silence, she coated his left nipple, then his breast-bone, then drew a rippling line down his belly. She stopped short of his thatch. His erection pointed sky-ward now, wavering with the flow of his blood and the periodic clenching of his buttocks. She looked at his balls, a neat plump package between strong, hairy thighs. He followed the direction of her gaze and started breathing faster.

Good, she thought, her own blood flowing strongly. She gripped the base of his balls between the fingers of one hand and squeezed, forcing them forward until the skin pulled taut around their heavy bulk. She poised the laden spoon above them and waited for the drip.

'Use your hand,' he gasped, then bit his lip. 'Please.'

Since he asked so nicely, she set the spoon aside and dipped her fingers in the jar. He groaned as she slath-ered the cool, sticky mass over his upthrust testicles. His thighs quivered as if her touch tickled, but he pushed himself closer with every swipe. When she released him, his sigh held both relief and longing.

'Now your cock,' she said. The word made him shudder, as did the slow trail of caramel up his raphe. She coated the underside first, then the upper, then gently, slowly dabbed the sticky mess over his glans. His eyes squeezed shut when she touched him there and she realised he must be very sensitive. Her pussy clenched and wept. She adored knowing a man's vulnerabilities.

His eyes were still shut when she straddled him. She

did not touch any part of his body, just loomed above him, his conqueror. His lids rose slowly. She put her fingers to his lips and, one by one, he sucked them free of sauce. He had a surprisingly gentle mouth. She was going to have to reward him. He shivered as she pulled the last finger free.

'Shall I lick you clean?' she whispered.

'Please,' he whispered back, earning a smile for his manners.

The caramel was sweet on her tongue, and salty with his perspiration. His heat was beginning to melt it. She suckled his sharp, tiny nipples, which inspired a series of long, breathy sighs. They deepened as she lapped down his chest, and quickened when she crouched over his balls. Again, she squeezed his testicles within their pouch, lifting them towards her mouth. He groaned at the first dragging lick.

She knew he'd need an incentive to hold on as long as she wanted.

'I'll make you a deal,' she said, between firm, slow licks. 'If you hold off coming through the rest of this, I'll untie you and let you fuck me.'

His thigh muscles tightened. 'You will?'

'My word of honour.'

He seemed to believe her because he set his jaw and clenched his bound fists. 'Do your worst,' he said.

'I will,' she promised. 'My very worst.'

His balls were clean now. Wanting the skin of his shaft as taut as she could get it, she made a V of her thumb and fingers and pressed his testicles down over his perineum. Most of the caramel sauce had melted off his cock but a thin glaze remained. She moved until she knelt perpendicular to his body. She pressed her mouth sideways across his under-ridge. With wet, sucking kisses she drew the swollen flesh against her tongue. Marty gasped, his thighs jerking and trembling. When she'd kissed her way to the flare of the head, she swept her hand down his belly and depressed his cock until it pointed towards his feet. Again she kissed the full length of him, stopping when she reached his glans. He squirmed against the checkerboard linoleum.

'Julia,' he said. He tugged at his bonds, testing their strength, but she'd secured them well.

She petted the tangle of hair beneath his arm. 'There's nothing you can do, Marty-boy. You're at my mercy. I can tease you all night if I want to. I can tease you till you cry.'

He gasped when she yanked one curly hair out by the root. 'I'm ready to cry now.'

'Your eyes are tearing,' she agreed. She blew the hair free. 'But your cock just got thicker under my hand. You know what that tells me?'

Marty blinked rapidly and shook his head.

She squeezed him until the skin beneath her fingertips turned white. 'It tells me you like this game. It tells me you especially like the fact that I'm running it.'

'Uh,' he said: not a denial.

His cock sprang upward when she released it, a column of hot, pulsing flesh. A network of veins gnarled the shaft. Only the cap was smooth. Even in the stove light she could see it was darker than the rest of him, a deep, russet red. She poised her mouth above it. Her braid fell over her shoulder, its end striking the pale skin beside his thatch. He grunted in reaction, delightfully sensitised. He was watching her with strained but eager eyes.

'Ready?' she asked. He caught his lower lip between his teeth. She knew the head games she'd been playing had him wound as tight as her massage. She kept him

60

hanging a second more, then sank down on his shaft. She relaxed her throat as she descended, letting him see how much she could take. All of him as it turned out, though her jaw ached from his girth. His reaction was worth it. His cock quivered like a harp string in her mouth.

'Oh, God,' he moaned. 'That is so fucking hot.'

She began to move. Her pulls were slow and tight and she turned her head at the end of each rise, adding a little corkscrew to the motion. She cupped his balls against the base of him. That earnt a whimper, as did the hand she wrapped around his shaft to follow her withdrawals. She would surround him in feeling. No inch of genitalia would go untouched. Deep-throating made a good visual, but a clever pair of hands were a fellatio artist's best friend.

Marty seemed to agree. His head rolled from side to side on the floor. She sucked faster, wanting to bring him to the very edge of panic. No moment was wasted. Every pause to catch her breath was an opportunity to run her tongue over the sensitive head. Her guess had been correct. Each time she lavished attention on his glans, his thighs widened and thrashed.

'I can't,' he finally said. 'Julia, I can't hold back.'

'You can,' she promised, pressing the words into his deep, shining come-slit. 'Breathe.' She kissed the slippery dome. 'Breathe slowly. That's it. Relax.'

He tried but, two pulls later, he was tensing again. 'I can't. I'm running fucking bond rates through my head but I can't.'

'Don't try to distract yourself. Concentrate on what you're feeling. I'll slow down. And don't hold your breath.'

She gave him a minute to slip back from the brink before she began again, slower now, lingering over the nerve clusters in the head and neck. He moaned in time to her thrusts but he held on; and moaning was an improvement over holding his breath. Finally, when he was trembling like a rabbit and bathed in sweat, she let him slip free of her mouth. Then she freed his wrists from the table leg.

At first he didn't move, but then his eyes opened and his fingers flexed. She smiled down at him. He could only blink.

'Want to fuck me now, Marty?'

He struggled on to his elbows and sat up. His chest rose and fell as his eyes moved over her naked body. He shook his head in disbelief. 'Mueller, you are so fucking gorgeous you bring tears to my eyes.'

Still sluggish, he wrapped his hands over her shoulders. He rose to his knees and pushed her on to her back. She parted her legs for him, waiting, wanting. He kissed her mouth first, his tongue working deep, his groans heartfelt. Obviously, he'd been wanting to kiss her for a while. His weight settled on to her breasts. He rubbed them with his furry chest. He strafed them with his nipples. They both caught a sharp breath.

She slid her hands down his back and cupped his broad, hard buttocks. 'I've got something for you in the pocket of my robe.'

Without so much as a curse, he reached over her head to grab the trailing hem, his cock springing up and down against her belly. He made quick work of the cellophane packet, then lowered himself between her legs. He pulsed against her lips again, thick and ready.

'Come inside,' she said. 'It's nice and warm.'

'No kidding,' he said. He wrapped his hand around

his shaft, adjusting his aim. 'I wish I could drag this out. I really do. But I fucking gotta fuck you.'

She laughed as he pressed inside, then groaned at the hot throbbing stretch of him. His cock was stocky like the rest of him, not so much long as wide. She writhed with an unaccustomed impatience. 'Give it to me,' she said, pushing up at him. 'Give it to me hard.'

Her order demolished his restraint. He lunged deep and gripped her bottom.

'Remember,' he said. 'You asked for it hard.' The words hadn't died before he was pumping into her, deep, swift thrusts that sent pleasure lapping outwards with every jolt. He seemed frantic to get deeper, as if more than pleasure depended on his penetration of her mysteries. But perhaps he feared she'd change her mind before he came. Every few strokes, he changed position, gripping her bottom to pull her more forcefully into his thrusts. She'd expected lots of 'fuck' and 'bitch' from him, but he muttered compliments as he drove himself in and out.

'Oh, yeah,' he said. 'That's good. What a sweetheart. What a gorgeous pussy. Oh, you're so good to me' and more of the same until she would have laughed if she'd had the breath for it.

Soon he was rocking in and out so fast she feared he'd beat her to the finish. She slipped her hand between their bodies to finger her clit.

'No,' he said, getting his hand under hers. 'Let me. You're so good. You're incredible.' His touch was firm and sure, a hard shimmying agitation that shoved her quickly to the edge of orgasm. The manipulation had little finesse, but it was effective. Her pussy tightened, her longing sharp and heavy. She blew out hard and rode the gathering wave.

'Hold on,' he panted, thrusting faster yet. 'I'm almost

there. We'll come together. That's it. I feel you. I feel you. God, you're so fucking wet. It's coming. Hang on. Not yet, I'm still – now, Mueller, now!'

Somewhere in the recesses of her mind a belt whistled and struck flesh. But she was laughing when she came. It bubbled up through her cunt and gripped his cock and shook them both into a cauldron of sensation. His hips jerked convulsively, drawing her orgasm into a second stab of pleasure. They sighed in unison and then he settled against her, his joints popping as he relaxed.

Julia kissed his raspy cheek. 'Thank you. That was lovely.'

'Oh, no,' he chuckled. 'Thank you. And it wasn't lovely, it was in-fucking-credible.' With a gratified sigh, he rolled her on top of him. 'Don't let go yet. I'm afterglowing.'

She rubbed her face across his meaty shoulder, unexpectedly touched. He was a nice sex partner, much nicer than she'd expected. But that didn't mean he wasn't a traitor. She drew a lazy circle around the small of his back. 'You know,' she said, 'Durbin really was upset about losing the Go-Tech account.'

'Was he?' Marty didn't tense a muscle, not even the one that nestled inside her pussy. 'I'm sure you could handle his disappointment. You never seem to get ruffled, no matter what he throws at you.' He yawned. 'To tell the truth, Mueller, I don't know what you see in him.'

'But he's your friend,' she said, her ears pricked for every nuance.

He shrugged. 'As much as he's anyone's friend. He's done a lot for me and I'm grateful. But if push came to shove, I know he wouldn't hesitate to stab me in the back.'

Did that mean Marty did it first? Did Santorini offer him something he couldn't resist? Money? A better title than senior VP?

'So tell me.' Marty gave her bottom a friendly smack. 'What do you see in that bastard?'

'Not what I used to,' she said, and let him make of that what he would.

Chapter Four

Marty shuffled back to his room, the image of a happy man: well fed and well fucked. Julia tidied the remains of their play and slipped on to the covered porch behind the kitchen. The air was frigid. She shivered in her velvet robe, but the stillness of the night was so seductively foreign she couldn't resist it. Gone were the rumble of traffic, the sirens, the hum of unknown machinery. Instead a soft rustling met her ears, the sound of feathery clumps of snow striking the eaves.

I'll be damned, she thought. The cowboy was right. As she peered through the fall, a flash of movement caught her eye. She leant over the smooth pine railing. Half-hidden behind a screen of evergreens, a deer lifted its head, its mouth working on something it had found beneath the snow. It appeared to be staring straight at her.

A tingle crept up the back of her neck. She stepped

on to the path that led through the yard from the kitchen stairs. The snow was cold and soft under her feet, an inch thick already. In the cloud-muffled moonlight she could see how hard it was coming down. The flakes melted on her skin and collected in her lashes. She laughed softly. The deer flipped its white tail and bounded away.

Goodbye deer, she thought, watching it disappear into the trees. She felt peculiar, as if a door were creaking open before her to reveal a strange and unexpected vista. Her encounter with Marty had been milder than her usual. She had laughed – with pleasure, not mockery – and so had he. She wondered whether having an affair with Durbin's protégé would anger him sufficiently to cast her off. Marty would certainly make a simpler partner. He wasn't obsessive. He didn't take life seriously enough for that. She hugged herself. Could breaking free be that easy? She had admitted what she wanted; had sent that desire winging into the universe, and here the ways and means were falling into her lap.

No. She shoved her hands under her arms. That was nonsense, wishful thinking. But she couldn't deny she felt lighter tonight, easier in her skin – and cold, of course. She was about to return to the warmth of the kitchen when she spotted a light in the stable. Zach had mentioned that he had horses. The closest she'd ever got to a horse was the mounted police who patrolled Central Park. She could change that now if she wanted. Surely there'd be no harm in taking a peek while they slept.

Zach had been brushing the same stretch of Starlight's withers for the past five minutes. Not that the mare was complaining. She loved being curried, especially now that her winter coat was growing in. No, he was the only one troubled by his distraction. He shook his head at himself. Twice now Julia's face had hovered before him as he shot his load, three times if he counted the fiasco behind the Coffee Stop. He'd come to the stable to puzzle out why he wanted this woman so badly. He'd wanted plenty of women over the years, but never with an eye towards keeping one. Usually, as soon as they got serious, he was ready to cut them loose. He shifted the brush to Starlight's back. He didn't think he wanted this one just because she didn't want him. As a rule, he wasn't so perverse, though some might call him harebrained, considering how slim the prospect of roping her seemed. She was a proud one all right. The memory of her scornful looks stirred a mixture of admiration and dismay. But as to why he wanted her . . .

His hand stilled at the mystery. Starlight shifted on her hocks, a gentle reminder to keep brushing. 'That's right, old girl,' he murmured, resuming the stroke. 'I haven't forgotten you.'

Maybe he wanted her because she gave off an air of live and let live. City girl or not, she wasn't a woman to crowd a man. She wasn't nosy. She was barely curious. Out here in Montana people sometimes lived so cut off they got starved to know every little thing about a person. Zach's family had given him a horror of too much closeness. From dusk till dawn, from birth till death, they did everything together on that blasted ranch: ate, slept, rode cattle, even fucked within a stone's throw of each other. Three trailer homes sat behind his parents' ranch to house his siblings and their mates. He could identify any family member by the sounds they made when they came. They thought he was crazy for closing the dude ranch now that he could afford to; said he'd go nuts rattling around with no one to talk to but Starlight and Buck and Gracie. But Zach was counting the minutes till he had the place to himself, which made the thoughts he was having about that tall drink of city water very strange indeed.

The stable was large and, while not warm, at least warmer than outdoors. The earthen floor had been swept and a queue of stalls marched down either side, all shipshape and empty as far as Julia could see. Clean as they were, the stalls seemed to be waiting, as if new tenants were expected at any moment. When she was halfway down the row, a scruffy black and white dog trotted out to greet her. She didn't bark, which Julia found strange, just snuffled a wet nose over her feet. She sat quietly when Julia knelt to pet the long fur between her ears.

An image of her younger self scrolled across her mind. She was reaching through the bars of a cage in a pet shop while an ecstatic Labrador puppy licked her fingers. Her mother stood behind her, patient but silent. Julia hadn't dared say please, but she knew her eyes said it for her.

'It would not be fair,' her mother had said in her crisp Swiss way, 'moving around the way we do.'

Julia had known she was right. The general always did the best he could for them, but sometimes they had a house with a garden and sometimes an airless apartment with barely enough room for the two of them. A healthy young dog couldn't live that way. Nonetheless, it hurt to leave that puppy behind. He'd never turn away, she'd thought. I could love him all I wanted.

Shaking off the memory, she gave this funny-looking dog a final scratch and stood. The dog padded after

Julia as she continued her journey past the neat, empty stalls. Finally, in a double-sized box near the end, she spotted a young horse – a colt, she supposed – curled up on a pile of hay. He was a rich chestnut brown with one white sock and a black mane and tail. His head was narrow, his legs gangly. They twitched as if he dreamt of chasing foxes. Julia wished she could climb inside and pet him, but she didn't have the nerve. Worse than getting kicked would be doing anything to harm the little horse.

She'd almost turned to go when she noticed a soft rhythmic noise, like an old-fashioned razor being stropped. Curious, she peeked over the wall into the next stall. There she found Zach stroking the sides of a large brown horse with what looked like a boot brush. His back was to her, but the loose fall of his shirt suggested it was unbuttoned. The plain blue cotton draped his shoulders, which rippled with muscle as he worked. His hair was damp from his exertions with Carolyn and a line of white skin marked the nape of his neck. He must have got his hair cut since the end of the summer. Her fingers curled with an inexplicable urge to explore the vulnerable stripe of skin. In fact, his whole neck was beautiful, tanned and strong, tendons moving beneath the close-cropped surface. She wanted to place her lips against it, to press her tongue to the shifting cords. Immune to such temptations, the horse half-closed its eyes, its ears flopped out from its head as if it were too relaxed to hold them up. It breathed out in what sounded uncannily like a human sigh.

'That's a sweetheart,' Zach said in a low, soothing tone. 'You don't care if I'm harebrained, do you?'

Julia didn't understand the words any more than the horse did. Zach had large, rough hands, red and chapped around the knuckles, but surprisingly clean around the nails. His strokes were so caring and steady that her chest tightened with emotion. The man and animal were at peace with each other, at one. The games she'd played with Marty, on which she'd so recently been congratulating herself, seemed worse than meaningless when set against a communication as honest as this.

A person like her didn't belong in this place. She was an artificial construct, a blight on the landscape. Never in her life had she used her touch as a straightforward expression of love. She had ordered others, whipped them, tied them, spanked them, made them cry tears of excruciating pleasure, but never had she touched another creature, man or beast, simply because she loved it.

She had no doubt Zach loved this horse. He declared it with his voice, with his hands, with the endless patience of his strokes. She wanted to turn away but the sight held her captive. Her lungs ached and her eyes stung with unsheddable tears. A sound caught in her throat. The horse jerked its head, ears plastered along its skull, teeth snapping the air.

'Hey there,' Zach soothed, catching its muzzle in a gentle hand. The horse snapped again and rolled its eyes. Julia's face heated, as though someone she admired had called her a bitch in the middle of a board meeting. She stepped back. Zach turned.

'Hey,' he said, surprised. The horse's head tossed between his hands, but its agitation didn't seem to alarm him. His eyes travelled down her velvet robe, warming with admiration. He broke into a smile that lifted his moustache and deepened the lines around his mouth. 'You must have crept up quiet as a bug.'

His twang made the words comical but she did not

laugh. She took another step back. 'Sorry. I didn't mean to scare your horse.'

'Aw, you can't scare Starlight here.' He patted the diamond-shaped star between her eyes. 'She's kid-broke.'

Julia didn't know what kid-broke meant but she could tell the horse didn't like her. 'I shouldn't be here,' she said, and turned to leave.

'Hold it right there,' he barked. Normally she was immune to the voice of authority, but something in his voice stopped her. 'You aren't going back outside dressed like that. No, ma'am.'

He took her wrist and led her towards a door at the far end of the stable. His hand was callused but warm. Its light clasp sent heat pouring to the soft, tender flesh between her legs, making her pussy feel heavy and full. She stumbled and he caught her elbow. He smiled at her, his eyes as blue as the Montana sky. His expression was so kind, so ordinary, that once again she had a sense of having stepped outside her rightful sphere.

'You're lucky I just mucked out,' he said. 'A stable is no place to be wandering around barefoot.' He wore a disreputable pair of cowboy boots, caked with mud and straw. Perhaps he saved the flame-sided boots he'd worn to the airport for formal occasions. He pushed a door open and flicked on a light. 'We keep extra duds for the dudes in the tack room.'

His tone suggested he meant to be humorous, but Julia was too dazed by her surroundings to smile. Leather filled the musty room: leather reins, leather saddles, leather crops. A worn bridle lay on a small desk, obviously awaiting repair. His stetson sat next to it, the crown scuffed and dented. She pictured him wearing that and nothing else. Oh, Christ, she thought, overwhelmed by a surge of lust. There was no escaping the arousal. The cramped room reeked of her favourite fragrance in all the world. Her limbs trembled. She pressed her thighs together and a trickle of warm, silky moisture squeezed between the lips of her sex. She'd loved the feel and smell of leather since she was a child playing dressing-up with her mother's shoes. The first time she masturbated, she'd been dragging a belt she'd stolen from the general between her legs. Sick, but true, and what's more she still had that belt. Over the years, so many erotic memories had become associated with the scent of leather that her response was very strong. She touched the bridle that hung from the nearest hook and ran her fingers over the curve of the brow-band.

Did Zach have any idea what a roomful of toys he had?

With an effort, she shook herself from her trance, though she didn't let go of the reins. 'You've got so much gear,' she said. 'Where are the rest of the horses?'

She almost jumped when he laid his hands on her shoulders. His chest grazed her back, warm and hard against her robe. 'My grandma and I hired horses from the neighbours if we got a big riding party. But there's no point keeping them around all the time, eating their fool heads off.' His hands stroked down her arms and up again. It was a liberty she shouldn't have allowed. His crotch brushed her bottom and for a second she thought she felt the ridge of a strong erection. 'I want to build a herd when I get a chance. Train 'em and sell 'em, you know. But for now I've got too many pots on the fire.'

'Pots on the fire?' she asked, her voice shamefully weak.

'Property management. I own a few lots in town. Here –' He reached above her head to pull something from the highest shelf. His groin touched her bottom again, and again her sex heated. He was hard. She was sure of it now. The knowledge unnerved and enflamed her. He handed her a pair of neatly folded, butter-coloured buckskin trousers. 'Try these on. I think you'll find they're more comfortable than those suits.'

She had to turn around to step into them. She expected Zach to look away but he didn't. Eyes focused on her hands, his lips tightened as she thrust her long bare legs into the trousers. In other circumstances she might have ventured a crack about cheap thrills, but his attention and the glove-soft feel of the leather joined forces to completely liquefy her insides. The cloth cupped her bare mound. She was going to get it wet. She was going to add her scent to the scent of the leather. Her hand shook as she pulled up the zip.

'Perfect,' he said, stroking his moustache. 'Those fit great.'

'I'm so gratified you think so,' she said, but the biting edge she meant to give the words was spoilt by their huskiness.

The sound brought him to attention like that funny dog of his. His moustache jerked up on one side. She ground her teeth. The stupid cowboy was grinning at her. He stepped closer. She lifted her hands to fend him off, but he'd already backed her into a wall of wooden shelves. He was heavier than she was, and broader. His chest wasn't bare as she'd expected – hoped, damn it – but covered by a thermal underwear top. Soft from many washings, the navy cotton hugged slabs of iron-hard muscle. They weren't the useless gym-bred sort Durbin and Marty sported, which did not excuse her complete lack of resistance. She'd let him back her into the shelves. She'd let him overwhelm her.

74

He slung his left arm behind her neck and pulled their heads closer. She meant to turn away but she was mesmerised by the approach of his eyes, his laughing, Montana blue, lash-starred eyes. She opened her mouth, one last chance to protest. He captured it before she'd made a sound and drove the wet spear of his tongue deeply, firmly inside.

A hum of pleasure escaped her control. He tasted of nothing but himself, slightly sweet, subtly metallic. His moustache was softer than she'd expected, almost silky. After the first deep thrust, his kiss softened, still greedy but playful, too. It was a kiss of surprising skill and charm. It reminded her of a square dance. Not that she'd ever been square dancing. But it had that sense of fun: light feet, light tongues. She responded almost without realising she'd done so, curling her tongue up the soft underside of his and sucking it gently deeper.

At once his kiss changed, like switching to a tango mid-dance. He made a hungry male noise, grabbed her waist and ground his hardened crotch over hers. He was taller than her but not by much. Their bodies fit together without a squirm. Oh, it felt good. The heat streamed out of his cock and up her cunt like sunshine in July. When he pulled his hips away she murmured in protest. Happily, the withdrawal was temporary, just long enough for him to fumble open her waistband and shove his hand between her legs. Her labia parted before his fingers, their rough length sliding through her lust-oiled folds. He groaned to find her wet, so wet his finger made a sticky, squelching noise as it eased inside her sheath. He drew it out and added a second, that entrance even noisier than the first.

She minded him knowing how aroused she was, but her body wouldn't let her pull back. Her body wanted more. Her body wanted to fuck him blind.

She breathed hard through the kiss, taking in the scent of leather, of man. Her knees began to give. She reached up to clutch his shoulders. Zach cursed softly against her mouth. He kneed her thighs wider and lifted one around his hip. Now his fingers moved freely, a steady, wet in and out. His thumb found the soft hood that covered her clitoris, pressing it over and around the little shaft. A ragged piece of skin scratched her with every pass. It felt so good she wanted to scream.

'Is that all right?' he whispered, the question panting hot against her lips.

She couldn't bring herself to answer, to participate any further in this stupidity. Besides, if she opened her mouth, she would order him to free that long thick cock and drive it between her legs. She closed her eyes and shuddered, her nails digging into him through his shirt, her head falling limply back.

She saw her mother's arm rise; heard the belt fall. The general cried out against his wrist and then, abruptly, the image was gone. The present jumped into focus. Zach's breath rasped in her ear. His legs sidled hers, the denim soft as velvet, the bulge of his cock pulsing on her inner thigh. She whimpered, a sound she couldn't recall making before. She was so close to coming that her sheath fluttered in anticipation.

'That's the way,' he said, cradling her neck more firmly in the crook of his arm. The pace of his fingers quickened, their rough spots jangling her nerves. 'That's the way. Ride it to the finish.'

Her stomach tightened and she gasped. So close. She seemed to ride a foaming wave, the anticipation as pleasurable as coming. Tingles swept her skin, hot alternating with cold. He licked a tendon at the side of her neck. His cheeks were damp, his mouth hot. He pressed his cock hard into the lee of her thigh. He rubbed it in tight, hungry jerks, not as if he were trying to come, just helpless to resist. Then he set his teeth against her skin and bit down.

She cried out at the love-bite but he didn't let go. His fingers worked her slippery flesh, lightning quick, diamond firm. Her cunt swelled, then drew in on itself. Her clit pulsed beneath the callused pad of his thumb. She quivered, her body escaping her control, and then she came, hard stabs of feeling that shot from her sex to the top of her head. The orgasm was better than anything she'd experienced lately, at her hand or anyone else's. The waves were hotter, more penetrating. They left an aftertaste of sweetness she could not deny.

He murmured endearments as she descended, the same way he'd murmured to the sleepy horse. The comparison returned her to her senses. No doubt he expected it was his turn now, but she was no dumb beast to be won over with a pat on the head and a handful of carrots. She was Julia Mueller, the hidden power at DMI.

She pushed him away so roughly he had to catch his balance on the battered metal desk. She yanked the edges of her robe together and cinched the tie.

'Very nice,' she said in her most condescending tone. 'I can see why that horse is so fond of you.'

His face darkened but he didn't say a word, merely folded his arms over his chest and rested his hips on the desk. His erection formed a monster arch she could barely tear her gaze from. As she strode from the room, his eyes followed her, prickling a spot between her shoulder blades. Despite the put-down she'd administered, she couldn't help feeling he'd got the best of the exchange.

He'd unsettled her.

'Damn,' she muttered, irritation warming her second barefoot trek through the falling snow. She didn't have time for this nonsense. She had less than two days to discover the culprit who'd betrayed DMI, less than two days to devise a sure-fire way to wrench herself free of Richard Durbin. Yes, she was interested in, some day, forming a more romantic attachment with a man, but not some stupid cowboy with hay in his hair and shit on his boots.

She stomped into the kitchen and shook the snow from her clothes. Her teeth were chattering, but she was too angry to care. She doubted the cowboy was looking for romance in any case. As far as she could tell, he'd screw anything that moved. He hadn't even waited to dry off from fucking Carolyn.

But it wouldn't happen again. From here on in she would focus on her purpose.

Her good feelings of half an hour earlier were history.

Zach's return to the house took him past the guest wing. He told himself he wasn't hoping for another glimpse of Julia, but in the end it didn't matter: her room was dark.

He shook his head at his own foolishness. But who could blame him? That kiss had been so promising, a sweet, aching, sinking together of mouths and bodies. She'd tasted so good. She'd fit him so well. Tall women were the best, tall meaty women with hair of gold and eyes like a mountain stream.

He rubbed the tightness at the centre of his chest. The imprint of her breasts and belly might have been burnt into his skin, so clear was his memory of it. He barely registered the light shining from the last window of the wing, except to wonder why one of the guests chose to sleep so far from the others. Then he drew up short. Had Julia changed rooms for some reason? Had she heard him and Carolyn making love? The possibility spurred a twinge of guilt. But the elegant young black man sat inside, his head bent over a scattered assortment of papers.

Few black people lived in Montana and he stood staring for a moment, rooted in place by curiosity. What was it like to walk in his boots? He'd barely said a word at dinner; barely looked up. Why was there such a distance between him and the others? Was the colour of his skin the cause, or some difference in temperament that none of them knew how to bridge?

He stroked his moustache in thought, jerking back to himself when he found snowflakes melting between his fingers. It sure was coming down. At this rate they'd get a foot, at least. This afternoon he'd welcomed the storm, but now he wondered if getting snowed in would do him a bit of good. He didn't know what he'd done wrong. Julia had enjoyed his kiss. She'd come so hard she'd squeezed his fingers to the bone. But as soon as she'd finished, she'd shaken him off like something she'd found stuck to her shoe.

She didn't strike him as the selfish kind, and he had reason to trust his instincts. He could always spot the yearling who'd hog the trough, who'd never be an equal partner to a man. But maybe her looks and manner had blinded him. Maybe her wrappings were so attractive, he hadn't looked hard enough at what lay inside.

No, he thought. I can't be that wrong. She is warm underneath. She is giving.

One thing was certain, though. Gentling a thorough-bred like Julia Mueller would not be a trot in the park.

* * *

Julia dreamt of the opening door. This time it lodged in the centre of her chest like a surrealist painting, full of clouds and mountains. A man on a horse rode down a distant peak and galloped towards the threshold. 'Yippee-ki-ay,' he shouted, waving a cowboy hat over his head. 'Crept up quiet as a bug!'

Julia bolted upright and pressed a fist to her pounding heart. Ridiculous. Utterly ridiculous. But she had a feeling the nightmare wasn't over yet.

Chapter Five

Saturday morning

Julia woke to a pearly grey light. Her body languorous, she indulged in a spine-warming stretch. Despite the dream that began the night, she'd slept soundly. Now a bone-deep relaxation weighted her limbs. If she hadn't had so much work to do, she might have lazed in bed, which was not a particularly productive impulse. Frowning at herself, she threw off the down-filled coverlet and padded to the window. Snow had blown against the panes during the night, leaving small portholes in their centres. Outside, white festooned the world. The ponderosa pines that bordered the guest wing were coated so thickly they looked as if they'd been dipped in meringue.

She pressed her nose to the glass. The snow continued to fall, slantwise now that the wind had picked up. This was nothing like snow in New York, which dirtied as soon as it fell, more nuisance than beautification. How wild this landscape seemed, how exhilarating and clean. A craving for hot cocoa made her stomach rumble. Definitely time to get dressed. Her glance fell on the buckskin trousers Zach had lent her the night before. If she wore them, would he take it as a peace offering? If she didn't, would he think her childish? She glared at the fan-backed chair on which they sat. To hell with it. Those trousers were more comfortable than her suits; he could think what he damn well pleased.

She dragged them on with a sense of rebellion, though what she rebelled against she couldn't say. Fortunately, she'd packed a turtleneck. Zach had left a hickey the size of Boston on her neck.

When she reached the kitchen she found everyone there except their host. The hour was early, but Carolyn and Ben were accustomed to being at work by eight. In recognition of his seniority, Marty generally arrived at nine and left at four. She deduced he'd been kicked out of bed by his stomach.

Her entrance provoked a wolfish whistle.

'I'll be damned,' Marty said, taking in her cashmere and suede. 'This makes twice in twenty-four hours I've seen you without your executive armour.'

Ben's gaze jerked from her to the senior VP, obviously jumping to the correct conclusion. He found his voice after a jaw-hanging pause. 'That outfit is flattering.'

Julia pressed her hand to her heart. 'Gentlemen, your approval overwhelms me.'

'Now if you'd just let your hair down,' Marty said, 'you might not frighten every man you meet.'

The banter would have continued if Carolyn hadn't cleared a circle in the window over the sink and announced she wanted to see the barn. Julia presumed she'd spotted Zach out there. Her stomach tensed. She dreaded seeing him again, though she'd be damned if she'd let cowardice dictate her behaviour. Perhaps she had put herself in the wrong by taking her pleasure and leaving him unrequited. She had not, however, asked him to kiss her in the first place, or do anything else for that matter.

She tugged the hem of her soft grey sweater over her waist. 'Yes,' she said. 'Let's all go see the barn.'

Marty led them into the hall. Of the four, Ben seemed the sleepiest. He rubbed his palms over his face and shook out his arms.

Julia handed him his coat. 'Up late reading?' she asked.

His exotic eyes warmed at the friendly question. 'Not too late. I'm afraid I'm not much good before I've had my coffee.'

'I guess the cowboy isn't used to early risers.'

'I guess not.' He smiled and Julia's heart tripped at the sheer force of his beauty. Such a lovely man. What a shame he was too nice to get nasty with. But at least he'd forgiven her midnight rendezvous with Marty. Ben was one of very few people whose good opinion mattered to her.

'Stop dragging your heels,' Marty urged, flapping Julia's coat behind her. 'I want to see the horses.'

'There's only two,' she said. The coat paused in its slide up her arms.

'Is that so?' He smoothed the collar around her neck. 'And when did Fräulein Mueller discover that?'

Julia didn't answer and Marty didn't press, though he did leer at her all the way to the stable. Unlike Ben, he seemed to relish the idea that she got around, as though in some convoluted way her conquests reflected well on him. She snorted to herself. She supposed that, to another male, the cowboy might seem a status-enhancing tumble: all that salt-of-the-earth, bucking-bronco brawn. Her relationship with Durbin, however, was a questionable addition to her cachet. But who knew what kink her bed habits had triggered in Marty? He had his secrets, too.

The scruffy dog met them at the door to the barn. She sniffed furiously at everyone's shoes, then barked once and plunked herself at Julia's feet. From there she stared adoringly up at her, wagging her feathery tail. Julia couldn't help feeling pleased at being remembered, though it was, perhaps, a silly thing to take pleasure in.

'That,' said Carolyn, 'has to be one of the ugliest dogs I've ever seen.'

Marty jostled her shoulder. 'Take care, Caro. Lots of men live by "love me, love my dog".'

Carolyn frowned, but he had worried her sufficiently to send her to her heels before the animal. 'I'm sure he's very bright,' she said, and reached out to pet it.

The dog growled at her. To Julia's surprise, Ben was the one to laugh. They all stared at him.

'Sorry,' he said. 'It's a she, though, and maybe she's jealous.'

Zach forestalled whatever quip Marty was going to make by appearing with a bucket of oats in each hand. He wore his grubby shearling jacket and a pair of equally grubby work gloves. His breath made clouds of white in the chilly barn. Carolyn waved, but his eyes went straight to Julia. She braced herself to face the questions in them, but whatever he wished to ask was hidden from her. His gaze slid down her legs and up again. She damned him silently for giving her a gift she couldn't resist. He didn't smile, but he nodded as if he, too, approved of her outfit.

'I see you've met Gracie,' he said, tilting his head towards the dog. 'Best cow-dog north of Bozeman.'

'She's adorable,' Carolyn said, and stepped forward to plant a kiss on Zach's startled mouth. She put some tongue into it, stroking the back of his neck with her slender, long-nailed hands.

Julia sighed under her breath. She suspected Marty's 'love me, love my dog' remark accounted for the public display of affection. Carolyn wanted to prove that this romantic encounter should be taken seriously and that she, Carolyn Q. Prentiss, had the power to drive men mad.

Her assertion would have been more credible if Zach had actually put down the buckets while she kissed him. Worse, Julia's sharp hearing caught the tail end of the plaint she murmured in his ear, something about not spending the night in her bed.

'Got my own room' was his matter-of-fact response.

Carolyn backed away. Cheeks flushed, she hid her embarrassment by making a fuss over the colt, which caused the little horse to dash around his box in what looked to Julia like panic, though Carolyn merely clapped in delight.

'Come away from there,' Julia said, braving the mare's teeth to pull her back. True to her fears, the older horse did try to take a nip at her, but got only air for her pains. 'You're scaring him.'

'Me?' Carolyn huffed. 'He's excited. He's playing.' She turned to Zach for support, but he shook his head and eased out of the mare's stall.

'Buck probably is a bit anxious, Ms Prentiss. He hasn't been around many strangers. Once he gets used to you, I'm sure he'll want to play.'

If Zach's failure to back her up disappointed her, his calling her Ms Prentiss was a slap in the face. She turned and walked stiffly towards the door, already patting her pockets for a smoke. Apparently, rejection had a bad effect on abstinence. Too focused on the horse to notice her departure, or her hurt, Zach stepped into the oversized stall. At once the colt stopped racing around. He crept towards Zach on trembling legs and butted his chest. He reminded Julia of a toddler clinging to his mother's legs. Zach stroked his glossy brown neck and spoke kindly. Seconds later the horse's nose was in the bucket and he was chomping away as if nothing had ever been amiss.

Julia was amazed and, though she fought it, entranced. No doubt the horse had known him since its birth, but even so the connection between them was magical. Zach's gaze caught hers as he left the stall. He stopped, struck by whatever he found there. His gloved hand rose to his moustache and for a second Julia felt his fingers between her legs again. The memory inspired a strident throb of arousal. She pressed her lips between her teeth, willing the feeling away, but her cheeks grew hot even as she did. She couldn't believe it. Of all people, Julia Mueller was being put to the blush by a five-minute hand job.

He touched her shoulder. 'You OK?'

Before she could stop herself she flinched.

'I'm fine,' she said. Flustered, and aghast at her loss of control, she turned to find Marty climbing the side of the colt's box. He reached down to pat its shoulders. A protest hovered on her lips, but the horse merely snorted and went on eating.

Marty flashed a delighted smile. 'You should try this,' he said to Julia and Ben, but Ben was peering into the tack room and Julia didn't dare, not even to overcome her disgust with her own spinelessness. Nor did Zach encourage her to approach the horse.

86

He crossed back into the stall lugging a bale of hay on a hook. 'Buck here has a partiality for men,' he explained. 'But I'll let him and Starlight into the pasture after breakfast and you can watch them run if you want.'

'You let them out in this?' Ben asked, nodding at the driving snow.

'You bet.' Zach forked a second load of hay into Starlight's feeding rack. 'I let them out in most anything. Horses get ornery if you keep them stabled all the time. They need to run.'

Just like people, Julia thought, then rolled her eyes at her fanciful turn of mind.

Finished with his chores, Zach slapped his hands against his thighs. 'Hope you're hungry,' he said. 'I've got a real ranch spread planned for this morning.'

As they left, he touched the small of Julia's back to usher her out. It was more a gentlemanly gesture than a pass, but she couldn't stop herself from jerking away again. He didn't take offence, though. In fact, he broke into a brilliant boyish grin. He looked as if he knew a secret: her secret.

Julia didn't relish that possibility one bit.

Zach's ranch-style breakfast provoked another of Marty and Carolyn's squabbles. She took him to task because he, the son of kosher parents, was eating pork sausage and bacon; he, in turn, accused her of cutting her food into such tiny pieces that her new boyfriend would conclude she had lockjaw. Since Zach had left them alone to their meal, Carolyn didn't pull any punches.

'Don't you worry,' she snapped, 'my mouth is big enough to cut you down to size.' Marty patted his crotch and volunteered to test her claim. Carolyn turned bright red and pointed her fork at him. 'You do that one more time and I'll have you up on sexual harassment charges.'

'Ooh.' Marty wiggled his hands. 'I'm trembling in my teeny-weeny jockstrap.'

Ben spit his eggs out on a laugh. Marty slapped his back.

'Watch out there, Ben,' he teased. 'Pretty soon we'll be thinking you've got a sense of humour.'

'You leave him alone!' Carolyn cried. 'He's twice the man you are.'

They were still sniping when Julia herded them into the conference room. The window-lined space contained an assortment of comfy chairs and low tables, all in shades of green and brown and gold. The effect was masculine but cosy, especially with the veil of snow falling outside. Marty immediately kicked off his shoes and stretched out on the couch. Julia knew the pose was deceptive. The others might resent him playing the grand pasha, but Marty's mind was as keen as it was ambitious. Of them all, he was likeliest to pull this strategy session out of the fire, which didn't mean the others couldn't help. They would help if Julia had anything to say about it. With that in mind, she handed each portfolio manager a leather-bound notebook.

'This is a collection of marketing ideas the three of you have run by Rich this year. They've been rejected for one reason or another, but they all have merit. Together you should be able to whip at least some into shape.'

Marty imitated a snapping cat-o'-nine-tails. 'Break out the whips,' he said.

Carolyn was not so sanguine. She tossed her copy on to the burled walnut coffee table. 'What's the point if Durbin has turned them down already? Besides –'

her cheeks pinkened '– you're not our boss, Julia. You're Durbin's secretary. Why don't you go make coffee or something?'

Ben gasped at the affront. Julia shrugged. A flyweight like Carolyn wasn't worth getting angry over.

'You can do as you wish,' she said. 'But I think you'll find this saves you time. Some of these ideas were never submitted formally, but merely mentioned in passing and perhaps not as persuasively as they might have been.'

'You've been collecting our ideas?' Ben asked, eyes wide.

'Only the good ones.'

'And just how would you know what the good ones are?' Carolyn demanded, still trying to put her in her place.

Marty sat up and clapped his hands to his forehead. 'Don't you get it, Prentiss? Don't either of you get it? Who do you think handles Rich's clients when he's golfing? Who interviews new hires before anyone else sees them? Who sets salary grades and decides what software our traders will use next year? Do you honestly think Durbin would waste his time on anything so unglamorous? Or, God forbid, bother to listen to any idea that doesn't come with a money-back guarantee?' He pointed a finger at Carolyn. 'Julia is the reason you weren't fired last month for slapping Mrs Harrington's nephew; never mind that he had his hand down your dress. And –' he shifted the finger to Ben '– she's the reason you were hired in the first place. Durbin didn't care how smart you are. He thinks black people belong on the basketball court.'

He sat back in his chair then, obviously embarrassed by his fervour. With a smile she couldn't contain, Julia kissed his raspy cheek. 'Now that you've whipped them into shape,' she murmured, 'I think I'll make coffee.'

As she made her way to the kitchen, she heard him call the others to attention.

'Let's get cracking,' he said. 'I know I can't afford to get sacked. I've got a mortgage payment you wouldn't believe.'

She was still glowing from his defence and it took a moment for the words to sink in. When they did, her hands stilled on the coffee maker. Did Marty have money troubles? Had he been vulnerable to a bribe from Santorini? She realised that her attitude towards him had changed. Marty might have his faults; he might even be her prime suspect, but she wouldn't enjoy turning him in.

After supplying her charges with adequate caffeine, Julia went in search of her second favourite tension-reducer. The cowboy claimed to have a gym. She hoped he didn't mean a broken Exercycle and a set of dumbbells.

Her expectations low, she descended the basement stairs. She found a surprisingly Gothic space. The walls and ceiling were constructed of smoke-stained brick, arranged in pointed arches like the vault of an old church. Some of the bricks had crumbled and been replaced. Zach's grandfather must have built his dream on the ruins of something older.

Don't we all, Julia thought, with a twist to her mouth.

The first door she tried opened on a wine cellar. Cool, dusty bottles lay in tall wooden racks. Curious, she stepped inside. To her surprise, the vintages were not restricted to Californian, and they were all first-rate. She touched a yellowing label, trying to adjust her presumptions. She didn't know which would have shocked her more: if Zach had amassed this collection, or if his grandparents had.

A laundry occupied the bay next to the wine cellar, followed by two communal showers. COLTS and FILLIES stated their heavy steel doors. That, she wagered, had to be Granny Taylor's doing. She peeked inside. The shower floors were tiled, but here, too, she found tall Gothic arches, their brick protected by a shiny, clear sealant. The effect was intriguing: debauched monastery meets sleek modern plumbing. A shiver of imagined possibilities raced down her spine. She'd return to this room, she decided, and she wouldn't return alone.

The next door opened on the exercise room. Julia's eyebrows rose. Zach had enough equipment for a professional gym. In addition to a wall of free weights, he had three kinds of bikes, a rower, a treadmill and a full complement of Nautilus machines. Her lips twitched as she envisioned his dear departed granny dusting these contraptions.

But perhaps his grandmother was the mastermind behind their purchase. You don't know, she reminded herself. You simply don't know.

She'd stretched upstairs so now she stripped down to her exercise clothes and did a quick set of pull-ups on the chinning bar. A few minutes on the rower got her pulse going, after which she switched to weight work. Her body began to hum under the workout, a sensual feeling that flowed outward from her sex in warm, blood-tingling waves. Julia was no body builder but she loved being strong; loved the sight of her body sheened in sweat or her muscles swelling into prominence as she worked.

She moved to the leg machine and watched herself

in the wall-length mirror, her eyes slitted with a mild endorphin haze. She wore a red sports bra and a matching pair of skin-tight, hip-high shorts. Her stomach muscles rippled with each disciplined breath, her thighs clenched, her calves rounded.

'You look as if you're enjoying yourself,' said a drawling baritone.

Julia's breathing faltered, but this time he did not make her jump. 'I am,' she said. She continued pushing, determined to finish out the set. A pair of long, callused fingers feathered over her shoulders. She shivered.

'I could put on some music,' he offered.

'No, thank you.'

He chuckled at her vehemence. 'Just a little jazz, Julia. I know how you city folks feel about the local tunes.'

She didn't answer and he left to turn on the audio system. Something sultry filled the room. It had a strong backbeat, but it wasn't fast. It made a tendon jump between her legs. She rolled her head against the padded bench, trying to stretch the tension from her neck.

Before she knew it, he was on her, swinging his leg over the bench so that he could straddle her belly. She immediately let the weights fall.

'What do you think you're doing?'

The cowboy grinned and that made her pulse race, too. Something had happened since last night to make him more aggressive, more confident. A considerable portion of his weight rested on her hipbones. She could feel the soft crush of his balls flattening across her pubis. He leant forward and braced his hands above her head. 'I'm just giving you a little extra resistance, darlin'.'

'Don't call me that.' She pushed at his chest but he wasn't budging. 'I want you off me.'

'But we have unfinished business, you and I.' He bent lower and nuzzled her sweaty collar bone. 'Mm, your pulse is racing, but I don't think you're afraid of me. No, I think you want to finish what we started last night as much as I do. You're just too proud to admit it. That's all right, though. I don't mind giving a skittish lady a little gentling.'

So that's what this was about. She'd shied away from him this morning, and he'd decided to treat her like his pals from the stable. She gritted her teeth. 'I am not a horse.'

'Maybe not.' He sat back and pulled his hands down her front. 'But I bet you could use a good rub-down.'

'You mean you could.' She stared pointedly at the ridge behind the fly of his jeans. She shouldn't have looked. Her mouth went dry at the thickness of the bulge, at the way it pulsed beneath the faded cloth.

'Oh, I definitely could,' he agreed. His thumbs brushed her nipples. From the twang that went through her, she knew they were hard. 'But I think you could, too.'

'I am not interested.'

His gaze moved from her breasts to her eyes. He smiled, a lazy crinkling of skin and lips. 'That was my first mistake, believing what your mouth said instead of your body.' He caught her nipples between his fingers and plucked them outward. A strangled sound escaped her throat. 'Glory be, Julia, was that a whimper?'

His teasing pushed her temper over the edge. Julia heaved hard and dumped him on to the floor. He hit the mat with a curse. She should have quit while she was ahead but she couldn't resist following him down to complete his humiliation. Too bad it turned into her own. All too easily he twisted free of her attempts to pin him.

'Oh, no,' he laughed. 'You can't pull that on me. I used to wrestle steers for a living.'

Then he sat on her and trapped her wrists.

'Fuck,' she said.

'My pleasure,' he responded, and swooped down for a kiss.

His mouth was as sweet as she remembered. 'No,' she moaned, tearing away, but her legs were parting for his hips.

His breath came faster. He pushed his crotch at hers. She pushed back. 'That's it, darlin'. Work with me. I ain't trying to break you. I just thought we'd both enjoy a ride.'

But they wouldn't enjoy anything if he didn't cut out the horse talk.

'Shut up,' she said, and buried her fingers in his hair. They writhed together, rolling back and forth between the machines. Their kiss was noisy, more greed than style. She clutched his back, then his buttocks. Her shorts were thin and she wore nothing beneath them. The shape of him branded her through denim and Lycra. He wriggled like a fish, trying to reach the fastening of his jeans. Too perverse to let him, she tightened her thighs.

'My zip,' he gasped.

'Aw, does it hurt?'

'Doesn't it hurt you?'

'I like it,' she breathed, and nipped his lower lip.

He winced, then nipped hers back and dragged her hands above her head. He rocked her hard, his erection mashing her clit dead on. He knew what he was doing to her. He watched her eyes as she climbed. She held

94

off, not wanting to give in, wanting to force him to come before she did. She kicked off her shoes; caressed his calves with her feet. His eyes narrowed. She craned forward and nuzzled his flannel shirt. She found his sharpened nipple on the second try.

'Oh, God,' he said, and she knew this was one of his sweet spots. His hold on her wrists slackened. She pulled them free and wrenched his shirt open. Buttons flew. 'Ah,' he sighed as she latched on to the tiny bud. She ran both hands around the curve of his buttocks and squeezed his balls. His cock jumped in its denim trap. He dug it into her, worked it over her, putting all his strength into each brutal jerk.

In spite of the vigorous treatment, she came before he did: twice. She'd never known a man to last so long. She lay under him, limp, drenched with sweat, and wondered what sort of a machine he was.

He didn't look triumphant, though. He looked desperate. He was shaking. His pulse beat visibly in his throat. He sat back on his heels as if unsure of his muscles' ability to hold him. When he rubbed his hands down his thighs, he left streaks of sweat on the worn blue cloth.

'Touch me,' he said, his thumbs stroking either side of his distended fly. 'I can't come unless you touch me.'

The confession perplexed her but, dom or not, she couldn't short him twice. She trailed her fingers down from his breastbone, savouring the firmness of his flesh. Every part of him was solid. He had a working man's muscle, a big man's bulk. Sweat sleeked the skin of his belly, matting the light covering of hair. She dipped a finger beneath his waistband to explore the hollow of his navel.

'Open the button,' he said, his voice rough, but vulnerable, too. 'Don't leave me hanging again.'

'I wouldn't do that,' she said and pressed the metal disk through its slit. She slid her hand behind the zip to protect him as she lowered it. His cock was hot against her skin. It pulsed with eagerness, then fell free. He sighed when she caught the heavy weight. She almost sighed herself. His cock was genuinely beautiful. Large enough to impress, but not to intimidate, it rose straight and tall from a bush of deep brown hair. She explored him slowly, finding her way through this lovely new territory. His skin was satiny smooth, and flushed a colour between old rose and russet. A single branching vein wound around the shaft, a graceful decoration, as if a Japanese painter had dashed it there for the sake of design. The crown was full, almost round, the two halves forming one mouth-watering whole.

Given his claim that he needed touching to come, she was surprised to find him so hard. She wondered if he had a problem with sensitivity, but as she began to stroke him in earnest it became apparent this was not the case. If anything, he was more sensitive than most men. The lightest touch provoked a dramatic response. He seemed alive to every nuance of every caress. She brought his inner thighs into her strokes, scratching up their hair-roughened skin. That made him quiver too.

A tiny thrill rolled across her shoulders as she imagined how he'd respond to a blow job. Very well, she thought. Very well indeed.

But touching him this way was a pleasure in itself. He was a fine, sensitive instrument and it was a joy to play on him. He shivered as she rubbed her thumbs in slow opposing circles over the hot zone beneath his glans. His neck sagged.

'Good Lord,' he said. 'You've got a sweet pair of hands.'

Still stroking with her thumbs, she added a rhythmic squeeze by compressing his shaft between the heels of her palms. His chest muscles tightened. He bit his lower lip so hard that the skin turned white. Any other man would have been coming. Any other man would have come twice over.

'What's wrong?' she asked softly. He focused on her with an effort. His face was dark with blood, his pupils dilated. 'Why can't you come?'

He groaned then pulled in a breath. 'My body's greedy,' he said. 'It likes to hang on to its pleasures. I –' He huffed again. 'I never did have the knack of coming quick. Not even as a boy.'

'Hm.' Julia's smile was just short of a laugh. 'I'm beginning to understand why you're so popular.'

'Are you? Well, that's something.' He closed his eyes at a subtle change in her stroke. 'Lord, that's perfect.' His buttocks tightened on her belly. He covered her hands with his own, more feeling their motion than guiding it. 'Yeah, that's – that's – ah, you've got such nice, big hands. Can you curl your fingers over the head? Can you? Oh, yes.'

He groaned his approval, his body rocking with pleasure, gently, dreamily. His expression was beatific. He wet his lips and rolled his head. His cock swelled between her hands and her pussy clenched in sympathy. Soon, she thought. Any second.

'Julia,' he said. 'God.' Then he came. The contraction was so slow his seed didn't spurt from his penis, it oozed. It flowed over her fingers and down his shaft and still he came, the pulses so pronounced she could count each one. They lasted a long time, at least a minute. Julia's mouth was hanging. Tantrists trained for years to come like this. How did an ignorant cowboy stumble on to the mystery, unless he came by it naturally . . .

His orgasm ended with a low sigh. He looked ready to keel over, so she tugged him forward, on to her. He was heavy but she was sturdy enough to support his weight. It seemed natural to put her arms around his back, necessary even. He was nice and warm and all this sweat was giving her a chill.

'Wow.' He turned his face into her neck. 'I've never felt anything like that. What did you do to me?'

'I – nothing.'

His chuckle rumbled against her throat. 'I understand. A woman like you needs her secrets.' He shifted higher and kissed the delicate hair that curled in front of her ear. 'You realise we're going to have to do this again, don't you? And next time –' his tongue crept out to wet her cheekbone '– I'm determined we'll both be naked.'

A sudden panic tightened Julia's chest. She should have fought it, but she didn't. She pushed him hard and squirmed out from underneath him. 'I need to shower,' she said. 'I'm getting cold.'

He was too sluggish to follow, though he did call out for her to wait. She didn't listen. The door to the ladies' shower had a lock. She used it.

There was only so much temptation a red-blooded woman could withstand.

His hand gripped the barred door so hard his palm hurt. He swore up a blue streak. He thought he'd had her this time; thought he'd finally found the answer. But here she was, shutting him out like before. He was hard again already. He wanted to slide inside her so bad he could taste it. She was naked behind this door. The water was pounding her lush pink flesh and he couldn't do a damn thing to join it.

He rolled his forehead against the metal. Patience, he told himself. Patience and courage were the primary qualifications of a good trainer. He was making progress. All he had to do was stick with it and eventually she'd come round. Eventually.

He tilted his head and stared at the arch above his head. If you love me, God, he mouthed, you keep that snow a-comin'.

Chapter Six

Saturday afternoon

Julia curled up by the fire with her biography of Alexander the Great, determined to spend a quiet and solitary afternoon. Alas, it was not to be. The wind picked up at one, wailing around the mountain like an army of lost souls. At two the power flickered. At four it died. Laughing and joking, the three portfolio managers joined her in the great room. Marty handed her the yellow legal pad on which he'd been taking notes.

'I've got writer's cramp,' he complained.

Julia took one look at his illegible scrawl and decided it was just as well.

Zach passed by with a torch and toolbox. He stuck his head in the entryway. 'Don't worry,' he said. 'I'll have the generator running in no time.'

Two hours later they were still working by firelight. Against her will, Julia found herself worrying about Zach. The cellar had to be freezing without any electric heat. She set her notes aside and stood up.

'Where are you going?' Carolyn asked.

'To rescue our host,' said Marty.

Carolyn popped up in her seat. 'I'll get him.'

'You're working,' he said, and tugged her back with one hand. He turned his eyes to Julia. 'Tell that cowboy to screw the generator. There are hungry people up here.'

As she'd expected, the cellar was icy. Zach had the generator in pieces on the floor. His lips were blue and the torch was dimming, but he was clearly reluctant to leave the enemy unvanquished. Such perseverance was admirable, she supposed, but stupid. A memory caught her blindside: the general sitting in the back yard repairing the chain on her bike. She couldn't have been more than twelve. He'd looked up at her and smiled. He had a dimple in one cheek and a cowlick where his hair parted. He'd seemed so normal, so much like any girl's father . . .

Rather than examine the sudden tightness in her throat, she planted her hands on her hips. 'Marty says he's hungry.'

Zach took one last reluctant look around. 'Guess this will have to wait till morning.'

'Guess it will,' she agreed.

They moved together to the stairs. As he had that morning, he ushered her up by laying his hand in the small of her back. Most men she knew wouldn't have dared. He had big hands. The chill of his fingers seeped all the way through her sweater. She fought an urge to either shake him off or chafe his cold extremities between her own. Rule yourself, she scolded, and managed to do neither.

But her control failed when they reached the kitchen. He'd been up since dawn, he'd spent the afternoon slaving in a frigid cellar, and now he had to cook dinner for four spoilt New Yorkers. Going soft was one thing. Being fair was quite another.

She followed him into the darkened room. 'I'll help,' she said.

He squeezed her shoulder, his smile brightening the gloom. 'Stove runs on gas, darlin', though I'd love the company.'

'I'm not company. I'm an extra pair of hands.' And I'm not your darlin', she almost added, except that she would have sounded snippy. Besides which, there was a tiny corner of her psyche that welcomed the endearment.

So I'm human, she thought, trying to throw off her irritation. This was not a surprise. The only surprise was that this particular man had inspired the weakness.

'I'd like to help,' she said more smoothly. 'You shouldn't have to do everything yourself.'

He laughed, the sound oddly joyous. 'Come on in then. We'll fire up this chuck wagon.'

He lit candles, more than they needed, and spread them across the tables and counter tops. Despite her resolve to remain aloof, she couldn't quite resist the mood he set. Even to a woman of her unorthodox experience, candles spelt seduction. When he handed her an icy German beer, her barriers wavered.

'Got to drink it before it thaws,' he said, and clinked her bottle with his own. 'Now.' He stared at the refrigerator as if reading its contents through the door. 'What do you think about three-alarm chilli?'

'I think very highly of it.'

He winked sideways at her, obviously attuned to her deadpan humour. 'Me, too. Especially on a snowy night. You can chop, can't you?'

'I can,' she said, 'and stir and measure, too.'

'Whooey.' He slapped his thigh. 'I knew you were a find.'

She laughed in spite of herself. The cowboy was cute when he loosened up. They worked in companionable silence until her curiosity got the better of her.

'Tell me about the rodeo,' she said as she stirred the cornbread batter.

He looked up from his pan of frying meat, his eyes shining with pleasure. 'You don't want to hear my ancient history.'

'I do,' she insisted. 'Tell me how many bones you've broken.'

'No more'n half a dozen.' He rotated one wrist in demonstration. 'Only got one pin. I know a rodeo clown who sets off metal detectors at the airport.'

'A clown?'

He tossed a bowl of onions into the ground beef. 'Clowns are the rescue workers of the rodeo. They pry riders loose if they get tangled in their gear. If somebody falls off, they distract the bulls so they don't get gored. They're the bravest, craziest men you'd ever want to meet. Braver than firefighters.'

She supposed this was high praise in a state with so much forest land. His hand stalled in the act of pulling a can of beans from the cabinet above his head. He was smiling faintly, his admiration for the men and his love of the sport written in his face.

After a moment, he looked back at her. 'You sure you want to hear this stuff?'

She nodded, feeling like a child waiting for a bed-time story. He must have read the sincerity of her interest, because he told her. He told her about bulls that tossed grown men over arena walls. He told her about horses that bucked so hard they'd go over backwards. He told her about roping calves with Starlight, and how Gracie the cow-dog once saved a junior rodeo champ from getting trampled by a sheep. Acts of bravery peppered his tales, and stupidity, and sorrow.

Finally, he covered the chilli pot and leant back on the counter, his thumbs tucked into the belt loops on either side of his crotch. 'You know what handlers say when you're waiting in the chute and you've drawn a hard ride, the kind of bronc that comes blowing out like Satan's minion?'

She shook her head.

'They say "cowboy up", which basically means grab your balls and hang on.'

'Gird your loins?' she suggested.

'Precisely.'

'But you want to draw a horse that bucks hard, don't you? So the judges will give you more points?'

He nodded in approval. 'A good stock contractor treats his animals better than his children. He won't ever try to break a rodeo bronc. A tame ride is a bad ride, and a bad ride won't bring in the crowds. Some folks say rodeo is hard on the animals and I don't deny that might be true in some cases. But I've drawn rides I knew were having as much fun as I was. When they toss you off, they'll prick up their tails and prance. King of the world. Bell rings after eight seconds, you know, and most riders have been bucked off long since. Cowboy might get the prize buckle, but the animal always wins.'

Julia paused in the act of chopping broccoli. 'You loved that life, didn't you?'

Zach grinned and blotted his forehead with his sleeve. The gesture half-hid his rosy cheeks. 'Yes, I did. But I've grown some since then. Now I'd rather have the horse working with me. Whew.' He coughed into the checkered flannel of his shirt. 'I haven't talked this much in years. You'll make me hoarse.'

'You tell a good story,' she said. 'I could listen all night.'

He looked down at his work boots, his cheeks flushing darker. Julia's heart beat out of time. He was going to ask her to spend the night with him. She could feel it. I want to make love to him, she thought, taking stock of her body, how warm it was inside, how easy and oiled.

He looked up and her heart stopped altogether. Could eyes really be that blue? Could they hold wisdom and simplicity and fondness all at once? The fondness surprised her the most. She didn't know what she'd done to earn it. She was sure he'd had avid listeners before. Unless, as he claimed, he didn't often talk this much. She could hardly hold his gaze it was so intense. Emotion glittered in his eyes. His hand moved. She knew he was going to touch her cheek; knew he was going to kiss her. What's more, she knew she was going to enjoy every second.

'Hey,' said Marty from the door to the kitchen. Zach's hand fell. Julia stepped back. 'What's all this laughing I hear? Who said you're allowed to have fun without the rest of us?'

'That's right,' Carolyn seconded, only her complaint wasn't so jovial. The gaze she sent from Zach to Julia was hard.

Zach patted Julia's shoulder. 'Julia here has been pitching in. She's earnt a laugh or two.'

Carolyn drew in a sharp breath. Before she could say she would have helped, too, Zach offered everyone a beer. Julia shook off her disappointment. The moment was over and good riddance. She had no reason for regrets.

* * *

They ate on their laps before the fireplace, washing the spicy chilli down with bottles of icy beer. Julia relaxed into the mellow mood. The VPs had progressed at their mission and the blizzard made everyone glad for shelter and company. Marty had thirds of everything and Carolyn actually emptied her bowl.

'This is nice,' said Ben. He sat on the braided hearth rug at Julia's feet, his long legs crossed, his elegant head resting on the couch cushion beside her knee. 'We ought to leave the generator off all weekend.'

Marty cracked another beer and passed it to him. 'I don't know, Ben. You may be singing another tune when you toddle off to your icy bed.'

'Guess I'll have to recruit a bunkmate.'

For a second everyone was speechless.

'Ben,' Carolyn giggled, too drunk to realise how silly she sounded. 'I didn't know you could be so naughty.'

Ben tipped his head back and winked at Julia. 'A lot of people didn't.'

Oh, Ben, she thought, stroking his temple with her thumb. If you only knew how tempted I am. She heard Zach shift in the opposite corner of the couch and knew he was watching her. She sat Indian style, but his legs were stretched out, his white-socked feet mere inches from her thighs. She fought an urge to check his reaction or, worse, reassure him that she had no intention of sleeping with the beautiful young man. Slowly, she pulled her hand back from Ben. She felt preternaturally aware of her own body, of the embrace of the leather couch, of her sex pulsing inside the soft buckskin trousers. She shouldn't have worn them again. She could still feel his fingers dipping inside her; could still taste his kiss. She curled her hand into a fist. She had to stop obsessing on Zach. She had to pull herself together.

'We should tell stories,' Marty said. Carolyn groaned but, as usual, he ignored her. 'Hey, what better way to warm up a cold night? We'll trade firsts.'

'Firsts?' Carolyn was curled into an armchair by Zach's end of the couch. Marty sat at her feet even as Ben sat at Julia's. 'You mean sexual firsts?'

'Exactly.' Marty's grin was pure mischief. 'And everyone has to tell something really intimate, so we'll all be equally easy to blackmail.'

'Hm.' Ben sounded doubtful. 'What if everyone tells their most embarrassing first and the last person chickens out?'

The senior VP had an answer for that, too. 'The least trustworthy person goes first.'

'Well, that would be Julia,' said Carolyn.

Marty and Ben both laughed. 'Like hell,' said Marty. 'That would be you.'

'Me?'

Marty squeezed her knee. 'Yes, little miss I-couldn't-keep-a-secret-if-you-paid-me.'

The fire wasn't the only thing turning Carolyn's face pink. 'I can too keep a secret.'

Marty shrugged. 'Now's your chance to prove it.'

'Fine. I'll tell you something so outrageous you'll have to work hard to top it.' She sat up straighter and stuck out her narrow chest. 'All right, listen and learn, Marty. This is the story of the first cock I ever saw.'

'Big deal,' he scoffed.

Carolyn smacked the side of his head. 'For your information, it happened to be my Uncle Biff's.'

Ben squirmed. 'Are you sure you want to tell us this? You have been drinking and maybe tomorrow you'll regret it.'

'Don't be silly, Ben. I can hold my liquor. Besides –'

she flicked a lock of hair from her brow '– someone has to get the ball rolling.'

Marty lifted his beer. 'Here's to rolling balls.'

'Stow it,' said Carolyn, and composed herself to begin. 'OK. When I was growing up, my family had a big beach house on Martha's Vineyard where we spent the summers. Between grandparents, parents, cousins and my six uncles there were almost thirty of us. Grandpa Herbert had married four times and had children by every wife, so by the time Uncle Biff came along, there were only five years' difference between him and the eldest child of Grandpa's first son, which was me.'

'Oy,' said Marty. 'My head is spinning already.'

'Ahem. Do you want to hear this or not?' Marty pretended to zip his lips. Carolyn resumed. 'Despite the measly five years' difference between us, Biff liked to lord it over me, never letting me forget that he was a member of the ruling generation. For sixteen years he made my summers hell until, lo and behold, the means to torment him fell into my lap.'

'When you blossomed?' Marty suggested, leering in anticipation.

Carolyn smiled down her nose at him. 'Yes, I blossomed and Biff noticed with a vengeance. He was mortified that I, his former victim, suddenly possessed the power to make him jump in his jock just by walking into a room. The fact that his desire was forbidden only made it worse. But even if he'd wanted to bully me into gratifying his unnatural longings, he couldn't with all those relatives around.

'So I could torture him as I pleased. I could wear my shortest shorts and my teeniest tops. I could sit on his lap when we piled into the car to go to the drive-in, and I was forever brushing against him "accidentally".

Unfortunately for Biff, on top of being a young man in his prime, he'd inherited Grandpa Herbert's sex drive. My cousins and I started placing bets on how quickly I could drive him to the bathroom to masturbate. Five minutes was the record, but I preferred those times when he could make no escape and I could force him to suffer for hours.

'This might have gone on all summer were it not for my staying home one day to nurse a younger cousin who'd taken a bad case of sunburn. The poor thing had finally fallen asleep when who should wander back from the beach but dear Uncle Biff. He pretended he'd returned for a book, but in truth he couldn't stay away from me.

'We sat in the kitchen talking about the universities I might go to. He wanted me to attend Harvard, like he did. I preferred Princeton, but I let him chatter and, as I did, I drew one foot up on my chair and pretended to scratch my knee. I had my usual short-shorts on. To make matters worse, for Biff at least, they were loose in the leg and I wore nothing beneath them.

'All of us girl cousins had taken to grooming our bikini hair that summer. I'd trimmed mine so close that poor Uncle Biff barely had a veil of smoke to shield his gaze from my bare pink pussy. His eyes kept sliding down my thigh to make sure he was really seeing what he thought he was seeing.

'Now Biff was a slim, lanky guy: good-looking in a preppy way and hung like a horse. All he had to restrain his giant organ was a pair of yellow Speedos. You can take it from me they weren't up to the task. He was so hard I could see the slit of his cock where it pressed the stretchy cloth. My sixteen-year-old eyes were popping, but I wasn't about to be distracted from my goal. I spread my legs a little wider and trailed my finger down the cleavage of my halter top. I was getting off on teasing him, of course, so my nipples stood out like bullets.

'As soon as Biff caught sight of them he stood, mid-sentence, and scurried off to the bathroom, so hard he was bow-legged.

'Well, the house was virtually empty and my curiosity was roused beyond resistance. I tiptoed after Biff and flung open the bathroom door. He had his dick in his hand and was pumping like mad, his face as red as if he'd been a sunburn victim. He turned when he saw me, said something like, "Oh, God, Caro" and dropped his quivering pole.

'It didn't drop far. In fact, it stood a little higher as I watched. I couldn't believe how huge he was. His dick was longer than my hand and thick around. The head was dark, almost purple, and a bead of clear fluid was rolling down the groove between the halves. The sight made my heart pound. Biff's, too. I could see a vein throbbing in his belly where he'd shoved his swimsuit down. His pubic hair was honey gold and not very thick. He was breathing hard. The noise of it filled the whole bathroom except for the sound of the tap dripping: drip, drip, like cream dripping from my pussy.

'His hand flexed at the top of his thigh and I knew he wanted to touch himself again; knew he could hardly bear not to. I was sure he wanted me to watch, but I had something even better in mind.

'"I could help you with that," I said, strolling into the room like a pint-sized Queen of Sheba. "But it would have to be a trade. You see, I need some help with this." I slipped my hand up the leg of my shorts and into my pussy. He moaned when he saw my fingers disappear. Before I knew it, he was on his knees eating me out. He was so sloppy it made me laugh,

110

but it was exciting, too. He ate me as if he really loved the taste, just sticking his whole face in there, you know? It didn't take me long to come and when I did there was no mistaking it. My body stiffened like a board and I moaned so loudly I could only hope our little cousin was a deep sleeper. Beads of sweat popped out on Biff's brow at the sound.

'"Now me," he said. I wasn't what you'd call sated, but what did I know about being assertive back then? What he'd asked seemed fair enough and I did want to touch him. Other boys had tried to get me to do it but, oddly enough, I never felt as safe with them as I did with Uncle Biff.

'"Like this?" I said, and took him in a grip better suited for opening pickle jars. Biff yelped and said, "Easy. Rub it easy. That's it." He clutched his balls with one hand and dragged my hand up and down his pole with the other. It was love at first touch, I think. I adored how hard I could make him, how he jumped in my hand and how, just by rubbing his dick, I could make my enemy beg for mercy. "Ooh, rub the head. Please, please," he said, sounding as if he'd sell his soul to have me do it. I wrapped my second palm over the helmet. It was slippery from all the pre-come he was leaking. He shuddered as soon as I moved. "Yes," he said. "Right there." Around and around I went, loving the satiny hardness of it, the fruit-ripe swell. Biff's knees started to twitch and his head fell to my shoulder. "So good," he said. "So fucking good."

'Poor Biff tried to make it last but his hormones were up and I'd been pushing his buttons for weeks. He started to whimper like the family dog when it needs to go out. He put his hand around mine again and squeezed it tighter. "Faster," he said. "Twist your palm on top. Oh, Christ." Then his cock got even hotter and

111

stiffer, and he started to thrust really fast through my grip.

'"Are you going to come?" I asked, because I didn't want to miss anything. But he could only groan because he was shooting into my palm already and dripping on the floor. I'll never forget how those little pulses felt, all warm and slippery. I'd always thought there'd be more but, even so, watching him come was very cool. I especially liked the way his body tensed, as if that much pleasure was hard work. He made noises, too, grunting like weightlifters do. As soon as it was over, I knew I couldn't wait to do it again.'

'So did you?' asked Marty, craning his head around to look at her.

Carolyn curled her hands over her knees and smiled. 'That,' she said primly, 'would be another story.'

Julia clapped, sincerely this time. 'Very nice, Carolyn. Marty will be hard-pressed to match that.'

Carolyn flushed with pleasure. Marty rolled his eyes and rubbed his stubbled cheeks. His knees were drawn up, but the shadow between them could not hide the bulge that Carolyn's account had inspired. A quick look around told Julia the other men were in similar straits. She felt nicely steamed herself. Someone was going to get lucky when this gab-fest ended. She could personally guarantee it.

'Well,' said Marty. 'I admit that was an arousing little anecdote, but it's nothing to the tales I could tell.'

'Oh, bull,' said Carolyn. 'Put your money where your mouth is.'

'I'd be happy to, my dear, if you'd be kind enough to reach me another beer.'

Carolyn grumbled, but she pulled a bottle from the snow-filled cooler. She opened it, too. Julia hid a smile beneath her downturned face. Carolyn really was born to serve.

Marty took a long swig and cleared his throat. 'I'm not going to tell you what kind of first this is because I'd hate to ruin the surprise. But this first came into being because my wife took a liking to the new pool-boy. We bought a place on Long Island last year. As some of you know, Didi has a competitive streak as long as the Great Wall of China. When she heard the neighbour ladies cooing over what a studly specimen the pool-guy was, she decided she would be the first to seduce him.

'It wasn't an unrealistic expectation. Didi's a good-looking woman: pretty face, great tits. Plus, she knows how to chat a guy up. Pretty soon the pool-guy's giving her special discounts on chlorine and shit, drinking her lemonade, staring at her breasts – all of which I gotta hear about *ad nauseum*, so I can be jealous, of course. Being the bastard that I am, and knowing my wife pretty well, I pretend I don't give a shit. But she's still got the neighbour ladies to impress, so she doesn't give up. Finally, she manages to lure the pool-guy into the house where he sees our wedding picture. "Ah, you're married," he says and naturally she uses that as an excuse to tell him what a skunk I am; how I cut up her charge cards the month before; how I go at her in bed till she feels like a hamburger, which isn't true, mind you. OK, once she got this cramp and I was, uh, too caught up in the moment to stop, but I swear it's not a regular thing. I would never –'

'We're sure it was only the once,' Julia assured him. 'You may continue.'

Marty rubbed his temples and sighed. 'OK, enough of the domestic discord. The thing you need to know about Didi is, she may be devious, but she couldn't

113

pull off a plot if Mussolini came back from the dead to hold her hand. Rather than *shtup* the pool-guy while she's got him oozing sympathy, she decides she's going to set up an assignation and then arrange for me to walk in on it. Then I'll be sorry, she reckons. Then I'll know she means business.

'Well, God knows how she convinces the pool-guy to come at the appointed time, but she does. Then she calls me at work saying the hot-water heater burst and I need to come home to help mop up. I'm not happy about it, but she's crying, so I say OK and head for my car. So far, so good – only Didi's forgotten it's not rush hour, which cuts my drive in half. She decides she has just enough time to run to Victoria's Secret for something to wow the pool-guy. Thing is, her luck being what it is, on the way back she gets stuck in traffic.

'Meantime, I get home, throw off my jacket, roll up my shirtsleeves and call out her name. No answer. Then I hear a voice from the bedroom. It doesn't sound like her but, who knows, she's been crying. Maybe she got froggy. I walk in and there's the pool-guy lying across my bed, stark naked, with his big, meaty *schlong* pointing at the ceiling. I see why the neighbour ladies think he's a stud. He's built like a swimmer, big chest, narrow hips, muscles so lean you'd think they were painted on. And that thing in his fist is nine inches, easy. He's working it kind of lazy, as if he's got all day and isn't worried about losing his edge. He's also got a dozen of my favourite Pierre Cardin ties scattered around the mattress. Well, I don't understand the ties, but I can add two and two, except I'm not adding it quite the same as the pool-guy.

'"Where's Didi?" he says. Well, if he doesn't know, I sure don't. Then he waves his hand. "That don't matter," he says. "I'd just as soon start without her."

114

Turns out, ever since this guy saw yours truly in the wedding photo, he's had a yen for me. For me, hairy old Marty Fine. Didi promised him a threesome. Guess she reckoned I'd walk in on them, blow a gasket, and she'd never have to pay up.'

'So what did you do?' asked Carolyn.

'I didn't know what to do. I'm standing there, my jaw hanging, kind of pole-axed, and the pool-guy – Barry was his name – rolls over and puts his hand on my crotch. That's when I realise I'm hard. I've got the Eiffel fucking Tower in my trousers and I don't even know it till he touches me. He smiles and his teeth are so white against his tan that he just about blinds me. "You know," he says, "you really haven't had a blow job until you've had a blow job from a guy." The words send this weird shiver through my cock. This Barry's no dummy. He can see I'm nervous but he knows there are plenty of guys who won't turn down a blow job, no matter who's offering, and, God knows, I guess I'm one of them. But "Is it really better?" I say, trying to sound sceptical. "It's better," he assures me. "A guy's mouth is harder and bigger. I can swallow you whole, Marty. And I won't be pissing and moaning about my jaw getting tired because I'll be loving every minute." "Well," I say, while what feels like a rumba band plays in my dick. "If you do me, I gotta do you. I may be a skunk, but I have my principles." "This is not a problem," says Barry, and he flashes that grin again, like an ad for a good orthodontist.

'So we get me undressed and we lie on the bed and he goes for it. It's everything he promised, only better. His mouth isn't just hard, it's soft, and – swear on my mother's grave – loving. I never felt as if anybody loved my cock before, but this guy worships it. He's got me so wet I'm dripping and I've only met one other person, who shall remain nameless, who used her hands the way this guy used his hands. He gave me a full cock-and-ball massage. Every time I got close to shooting, he'd back off and start again. I'm not ashamed to say that after the first couple of times I was crying like a baby. "Please," I finally say. "Please let me come." Then I see what he means by having a strong mouth. He sucks me so hard I can feel my skin stretching. He's got his thumbs on my balls and his fingers kneading my thighs, and I feel this tingle start in my toes. It races up my legs and into my tailbone and, whoom, I'm shooting my load down his throat. The orgasm is so strong I feel as if my eyelashes are coming. "Oh, God," I think as I'm lying there like a dishrag. "Now I've got to do him."

'But he don't want me to. He wants me to kiss him which, to me, seems harder than giving him a blow job. But I believe in fair play so I give it a go and, what do you know, soon I'm getting into this, too. He's a beautiful kid. Maybe it's a narcissism thing or maybe I'm not as straight as I thought. Whatever, I'm liking the feel of him in my arms. It gives me a kick that I can arouse him, as if I've got this power I never suspected I had. I mean, I'm used to turning women on, but men, this is new to me. Anyway, after a bit of rolling around and kissing, I'm hard again myself. "Take me in the ass," he says. Whoa. My eyes are bugging at this. I've never even taken a woman that way. But Barry's a persuasive guy and between the novelty of it and the second massage that he gives me rubbing the KY jelly over my cock, I'm pretty well up for it. So he lies down on the bed with his butt in the air and his legs bent up like a frog's. "Take it slow," he says. "You're thicker than I'm used to."

'Damned if I don't feel flattered. It takes ten minutes

to get me in and we're both laughing. That's weird, too, 'cause it's like two guys laughing over beers or something. A new twist on male bonding. I didn't expect it to be fun and I feel, I don't know, excited as hell, but relaxed, too, 'cause it's just us guys and who cares if I fuck up. He's feels incredible down there. It's smooth and tight and it moves like a woman moves inside. I guess Barry likes the way it feels, because he's groaning and saying, "Thrust, Marty, thrust!"

'I do, of course, and it's incredible. Soon we're huffing and puffing and sweating like pigs. The bed is making this God-awful racket and I'm praying Didi won't come back from wherever the hell she is, because I really want to see this to the finish. Barry's starting to sound pretty desperate himself, so I reach under him and grab his cock. He's hard the way only twenty-year-olds get hard and hot enough to burn my palm. He shoves himself into my hand and on to the mattress with so much force my wrist goes numb. "Yeah," he says. "Oh, fuck, yeah," and a second later we're both blasting off. I mean, the first time we ever screwed and we're coming together like Romeo and fucking Juliet. "That's the first time that ever happened to me," he says. "But I hope it won't be the last." God help me if I know what to say to this. I'm still shaking. I don't know what I want, so I say: "Tell me one thing, Barry. What are the fucking neckties for?" "Ah," he says. "That was your wife's suggestion. She says you like being tied up."'

'Do you?' Carolyn asked.

'Hell, no. That was probably Didi's idea of a joke.'

Ben turned and draped his elbow over Julia's leg. 'So what did Didi do when she got home?'

'Nothing. Barry was long gone by then. Didi probably decided he'd never showed, so she made up some story to explain why she'd lied about the hot-water heater. I pretended to believe it and we went out for a nice dinner.' Marty grinned. 'As you might imagine, I'd worked up an appetite.'

Carolyn couldn't contain her curiosity. 'So did you see Barry again?'

'That,' Marty said with an echo of her own finish, 'would be another story.'

Carolyn glared at him, then reached over to pat Zach's arm. 'You next, Zach. We want to hear your story.'

'Um,' said Zach. The leather creaked as he shifted in discomfort. Julia looked at him, wondering if he'd open up to everyone the way he had to her in the kitchen. She wanted to hear his story, but she also wanted those moments to be special. His eyes lifted and found hers. His smile woke a hidden fan of wrinkles. Something hot and sharp pricked her breastbone. A flush crept over her cheeks. He couldn't know what she was thinking. He couldn't.

'I'm just an observer here,' he said.

'No, no,' said Marty. 'You've broken bread with us. You're one of the gang now. You've got to spill your guts.'

Zach shook his head, his eyes still warm on Julia's. 'I don't mean to be rude, and I appreciate your letting me sit in, but I don't have it in me to tell a story like that.'

Julia knew he did but she didn't say a word, not even when Carolyn and Marty set up a chorus of pleas.

'I'll go,' said Ben, probably more out of sympathy for Zach than any desire to be the centre of attention.

His offer distracted Marty. 'Ben-ster!' he said. 'Reveal your mysteries. Invite us into the seamy, steamy world of the private Ben Isaacs.'

Ben's chuckle sounded embarrassed, but not painfully so. 'I don't know how seamy this story is, but it definitely was a first for me.' He drew his long legs up and wrapped his arms around them. His eyes glowed in the firelight, green as glass. Ben's mother had come from Jamaica and his faint, second-hand accent made the words flow like music. 'All right,' he said. 'A few months ago I went to a club in my old neighbourhood. It's not a bad neighbourhood, but it's not a great one, and the Blue Note is strictly low rent: the kind of place you don't want to see in the light of day. At night, though, with candles on the tables and fans turning the smoky air, it can stake a claim to ambience. Sometimes the floor is sticky, and sometimes the smoke isn't all tobacco. But the food is always good and the music . . .' Ben shook his head. 'The music is a beautiful secret whispered in the dark.'

'Old timers play there, old jazz greats no one ever heard of and no one ever will, because they can't get out from under bad breaks and worse habits. Sometimes, in the middle of a set, one of the musicians will nod off under the influence of his personal poison. Nobody's surprised. The manager walks over and shakes him awake. No big deal. It's a sad place, I guess, but when those old guys play you can hear devils and angels falling in love. I go there to remind myself where I came from; of the pitfalls I want to avoid and the riches I can't bear to lose. I never hear the same riff twice at the Blue Note, but I always know what I'll find.

'Not this night, though. This night there's something different. A woman is dancing in front of the stage, a customer, not a performer. Everyone's watching her because people don't dance at this club. They drink their drinks and they smoke their smokes, and they sit real quiet and listen.

'I can see this woman is stoned out of her mind: drunk, it looks like. She's wearing a skin-tight red satin dress and a couple of carats' worth of diamonds around her neck. She's got the body of a geisha, slim, firm, girlish curves. And, man, can she dance. It's a slow, snaky kind of dance, with her body curling out and pulsing back like Eve in the garden. Her eyes gaze off into the distance. She's the only white woman in the place and I know there's going to be trouble. It's not a bad crowd, but it's not Sunday school and she stinks of too much money and booze.

'The crowd knows there's going to be trouble, too. They're holding their breath as if they're waiting for a car wreck. Then the woman turns and I realise I know her. I can't remember her name, but she's the wife of someone I met at an office party. She's got the eyes of a wounded doe, like bruises in her face. You know how some women seem to ask for trouble just by breathing? As if there's a sign on their forehead that says: I've been hurt before and now it's your turn?'

Ben paused. The fire crackled in the hush. He pressed his fingers into his thighs, steepling them until the pale ovals of his nails turned white. He didn't look at Carolyn, but the omission required such force of will that both Marty and Zach turned their eyes to her. If she noticed any parallels to her own character she didn't show it. She was listening so raptly her delicate pink lips were parted with anticipation.

'What next?' she whispered. 'Did you go to her?'

'Well, I couldn't just stand there and watch. I squeezed through the tables and said, "I'm Ben Isaacs. Do you remember me?" "Oh, Ben," she says in this whispery, girlish voice. "You'll dance with me, won't you?"

'I guess I got mad, or maybe I was afraid she wouldn't listen if I was polite, because I said, "Don't be a stupid cunt, Mrs X." I remembered her name then. I remembered it as soon as I heard her voice.

'She looked like a little owl blinking at me, as if she'd never dreamt anyone would call her a stupid cunt. Before she could get into any more trouble, I grabbed her arm and dragged her out of there. Nobody stopped me. I guess they didn't want to see a car wreck after all.

'When we got to my Audi, she wouldn't tell me where she lived. "Take me to your place," she kept saying. "Take me to your place, beautiful Ben, and we'll fuck until the sun comes up." She thought this was funny. She had this husky little laugh with a catch in the middle. The sound of it was making me hard. She'd squirmed over to my side of the seat and she ran her hand up and down the inside of my thigh. She didn't touch my cock, but that was worse somehow, because then I wanted her to touch it even more.

'She was gorgeous with her hundred-dollar haircut and her red satin gown and some stinging sweet perfume, like a hothouse orchid set by a fire. I couldn't drive around for ever so in the end I did take her to my place.

'Cute, she called it, and I knew she had bigger closets. I wouldn't let her drink any more so she started to undress. I couldn't take my eyes off her. She was so fucking pale she glowed. I'm going to touch her, I thought. I'm going to put my black hands on her pale white body. Stupid, but that was all I could think of: how my hands would look on her; how her hands would look on me. I was so hard my teeth were chattering.

'"You've never had a white woman before, have you?" she said. I shook my head. She beckoned me closer. Then she undressed me. I didn't lift a finger. I watched her. When all my clothes were gone she drew me down beside her on the fake Persian rug. She put my hand on her breast and sidled her leg between my thighs. "Aren't we beautiful?" she said. "Aren't we the most beautiful thing you've ever seen?" When she said it, it seemed to me we were. Her skin felt different from what I was used to, and it smelled different: more fragile, less rich. Shivers ran down my spine when she trailed her long white finger down my cock. "Fuck me," she said, and I knew I was going to.

'She didn't have a condom. I knew she wouldn't. I got one of mine and made her put it on me. She thought that was cute, too. Dudley Do-Right, she called me; said a man like me could reform a woman like her. I knew better but I didn't care. I'm going to fuck her lily-white pussy, I thought. I wanted to stop myself from thinking that way but I couldn't, like a song that's stuck in your head.

'"Ride me," I said because I wanted to watch and because you can't trust a woman like that not to go round the bend if you make a wrong move. Let her make the moves, I thought. It's worked out fine so far. She lowered herself on to me real slowly, as if she knew I wanted to see my cock disappear inside her. It was something to see. I'd never felt so big, so dark. She rode me in waves, one curving rise at a time. Her movements were so much like her dance at the Blue Note, I thought she must be hearing the music in her head: the musky smooth sax, the throaty, thrumming bass.

'"Put your hands on my tits," she said. Her breasts were round and high and small. I could cover them when I splayed my fingers. I squeezed the peaks between my knuckles and she moaned. That must have been all she wanted because she didn't say anything after that. She rode me until I saw stars, little flashes of white popping in the air before my eyes. I tried to wait for her to come, but I thought I'd die if I didn't let go soon. I slid one hand to her pussy and rubbed her clit. She still didn't go over. I guess she was too drunk.

'"I can't wait any more," I finally said, feeling as if my skin were going to split. "I've got to come." She just smiled and nodded, and the feeling rushed out from my cock like a rocket shooting through the night, a velvety whoosh of air and fire. It was sweet and sad and when it was over I almost wanted to weep.'

Ben rested the back of his head against the couch and closed his eyes. 'She made me breakfast the next morning. Burnt the toast and boiled over the coffee. We fucked in the shower and I found out she bites her lip when she comes. She never makes a sound until she's finished and then she sighs, as if Christmas is over for another year.' Ben sighed himself and opened his eyes. 'And that,' he said, 'is the story of my first white lover.'

'That was beautiful,' Carolyn said, without her usual gush.

Julia stroked the tightly curled hair of his head. 'Yes,' she said. 'Thank you for sharing that.'

He reached up and squeezed her hand. His palm was warm and slightly damp, his grip too intense for anything but intimacy. Julia's insides quivered. He hadn't given up on her. He still wanted her. Part of her didn't know how to be sorry.

'Your turn,' he said, his gaze steady on hers.

123

'Yes,' said Marty. 'Last but we hope not least.'

Julia turned her gaze from Ben's glowing green eyes to Zach's brilliant blue ones. She found no jealousy there, merely interest and warmth. Nothing threatened in that calm, weathered face: no expectations, no hopes; none that she could see, anyway. There was no earthly reason for her to be disturbed and yet the back of her neck tightened all the same. Maybe his calm was patience. Maybe he was so sure he'd win her in the end he didn't need to be jealous.

She withdrew her hand from Ben's hair. Marty threw another log on the waning fire. As he bent forward, orange light licked his blue-black curls. She watched the flames leap up, greedy and beautiful, flickering over the rough, river-stone hearth. She couldn't recall experiencing a moment like this before. The combination of camaraderie and isolation, of fear and desire, of hope and dread, was unprecedented. Almost without conscious thought she decided on a course of action. This once she would bare her soul, but not for the purpose of strengthening ties with these people.

Burn your bridges, she thought, and never look back again.

Chapter Seven

Saturday night

Julia settled more comfortably into the corner of the couch. Deep inside she was shaking, but she knew it didn't show. 'Do you mind a long story?'

'Not at all,' Marty said. 'The longer the better.'

She permitted herself a smile. 'Very well. This first begins with the general. He was not my lover, but my mother's. My father was an army aviator, a dashing, handsome fellow. He was my mother's last hope for escaping the general's allure, but twelve days before I was born his plane took a nosedive into the Arizona desert and that, as they say, was that.'

Ben and Zach gasped, surprise and pity mingling in the sound. Marty, however, nodded as if he'd expected something of the sort. His reaction was by far the more comfortable for her. She smoothed her hair back with both hands. Her father was a shadow figure to her. She'd never known how to acknowledge sympathy for his loss, and she didn't now. She continued.

'The general was a bluff, kind man; the best sort of army man: competent, hard-working, punctilious in matters of ethics, but not without mercy when the situation called for it. He was fifteen years older than my mother. They met when he was stationed in Heidelberg. She was a Zurich schoolgirl, of legal age but barely. At the time, he was only a lieutenant-colonel, though to her that seemed lofty indeed. Their acquaintance was brief, but during his leave in Switzerland they discovered they had interests in common that were near and dear to their hearts.

'The general, you see, was a sexual masochist. My mother, while not a sadist in the strictest sense of the word, had a dominating personality. Even at the age of seventeen, her gift for mastery was so pronounced that the general was unable to forget the experiences they'd shared. She became the benchmark against which all women were judged. Needless to say, the others fell short, both in skill and in trustworthiness.'

Julia bent forward, her hands locked together in one joined fist. The others leant closer as well.

'I should explain that the code of the army officer prohibits intemperance of any kind: drinking, gambling, fraternisation with officers of the opposite sex; even foul language is considered a transgression. How much more the general's particular vice! Fortunately, being Swiss, my mother was as close-mouthed as she was self-controlled. Even if the general had been capable of forswearing the whip, my mother's reserve proved too great a temptation. With her as his partner, he could indulge without fear of betrayal. As soon as he was in a position to do so, he arranged her passage to the States and established her as his secretary.

'You may imagine what indulgence followed her arrival; their appetites were all the stronger for being repressed. Things reached such a pitch of depravity that my mother, despite her pragmatic nature, began to fear for her soul. This fear led her to marry my father, a decent man, if lacking in imagination. The marriage was not a resounding success for either party, but amicable enough to result in my birth a year and a half later. From a survey of my mother's papers I have deduced that her affair with the general resumed when she was four months pregnant, so it may be said that I made the general's partial acquaintance early on.

'In any case, such were the undercurrents with which I grew up: the starched khaki discipline of the army coupled, or coupling if you prefer, with the secret sybaritic discipline of the whip. I did not discover the truth of what was going on until I was fifteen, but there were hints: doors locked against my entrance; strange objects kept in boxes at the back of my mother's closet; their banked excitement whenever they were together. For years I, and many others I'm sure, thought the general must be prodigiously well hung. He was invariably erect in her presence and had to wear binding cloths around his genitals to avoid giving himself away. The constant swelling misled people as to his size, though in truth his size was not inconsiderable. The bindings may also have been part of their game. One can only imagine the discomfort involved. Of course, to a man of the general's bent, discomfort gave as much pleasure as relief. Intentionally or not, I have no doubt those bindings became, in the end, as eroticised as his belt.

'He had a particular belt, you see, that my mother used to punish him. He wore it with his army-green service uniform, which is the normal duty dress. It was thus available on a daily basis for whenever they were able to steal a private moment during the long army day. I developed a fascination for the belt myself; it seemed to hold such power, as did the general. He was the closest thing I had to a father figure and, despite his sexual obsession, there was much to admire about him. By the time I was sixteen, he was spending nights at our house. My mother and he had realised I knew what was what. Since I was no more confiding at that age than I am now, they trusted me to keep my mouth shut. I imagine they relished the added time together, though their continued need for discretion saved their passion from any diminution by being over-gratified.

'Sometime during this occasional cohabitation, I snuck into my mother's room while they slept and stole the general's belt. I'm not sure I can describe the thrill it inspired in my dewy sixteen-year-old breast. Anger played a part in it. The devotion they gave each other could not compare to the mild affection they seemed to feel for me. On top of anger was added a fear of discovery, a sense of triumph at my own daring, and a deep vibratory lust I did not completely understand. What others feel for a first lover, I felt for that belt. Quivering with excitement, I returned to my room and stripped off my clothes. Over my now naked body I rubbed the well-worn leather. I smelled it; I licked it; I wrapped it around my waist and shook so hard I could barely stand. Finally, I knelt down by my bed with my forehead resting on the mattress and drew the belt between my legs.

'The first touch of that thick brown tongue sent a jolt of sexual energy through my cunt. Its intrusion into my private flesh was more intimate to me than a human hand, more emotionally penetrating, more forbidden. With a moan I attempted to muffle in the covers, I jerked the belt taut and pulled it back and

128

forth between my cream-drenched lips. Back and forth I worked it, back and forth, ever harder, ever faster, until I thought I would die from the intensity of the sensations ricocheting through my body. But I would not stop. Indeed, I could not. I bit the edge of the mattress and groaned. I spread my legs wider. I wrenched the belt closer to my clit and gyrated against it as if that strip of leather were something I could fuck. Fuck it I did until I feared someone must hear my ecstatic groans.

'I did not know how to come back then. I barely knew what coming was, except what I'd read in various novels. I did not believe I'd achieved orgasm yet, though, because the suspense was unbearable. I closed my eyes and re-created the most arousing image I knew: that of the general leaning over his desk with his khakis shoved to his knees while the belt, doubled over in my mother's hand, swept through the air towards his ass. His poor, happy, tortured organ had been freed from its bindings. It thrust through the tails of his shirt like a policeman's baton, jerking higher with every slash, reddening, swelling and finally jetting out a forceful spray of white.

'I came to the image of his seed dripping down the drawer that held his pencils, came like the drawn-out wail of a bugle playing "Taps". The orgasm was a revelation, a violent squeezing together of muscle and bone. I came for minutes, it seemed, shaking under the sweet attack of the nerves between my legs.' Julia drew a deep breath. 'And so ends the story of my very first orgasm.'

'No, no, no,' Marty cried, his face both red and pale, his hips shifting under the bulk of his erection. 'You can't leave it there, Mueller. That wasn't a long story at all.'

'No, not long at all,' Ben agreed. He looked far more composed than Marty, though the bulge in his crotch was equally large. Even Carolyn was pink in the face, her nipples forming distinct protrusions beneath her snug angora sweater. She looked as if she wanted to hear more, though it would have galled her to admit it. Their eagerness surprised Julia, their seeming lack of disgust.

'Very well,' she said. She risked a brief glance at Zach. He was stroking his moustache in what appeared to be bemusement. At some point during her account, he'd resettled so that his feet brushed her leg, as if she needed support, as if she deserved it. Against her will, her eyes slid downward. He was as hard as Marty or Ben. His thigh muscles were tense with it, his breathing carefully controlled but clearly altered by arousal. Why wasn't he horrified? Had she not been frank enough? Had she told the wrong story? 'Very well,' she repeated. 'I'll tell the tale of the first time I used the general's belt on someone else.'

'I knew it,' Marty said with the sharp chuckle of someone who's won a bet with himself. Carolyn back-handed his shoulder and he motioned for Julia to go on.

'There was a drill sergeant at Fort Benning,' she said, 'who was known as Hothead Hopkins. Not long after my discovery of the general's belt, he discovered my skill for fighting. When you work for the military you move around a lot. When you move around a lot, you get to be the new kid on a regular basis. I was never small, never an easy mark, but my mother had taught me to hold myself with pride; with arrogance, I suppose, and there was always one kid, usually an older boy, who wanted to put me in my place.

'One day, after watching me bloody three noses in

succession, old Hothead decided he could make use of me. He asked if I wanted to learn to fight like a soldier. When I convinced him I did, he gave me my first taste of disciplined combat. He taught me how to take someone down without spilling blood; how to get back on top when any normal person would give up. Balance was his secret, cultivated through a mélange of martial arts. Size means nothing, he would say. The fighter who controls the balance controls the outcome. Then he turned me loose on the new recruits. The administration didn't know about it, of course; they'd have tossed him out on his butt. But Hopkins thought it worth the risk. He wanted to use a pussy to beat the pussies, as he liked to call his charges; the theory being that if you break a man's pride before building it up, he owes his pride to you.

'Hopkins did not, however, realise that young men entering the military, going through basic training, sometimes discover things about themselves the army would just as soon they didn't. Even today, the military is an intense and intensely male culture. Sometimes the experience forces soldiers to acknowledge latent homosexual tendencies. Sometimes it brings out the sadist in a man. And sometimes it teaches him that being the object of rigorous, authoritarian discipline affords a thrill far beyond the thrill of measuring himself against adversity. In my case, a pair of rangers in training discovered they enjoyed being whipped by a pussy best of all. For them, my gender heightened the sexual component of the process because it introduced the possibility, however remote, that their frustration might one day be consummated.

'Hopkins ran these unorthodox pussy-whipping sessions in the back of an old supply depot. He had a wrestling mat and a chalked circle, outside of which we could not step without admitting surrender. There were no rules except that I could not break bones. Given my aptitude and his training, there was little chance of anyone breaking mine. I was permitted to draw a small amount of blood if it appeared that my opponent was pulling his punches. Some did. They could not get beyond their childhood training. I was a female and they would not hit me, no matter what I did. Their attitude was impractical, but I admit I admired them for it. Hothead could be a vengeful bastard. Refusing to fight me took as much courage as agreeing.

'I had no such trouble with the two rangers. I'd noticed they kept being singled out by Hopkins for my special brand of discipline, as if they'd screwed up on purpose in order to face me. Both were a good match for me. They fought well enough to prolong their defeats and both, especially the larger of the two, liked to get me in a clinch so that I'd have to wrestle them to the mat. This predilection proved their undoing. Old Hothead wasn't blind. Even in camouflage trousers and jockstraps, it was hard to hide the level of arousal they were experiencing.

'He called an end to the fun soon after our fourth match. He didn't say why, but I knew. I'd seen the glitter in the rangers' eyes when we faced off, the flush in their cheeks, the near sexual squirm if I pinned their bodies under mine. I'd seen these responses in the general, as I'd seen my own heightened excitement in my mother. A new flow of vitality seemed to run through my spine. I stood taller and straighter. I felt invincible.

'I wasn't surprised when the rangers began following me, discreetly, of course. I'd spot them outside the commissary or the post exchange. If their duties permitted, they'd drive by the local high school when classes were let out. They'd offer me a ride and drop me at the door to our house. They were very polite, very well behaved, but I knew why they were dogging me: I had something they wanted, something that by now they needed. They just didn't know how to ask for it.

'Unfortunately, time was of the essence. Ranger training lasted nine weeks. Once it ended, they might be posted anywhere and who knew when they'd get another chance to explore this dangerous thrill? The question was, could they trust me not to report them? That would have ruined their careers almost before they'd begun.

'I let them sweat for seven long days after Hopkins stopped the matches. Then I invited them in.

'Our house was ideally situated for private games, located off the base and separated from its neighbours by a thick screen of magnolias. It was a hot May day, insects droning, pavements baking under the Georgia sun. I offered them a glass of lemonade, freshly squeezed. We sat in the kitchen as they drank it down. We spoke of inconsequentials: school, life at the base, the last films we'd seen. Despite the calmness of the conversation, the men grew increasingly agitated, fidgeting in their chairs and reddening each time my gaze swept theirs.

'Finally, one of them, the tall redhead who liked to make me pin him, said, "We were wondering . . ."

' "I know," I cut in. "And I'm prepared to give you what you want, now, today, if you think you can take it."

'Their mouths fell open. The smaller, dark-haired one, recovered first. He had the face of a sullen angel, and a taut, wiry body. He emptied a small paper sack

133

on to the table. Out spilt a box of condoms. "We can protect you," he said.

'My response was as icy as I could make it. "That was considerate. In the future, however, do not assume I haven't already provided for every contingency. If I wish you to perform a service, I will request it."

'He hung his head, but a quiver of excitement ran through his torso. "Yes, mistress," he said.

'It was the first time, apart from my fantasies, that anyone had called me that. It sounded very sweet to my ears. It was, however, what the general called my mother. I wished an honorific of my own. "You may call me Ms Mueller," I said. I liked the idea of making an older person refer to me the way I had to refer to my teachers. "Ms Mueller," said the young man. I knew the title was just right. It rang through my cunt as if a tuning fork had been set to the individual frequency of my lust.

'My body humming with pleasure, I directed them to my bedroom. I pulled down the shades and ordered them to undress. The air smelled of my baby powder and their sweat. The redhead was wearing Old Spice cologne, the scent of which makes me wet to this day. They folded their clothes as they progressed: shoes, socks, khaki T-shirts and camouflage trousers. I loved the respect inherent in that neatness. The army had prepared them for me in many ways, a fact that became apparent as soon as their clothes were gone. They were hard beneath those simple uniforms, hard of muscle and hard of cock, two beautiful male specimens in their prime.

'I'd never seen completely naked men before. My sense of discovery was keen. I circled them, the way a drill sergeant will, but I circled them in silence. They remained eyes and face front, as they'd been trained, and they broke out in goose-flesh under my gaze. When I'd finished my survey, I removed my school clothes. That startled them, until they saw I had my own uniform. Beneath my T-shirt and jeans I wore a black merry widow. You know, the racy undergarment with the push-up cups and lace around the edges? It was satin and snugged at the waist by an arrangement of eyelets and leather laces, like an old-fashioned corset or a boot. I looked much as I do now, full-figured but strong. The redhead moaned. Then I slipped into a pair of five-inch patent-leather heels.

'"Oh, God," said the black-haired one, overcome by the sight.

'I slapped him sharply across his cock. "Don't speak unless you're spoken to," I said, then turned and slapped the redhead for good measure. "Equal punishment, boys. What one suffers, so shall the other."

'"Yes, Ms Mueller," they said, their cocks throbbing even more forcefully from my blows. A thread of pre-ejaculate stretched downward from the dark one's helmet, glistening in the soft golden light. His fingers twitched as if he wanted to wipe it free. Catching the movement from the corner of his eye, his partner shivered in sympathy. Neither man moved.

'My heart melted and my pussy. They were so lovely, so good. But if I softened now, it would be no kindness. I reached beneath the mattress and removed the general's belt, the same belt I had stolen from my mother's room, the companion to countless frenzied orgasms. I pressed it beneath the redhead's nose. His nostrils flared, smelling the leather, smelling me. He made a sound, small and mournful, but he did not speak.

'"Good," I said and bent forward to nip the pebbled tip of his breast. "Very good."

'I repeated the favour with my black-haired angel, then shoved him until he half-fell across my bed. Before he could regain his feet, I began whipping his buttocks with the doubled belt. He had dark olive skin and his bottom was firm. He could withstand a great deal of force, but I didn't want to leave marks that would not fade within the hour. I didn't want him to get caught. Because of this, I spread the blows over his buttocks, the sides of his waist, the back of his thighs. He could not bear the excitement this caused. His hips lurched forward. He rubbed his cock against the side of my box-spring.

' "No," I said, harsh and low. I wedged the pointy toe of my shoe between him and the bed to pull him back. "I say when you take your pleasure, not you."

'He begged my forgiveness and I slapped him with the belt again, lightly this time. I caught him beneath the balls, though, so the blow genuinely stung.

' "Turn around," I ordered. "Put your hands behind your head and watch."

'His cock was so hard now it strafed his belly. The head was wet, the veins ropy and dark. Pink stripes marked the sides of his waist. The sight of them made my pussy quiver. I wanted to draw the marks across his stomach as well, but the other waited, my other, untouched servant.

' "Kneel as he was kneeling," I said.

'The redhead complied without hesitation. He stretched his arms across the mattress and gripped the covers in his fists. He had a beautiful back, broad in the shoulder, cleanly muscled under satiny skin. The crease of his buttocks was shadowed with a lick of bright-red hair. I set about bringing his skin into harmony with it.

'The other began to cry as he watched, silently,

shuddering in an ecstasy of envy. His misery enchanted me. This one has earnt a special reward, I thought. This one will take me first.

'He was ready by the time I finished marking his friend, more than ready. His balls were drawn up against his body, plump as a Georgia peach, ripe as a hothouse tomato. A steady flow of fluid drooled from his cock; there simply wasn't another word for it, the stream was so copious.

'He seemed to feel this required an apology. "I'm sorry," he said, nodding red-faced at his dripping member. "I can't help it. This makes me so horny. I haven't let myself come since the last time we wrestled." His voice dropped till I could barely hear it. "I've been wearing a special ring at night so I'll wake up if I'm about to have a wet dream."

'His confession sent chills of excitement down my neck, but I knew better than to let on. I took the flange of his cock between my fingers and pinched until his slit gaped wide and a bubble of pre-come rolled out. He made a choking noise, caught between pain and ecstasy. I put my face right up to his, drinking it in. "I didn't say you could speak, did I?" He shook his head, his cheeks gone blotchy with embarrassment. Jealous tears shone on his skin. I couldn't resist him. I pressed my lips to his trembling mouth. He didn't dare kiss me, but I knew he wanted to.

'"You may kiss me," I whispered, "and you may take me. But if you come before I do, this will never, and I mean never, happen again."

'His breath rushed from him in hot, anguished longing. "I want to, Ms Mueller," he said. "But I'm afraid the first stroke would make me come. The first touch."

'This confession pleased me as much as the other. Unable to hide a smile, I lowered myself to the floor before him, my thighs spread, my elbows supporting my upper body. The merry widow fastened between my legs with a single snap. My new slave licked his lips at the dampness of the cloth. I undid the snap and peeled the satin away, baring my secrets to his gaze. He blinked rapidly and one last tear rolled down his cheek. With two careful fingers, I pinched my clit out for him to see.

'"I said you could kiss me," I reminded him. "Or don't you know how?"

'He answered with a groan, already falling towards me. "Yes, Ms Mueller, yes."

'He did know how. He knew how very well. He spread me with his fingers and worshipped me with his mouth. He lingered over the spots that made me moan the loudest, but he did not neglect the rest.

'"May I help?" pleaded the other. Before I could answer he claimed my breasts, suckling the hard, hurting tips against his teeth. I pinched him for his insolence on the well-warmed skin of his bottom. Naturally, he wriggled with pleasure and moaned for more. Laughing, I obliged him, feeling freer and more joyous than I had in all my life. Sensations overwhelmed me: the mouth at my breasts, the tongue at my clit, the overwhelming champagne fizz of power. For all my confidence, I had never been touched so intimately. I came in a series of sharp, deep beats, my whole body clenching, my whole body pleased.

'"Now," I said, stroking the hair of the dark-haired one. "You may take me."

'He rose between my legs, his body hot and slim. He rolled on the condom with a flair I shall never forget, like a magician with a deck of cards. One second the latex was housed within the packet; the next it sheathed his cock. His hands came down beside my shoulders, supporting his weight for entry. He did not guide himself, but let his cock find its own slippery way between my lips and to my gate. I held my breath and bit my lip. I think that was when he realised how inexperienced I was, because he smiled reassuringly.

'Even so, he was surprised to find me a virgin, surprised and touched. "Oh," he said, halting at the thin barrier. "Oh, Julia."

' "Do it," I said, but it was as much plea as order. I slid my hands down his back and stroked his burning buttocks. "Do it, slave."

'He thrust hard, taking me in a single stroke. His cock seemed enormous. My insides were on fire, but pleasantly so. A brief sting was all I'd suffered for the loss of my virginity. Already my sheath was beginning to undulate around the intruder, hungry for more stimulation. My lover shuddered and held fast, his head dropping towards mine until our temples brushed. His was sweaty, mine throbbing. "All right," he said. "Don't move. I think I can hold on. I think I can make you come while I'm inside you."

'I let him do as he asked, but even lying motionless I tortured him. His every thrust inspired a groan, my every sigh a tremor. The redhead knelt on the floor to watch us, his breath mirroring ours, his eyes hot. After a minute, he pressed the belt into my hand. If he couldn't do, he wanted to watch, and he wanted to watch more of what had brought us to this point. I could not scold him, because I wanted the same. I looped the belt behind my lover's back, first just tugging his waist, then pressing the stripes that flamed across his rolling bottom.

'The touch was enough to arouse him beyond control. He screwed his eyes shut and began to pant, hard, as if he were engaged in a gruelling race. His pace increased and I pushed up to meet him, my cunt swimming at the thought of what he must be feeling: the sting and burn of his ass, the wet, squirming clasp of my sex, the hard edge of the leather. My excitement rose and with it the first ache of orgasm fluttered through me. I snapped the belt against his skin, as sharp as a spank. He cried out. He thrust faster. I came once, deeply, and immediately rose again. My need to climax was immense. I caught his mouth with mine and kissed him wildly. I slapped him again. Our tongues battled, trembled, and then we both shuddered together. This time the spasm seemed endless. I swallowed his moan; I drank in his sigh. He thrust once more, to the very depth of my sheath. I felt a final pulse, his cock spitting the last of its pleasure. Then he pulled carefully out. "Thank you," he said. "Thank you very much."

'And thus began my career as a dominatrix.'

The room was silent except for the crackle of the fire. Marty rubbed his stubbled face. Ben shifted against her knee and Zach was entirely still, his hands steepled before his mouth, his eyes wide. Julia told herself she was glad she had shocked him, glad she'd shocked them all.

'Jesus,' said Carolyn, the first to regain her powers of speech. 'I had no idea. We made jokes about you cracking the whip, but I had no idea.' She rubbed her hands down the front of her thighs and Julia realised she was aroused. The story might have shocked her, but it hadn't turned her off. 'You did see those men again. I know you did.'

'Yes, I did,' Julia admitted, her voice sounding distant even to herself. 'And I do. Every year on our anniversary, they visit me. I count them among my oldest friends.'

'Wow,' said Carolyn.

'Wow,' Ben agreed. He seemed shocked in a different way, more stunned than titillated.

Marty broke the tension by chuckling. 'I don't know about the rest of you guys, but if I don't get lucky tonight, I may need medical attention.'

'Amen,' said Carolyn and, with a musical giggle, she dragged an unresisting Zach from the room.

He didn't know what to think of Julia's story; didn't want to know what to think. He held his judgment back like a wild mustang he'd roped and hobbled. He didn't want to come down on one side or the other. He didn't want to judge.

The more he learnt about Julia, the more she fascinated him. What was this world she lived in, this Tibet of sexuality, this erotic Timbuktu? As she'd spoken, he could picture himself with the belt, could almost feel it in his hand: he, who refused to wear spurs in competition, who never slapped a horse except with the flat of his palm. Stranger still, he could also picture himself kneeling before her. She exerted such a pull on him. His heart was so full. She'd had a mother who didn't know how to be soft, and a father who'd died before she was born. This control she loved: it was herself she was trying to master, her own inadmissible hurt she was trying to whip behind its barrier. He could see that as clear as the nose on his face.

But he didn't want her any the less for it. He would have kissed her feet himself if he'd thought it would ease her pain. The impulse to go on to his knees for her was so strong, so foreign, it frightened him. So he held back his judgment on that as well. When Carolyn took his hand and pulled him away, his brain was too rattled to stop her.

* * *

141

Julia sat for a long time staring at the dying fire, trying to be glad for the bridge she'd burnt, trying to pull the walls of privacy back around her soul. Her psyche felt raw. She didn't notice when Ben drifted away, though he must have said something in parting. She came aware again when Marty knelt before her and placed a hand on each of her knees.

'I want you to show me,' he said with unaccustomed seriousness. 'I want to taste what it's like.'

'Oh, Marty.' She felt as old as the hills and as sad. Despite which, part of her unfurled at the thought of a new challenge.

He took her hand and kissed its palm. 'Do you think it's wrong for me to want that? You, of all people?'

'I'm not always kind,' she warned.

'But you'll be kind to me, and at least you know kindness should rule it. Didn't you hear your own story? You're still friends with those men. They still love you.'

'They love what I do to them.'

He shook his head. 'You know, Julia, for a smart woman, you can be pretty stupid. You've got a heart the size of Texas.'

'I don't.'

'You do.' He squeezed her hand. 'I've known that since you campaigned for Rich to hire Ben. Since two years ago. Do you think I want to fuck you just because you're a goddess? I admit that's a good reason, but I want to fuck you because I like you. And I want you to give me a taste of the whip because I trust you to do it right.'

She looked at him. He seemed so sure of himself – confident, excited, curious – exactly what a sub should be.

'Very well,' she said. 'If you're going to do it, you may as well do it with me.'

She led him to her room. She pulled the steamer trunk out from under the bed and unlocked the second compartment. Her toys lay neatly inside. Whips and paddles nestled beside cock rings and nipple clamps. The costumes sat folded to the right. The scent of leather rose from most, but there was silk as well, and lace. The power of classic femininity received its due.

Marty craned around her shoulder. He touched a cock-and-ball harness, thick fingers stroking the sturdy leather. Julia filed the reaction away. 'Jeez, Julia, you brought all this stuff on a business trip?'

'My last business trip.'

He stopped breathing for a moment. 'You're not going back to DMI?'

'I'm burning my bridges, Marty.'

To her surprise, his eyes filled. He hugged her. 'I understand. Rich is a Class-A Bastard. I'm amazed you lasted as long as you did. But, damn, I'm going to miss you.'

Julia patted his back, more awkward with this embrace than with an intimate one. When he pushed away from her, teary and tender, she could barely meet his eyes. She'd just lifted her hand to cup his cheek when the door slammed open. Carolyn stood on the threshold, mascara running down her cheeks, fists clenched in anger.

'Teach me what you know,' she said. 'Teach me how to master them.'

Julia realised Zach must have rebuffed her. For a moment she was happier than she had any right to be. Then she remembered. Carolyn must have fucked him seven times by now. Zach hadn't sent her away out of

143

concern for Julia. He'd sent her away because she'd exceeded his quota.

'What are you talking about?' she asked, stalling for time. This was the chance she'd been angling for ever since Carolyn had told her to get her own man. But now she had the means for payback, she wasn't sure she wanted it.

Carolyn stepped into the room and shoved Julia's chest. 'I want them on their knees to me. They're never going to break my heart again.'

After a two-day romance, Julia doubted her broken heart was serious. 'You mean men?'

'Of course I mean men. I want you to teach me to be a dom. I'll pay whatever you want.'

At a loss, Julia turned to Marty. He lifted his hands and backed away. 'Oh, no. I said I wanted a taste of the whip, but not if Nelly Neurotic here is wielding it.'

In spite of herself, Julia laughed. 'Don't be silly. I can't teach Carolyn to be a dom. She doesn't have it in her.' She turned back to his nemesis, the way suddenly clear to her. She would teach Carolyn a lesson all right, but a lesson she could use. 'If you want, I'll teach you to be a better sub.'

'What?' Carolyn's eyes went round. 'You want to teach me to be a better doormat?'

She did indeed have a lot to learn. Julia rubbed her arm. 'You're a naturally giving person, Carolyn, not a doormat.'

'Then why do I always lose them?' Her voice broke under a renewed threat of tears. She pressed her fist beneath her nose. Julia knew better than to offer sympathy.

'You can't lose what you've never had,' she said. 'Those men never belonged to anyone but themselves.'

'That makes me feel a hell of a lot better.'

144

'Don't fight your nature. There's as much power in submission as there is in dominance. You simply need to learn to surrender power by choice.'

Carolyn shook her arm free. 'I'm supposed to believe all those men who beg to lick your boots are powerful? What a load of crap. You don't know anything.'

'Then why are you here?'

'Because I'm an idiot.' She wiped her cheeks with her hands and stepped back towards the door. 'Never mind. I'll toughen up without you, Mueller. You wait and see.'

Julia did not protest when she left, though she knew Carolyn would fail. This was the same tone she took after every lost-another-boyfriend crying jag. 'Never again, never again,' she'd say ... until the next time. She never learnt. She never changed. 'Men are bastards' was all the wisdom she'd managed to garner. Wearily, Julia covered her face and shook her head.

Marty squeezed her shoulders from behind. 'I suppose the mood is ruined now?'

'Yes, I'm sorry. I just can't tonight.'

He eased closer and wrapped his arms around her waist. 'It's still as cold as a witch's tit in here.'

She smiled. 'Are you asking to stay?'

'Would you kick me in the balls if I were? Oh, right, you're not in the mood.'

She turned in his hold and ruffled his curls, weariness fading in the face of amusement. 'You're welcome to stay, Marty. I could use the company.'

Zach's hand froze in the act of rapping on her door. He heard the soft, wet moans of people kissing inside. He backed to the opposite wall and closed his eyes. He'd let her do it. He'd let Julia scare him off and now he'd lost precious ground he might never regain.

He knew better. The wildest horses always tested their handlers. Half the time their wildness was fear. They'd been mistreated, or sometimes just misunderstood. Horses had quirks, like people did. You had to work to understand them. You had to be patient, and persistent, and you couldn't let them scare you off. Julia wanted him. He could feel it, and it was more than a wanting of the body. She might not care to admit it; it might frighten her, but she yearned for him the same way he yearned for her.

But now he might never have her. Time was short. This blizzard couldn't last for ever.

Chapter Eight

Sunday morning

*S*he woke before dawn. Marty lay beside her in the double bed. She'd assumed he'd snore, but he slept as peacefully as a child. What was that like, she wondered: to see what you wanted and feel justified in taking it, to harbour no regrets, no second thoughts?

She eased out from under the covers and pulled on a robe. The room was warm. The power must have come on again. She padded to the window. The snow still fell, but gently now. In the pre-dawn light she saw drifts reaching past the sill. No way in hell would they make their scheduled noon flight.

I'm glad, she thought, facing the weakness. So much remained unsettled: Zach, Carolyn, the DMI traitor, her life. She knew she wanted to part ways with Durbin, but what about her life as a dominatrix? Did she, as Marty claimed, believe those games were wrong? And if she did, was she capable of leaving them behind? Even now, a corner of her mind was juggling the possibilities, intrigued by the thought of initiating Marty and Carolyn together. Those two had an interesting dynamic. She was sure she could use it to advantage, if she chose to.

'What do you want?' she whispered, a hiss as soft as the falling snow. 'Who do you want to be?'

That was the heart of it. Who did she want to be? One thing was clear. She couldn't be who she'd been with Durbin. That door had closed. But which would open? Was the answer taking a new sub, one she liked and respected, one she could be tender with? Tender. She cast her eyes to heaven. Did she even know how?

She thought of Zach's beloved horse, the one that snapped at her every time she went near it. The mare seemed to know hers was not a gentle spirit. On the other hand, the animal's rejection had hurt her. Surely she couldn't be hurt if she didn't have a heart, and if she had a heart, she could learn to be tender.

She clasped her hands at her waist. She could learn, and she would. What's more, she would begin today.

Zach walked in around the dozenth time that the horse nipped her hand. She spun around, then spun back again, her eyes brimming with tears of frustration. 'I'm sorry. I thought she'd get used to me. I didn't mean to upset her.'

Zach chuckled and emptied his bucket into Starlight's manger. The mare immediately fell to it. 'A full stomach might improve her disposition,' he said, seeing to the colt as well, 'but it wouldn't hurt to learn how horses think.'

'Obviously, they don't think much of me.' Her voice was too sharp. She blinked hard, her vision swimming.

'Hey, hey.' Zach set his bucket down and wrapped his arm around her shoulder. The embrace felt good, too good, but she couldn't bring herself to move away. 'Horses sometimes dislike a person for no good reason. They don't fancy their perfume or their voice, and they get jealous, too. Starlight here considers me her personal property. Perhaps she's realised she's got a rival.'

'I don't know how she could tell,' Julia muttered. Zach went still. Good Lord, why had she said that? She sounded like a sulky teenager pouting for attention. If this was what Zach brought out in her, she'd do well to keep him at arm's length.

Recovering from his surprise, Zach rubbed the back of his neck. 'Ah,' he said. 'Is that how your wind's blowing? Well, let me tell you, Miss Julia, you haven't given much indication you wanted to be a rival.'

'I don't.' She pinched the bridge of her nose, willing the lie to be true. 'Not really. I'm just being childish.'

'It isn't childish to want an animal to love you,' he said. 'That's something God put into us humans so we wouldn't be a bunch of bastards, at least not all the time.'

Julia pinched her nose harder and pressed her lips together. She'd be damned if she'd cry in front of him. 'Can you show me?' she asked, her voice as firm as she could make it. 'Can you teach me how to make her accept me?'

'Sure can.' He led her to a hay bale to sit down. 'Nothing easier. Only we'll wait till she's finished her breakfast.' He patted her thigh. 'You need a hankie, Julia?'

'No,' she snapped, then held out her hand for it.

Once she'd blown her nose, they sat in silence. A few times she thought Zach was about to speak, but in the end he held his peace. Smart man, she thought, though part of her was disappointed. Most men would have jumped on her admission that she and Starlight were rivals for his affection.

When the horses had finished eating, Zach led them into the paddock that adjoined the barn. As soon as he released their halters they took off for the opposite fence. The colt seemed delighted with the snow. He danced through the drifts with his tail held high, nickering at his mother as if to say, 'Look, Mummy, look!' While his show was entertaining, Julia didn't see how she was going to make friends with his mother from over here.

Zach's voice came inches from her ear. 'Horses are flight animals,' he explained. 'She'll feel less cornered if you give her room to run.' He put his arm around her back again and led her slowly into the paddock. 'What you want to do is talk to her, kind of sing-song, so she gets used to the sound of you. Tell her she's a pretty horse, a good horse. She's got a swollen head, Starlight has, and she falls for that sort of thing.'

'Does she?' Julia's smile was sceptical.

He released her and gave her a little push. 'Try it for yourself. Don't look at her eyes, though. She's apt to take that as a threat and hare off. Keep your head down and walk slowly. If you get behind her, she'll run forward. If you move towards her head, she'll go back. So aim for her belly. That's her neutral point. And don't forget to sweet-talk her.'

Julia felt foolish, but she told Starlight she was a pretty horse, a good horse. The mare flicked one ear at her.

'That's good,' said Zach, plodding through the snow a short distance behind her. 'She's listening to you. Keep it up.'

She looked bored to Julia, but Julia kept it up. 'Beautiful Starlight,' she said. 'Good Starlight. Nice

Starlight. I'll give you a carrot when this is over. In fact, I'll peel you a whole bag.'

One horse-length from success, Julia made the mistake of meeting Starlight's eye. The horse snorted, shook her hide and raced off to the opposite side.

Julia stomped her boot in the knee-high snow. 'Hell.'

'No, no, no,' said Zach. 'That was pretty good for a first try. When I'm breaking a new horse, we can go on this way for hours.'

'Hours!' Julia moaned.

He grinned. 'You can give up if you want. But I wouldn't advise it. With horses it's best to set a small goal and stick with it. Otherwise, they learn they can get the better of you. Besides, today's a good day to do this. The snow will tire her out pretty soon.'

'It'll tire me out, too,' Julia grumbled, but she began the slow trudge back. 'Good Starlight. Beautiful Starlight.'

She heard Zach laughing softly behind her.

On the fifth try, she got within touching distance. The horse turned one ear towards her, but other than that she didn't acknowledge that Julia was there.

'Oh, God,' she whispered. 'What now?'

'Now, reach out, nice and easy. You want to put your fingers together and pretend your hand is a horse's nose. You're gonna touch her side with the tips of your fingers and rub it in a circle, as if you're nuzzling her.'

'Nice Starlight,' Julia said, her hand creeping out, her voice shaking. 'Nice horse. Pretty horse.' Her fingers touched the horse's side. Starlight's hide shivered and she shifted her weight, but she didn't move forward. Julia drew a little circle with her hand. 'Oh, oh, Zach, her fur is so thick. It's so soft.'

'That's right,' said Zach, behind her shoulder now.

151

'She's got her pretty winter coat. Don't you, girl?' Starlight whuffled at him in answer. 'What you're doing, that's what mothers do to reassure their colts. It's basic horse talk. It says, you're all right. There's nothing to be scared of.'

'No,' Julia crooned. 'There's nothing to be scared of.'

'That's good. She's standing nice and calm. You can put your whole hand on her. Just stroke her nice and slow. Work up around her neck there. That's it. She likes that. Now step up close so that she can feel your whole body next to her.'

Julia moved closer and inhaled the mare's wonderful horsy smell. She was warm and solid. Her neck came around and she snuffled at Julia's coat, but there was nothing of fear in the sound, nothing of anger. Julia buried her face in her thick black mane. 'Beautiful Starlight,' she said, her throat tight with love for this big wild creature who'd given her a second chance. 'Beautiful Starlight.'

Suddenly tears were running down her cheeks. She didn't try to hold them back. This was what she'd been searching for, this sweet emotion, as strong in its way as her love of power. Waves of tenderness flowed through her as she stroked the mare's muscular neck. Something bumped her from behind. She thought it was Zach, but when she turned, the gangly colt was there. He butted her chest as if he wanted attention, too. 'Oh, you're beautiful, too,' she said, sliding her hand over his velvety muzzle.

Like any adolescent, he wouldn't stand much fussing. Soon he was dancing off again, kicking up snow with his sharp black hooves. He bounded through the drifts as if his legs were made of springs. She watched him for a moment, then turned to Zach. He was smiling, but his eyes were as full as hers. She couldn't help wondering – hoping – that his expression held more than a teacher's pride.

'Thank you,' she said from the bottom of her heart. 'That was wonderful.'

His moustache twitched up on one side. 'Wasn't my doing,' he said. 'Anybody would love you if you gave them a chance.'

She pressed her fingers over her mouth, afraid she was going to break down, then sure she was. He opened his arms. 'Oh,' she said, 'oh', and stepped into them.

He held her tightly, rocking her back and forth and kissing the cold curve of her ear. 'You are something, Miss Julia. You got me all turned upside down.'

'I didn't mean to,' she said, even as she hugged him back and nuzzled the warm skin hidden beneath his collar.

'Doesn't matter. You did it anyway.' He turned his head and their mouths found each other.

The kiss was tentative. Tongues stroked lightly; lips brushed softly. Their breath rose in clouds between their glancing faces. For once in her life, she welcomed tenderness and offered tenderness. Like Starlight, Zach was one of God's darlings. Julia felt more gratitude than she could express. She wove her hands through his short, silky hair, caressing the bare spots at his temples, the strong line of vertebrae behind his neck. Zach's hands flowed over the back of her coat, pushing the leather closer, pushing their bodies closer.

Hunger rose like the thumping approach of a steam engine. She clasped his cheeks even as he cinched her back. Their mouths closed together, greedy and impatient. They reached deep and sucked hard until Zach broke free with a ragged gasp. 'We keep this up, we're gonna make Starlight jealous again. Come on.'

He nodded towards the stable. 'I've got a bale of hay with your name on it.'

She followed him eagerly, laughing as he tugged her through the drifting snow. He slid the barn door shut behind him and smiled at her. 'Oh, darlin', have I been looking forward to this. You have no idea.'

'I might have some idea,' she said, returning his smile. What was the point in lying now, either to herself or to him? Happiness bubbled inside her. She felt as fresh and clean as the snowy world outside.

Something in her expression brought a flush to his rugged face. He pointed towards the ladder to the loft. 'You'd better climb up there before I throw you up.' With a swiftness that conveyed his desire to waste no time, he gathered an armload of blankets and followed her up the ladder. He spread them haphazardly over a loose pile of hay. 'Wouldn't want you to get prickled to death,' he said in his most humorous twang, but his voice was rusty and his cock a thick ridge at the front of his jeans.

He undid three buttons of his shirt and wrenched it over his head, cursing when the cuffs caught on his hands. Julia dropped her coat over a bale of hay and sat to remove her shoes. The top of his thermal underwear flew in the same direction as his shirt. She rolled her leggings to her ankles, her eyes on the show. She'd been wrong to deny herself the pleasure of seeing him naked. He had a good chest: well muscled, broad in the shoulder, firm at the waist. Tiny rose-brown nipples peeped through his light chest hair, their centres sharply erect. Reluctant to lose the sight even for an instant, she peeled off her sweater and tossed it into the growing pile of clothes. Zach's hands were fumbling over his jeans front. He stopped when he saw her sweater fly. He turned his head to her. His eyes widened.

Her brassière and panties had been custom-made in Paris. The silk was a pale, icy pink, the lace a mellow cream. Julia smoothed her hands over the front of the bra cups. He rewarded her with a sharp intake of breath.

'Lord, that underwear is pretty,' he said. 'If I didn't want you naked so bad, I'd let you keep it on.'

'Let me, like hell.' She unsnapped the front catch and shrugged the lacy bra off her shoulders. Her breasts spilt free, full and tipped with fire.

Zach's pupils dilated. He took one step forward as if he meant to grab her, then shook his head. 'Naked,' he said. 'I want both of us naked.' He slid one hand down his half-open jeans, covering his erection, then yanked the zip down. With his thumbs he gathered both long johns and denim together. He pushed them down his legs in a single sweep.

Julia couldn't help sighing in admiration. His body was sturdy, but lean; strong, but graceful. His cock was as beautiful as she'd remembered, as hard as she could have wanted. It angled up towards his rippling belly, the shaft curving slightly, the tip swollen to a ripe, seeping mouthful. She licked her lips. Zach didn't miss the instinctive reaction.

'Take your panties off,' he said, his voice even hoarser than before.

She wriggled them over her hips, then stood with her arms at her sides, her skin pulsing with awareness as she let him look his fill. His cock jerked and a tiny spurt of clear fluid jumped from the deep-red slit at its top. Oh, he was too tempting, too responsive. She stepped up to him. She clasped his neck with one hand and his cock with the other. It leapt in her hand and spurted again. She rubbed its agitated glans around her navel.

He groaned as if the world were ending. His mouth caught hers in a greedy kiss, his hands roving her curves and swells. His fingertips played over the crease at the top of her thighs, then tightened on her bottom. He lifted her off her feet. His hips jerked back, pulling his cock free of her grasp. He hitched her higher and shifted his hold. His fingers wrapped her thighs in bands of steel. She hadn't expected him to use such force, but she honestly didn't care. She wanted him inside her now, immediately. The head of his cock probed her swollen lips. She gasped at its slippery heat.

'Now I've got you,' he growled against her mouth. 'Now you're in my arms.' He didn't wait for her to lift her legs around his waist. He pressed into the narrowed entrance. The fat bulb slipped inside, then an inch of throbbing shaft. She moaned and felt herself tipping backward on to the blanket-covered hay. Suddenly it was too much, too out of her control.

She heaved upward, digging her heels in, but that only pressed him deeper. He still had her thighs trapped between his and the feeling of being filled to bursting made her head spin. He grunted and shoved further. Her sheath let down a warm gush of cream. His tongue quivered inside her mouth, then withdrew.

'All right,' he panted, his hands sliding up her torso, over her heaving breasts. 'All right, I'll slow down. Promise.' He kissed her cheek. 'You're where I need you now. I'll slow down. Oh, darlin', you don't know how good it is to have you in my arms. You don't know how hard it's been to wait.'

'Let me –' she began, then lost what she'd meant to say as he began to thrust, slowly, gently into her constricted passage. He couldn't thrust far in this position but it hardly mattered. Her nerves were squeezed so sweetly to his hardened flesh that she could almost forget he'd taken control. The easy rock and pull of his cock lulled her, enchanted her. The hay rustled beneath them, its summery scent as provocative as leather, as horse. His hands slid along her arms until they reached her wrists. He cuffed them with warm, hard fingers and dragged them over her head. She thought of stopping him, but he seemed so gentle now, so safe. Soon it was too late. Her arms were held taut, her body stretched. Strange feelings swirled within her, dark ink curling through murky water. She couldn't say if it was fear or excitement. Then her sex released another flood of moisture. A shadow of panic prickled across her scalp. She shouldn't be reacting this way. She'd never liked being overpowered.

'No,' she said, but her cunt said yes, jerking upward and tightening around those lazy thrusts.

'You're not enjoying this?' he whispered, his expression stricken. She couldn't answer, not in word or deed. His thrusts stopped for a moment, then began again, more shallowly, as if he knew he ought to stop, but couldn't quite bring himself to. His hands loosened on her wrists, then tightened. Julia moaned, wanting more, fearing more. He bent to kiss the tip of her breasts, playing his tongue over the sharpened nipple. 'Tell me what you want. Anything. I'll do my best to give it to you.'

'Suck my tit,' she said, trying – and failing – to make it an order.

Plea or order, the words broke his hold on himself. He shuddered. His mouth opened and drew her in. She cried out at the strength with which he pulled, swells of delicious pain-pleasure washing through her

157

flesh. The edge of his teeth scored her breast. His tongue rasped like sandpaper. She could feel how much he wanted her; could hear it. He whimpered with hunger, low puppyish sounds that called up an involuntary echo from her own throat. The ache of wanting him literally hurt. This slow slide and draw was not enough to soothe it. She wrenched one hand free of his hold. She had to come; couldn't bear to wait. But he anticipated her, increasing the speed of his thrusts before she could. In a move too quick to counter, he whipped one leg between hers and pressed her thigh outward, trapping it beneath his bent knee.

She clutched his thigh, meaning to push it away but instead found her hand sliding up the labouring, hair-covered muscle. Sweat rolled down the crease of his buttocks. His sac spanked her fingers as he thrust. He muttered something against her breast, then released it.

'I've got you,' he said, catching up her stray hand. He dragged it over her head again. 'Don't worry, I'll take care of you.'

This time she couldn't twist loose. He held her too tightly. He'd trapped her. He hadn't even slowed his thrusts to do it. She quivered deep inside, her sex clenching and weeping with excitement. She didn't want this to stop. She was loving it. His words spiralled in her head: I'll take care of you. I'll take care of you. They stabbed her pussy with knives of heat. Oh, God, what was happening to her?

'Deeper,' he said, gasping for air. 'Got to get deeper.'

She struggled beneath him as he humped her faster, harder. She could not get free. She could only thrash from side to side. She could only dig in with her one free leg and thrust at him and wail at him, while pleasure sang through her at every pound of his cock.

Her reactions careered out of control, immense, unstoppable. She came with a low groan. He sank his teeth into her shoulder and she came again. Her whole body shook with the strength of it.

'Julia,' he cried, his hips beating white lightning through her sex. 'Julia. Jesus. I'm going to come. Hold me. God, hold me.'

Suddenly, her hands were free. They fell to his back and clutched his sweaty muscles. She held him, tightly, desperately. He shifted his second leg between hers and yanked her thighs up and wide, pinning them under his forearms while he thrust ever deeper. Now she could move even less than before. His cock seemed to pummel her womb. The muscles at her groin stretched and, oh, Lord, another orgasm rose, this one building ache upon bone-deep ache. She could not draw it nearer. She could not push it away. Her pleasure was all in his power, in his frantic, heavy drive.

Please, she mouthed, though no sound emerged. Please, Zach.

'Julia,' he gasped, his face a mask of torment. He wasn't going to take for ever to come this time. His cock swelled inside her. He drew back and slammed forward, grunting with effort. He held fast, his pubis grinding over hers, the root of his cock mashing her clit. Their hair rasped like silk. She tensed, dying for release. His head dropped back, throat bared, veins pulsing. He came. The first spasm rolled down his cock. He grunted, relief in it and awe. Then her climax broke. She'd never felt the like. She wailed as her back arched off the ground, as hot arcs of pleasure made the world disappear. Her awareness shrank to her own shudders of ecstasy and to him: his hard, shooting cock, the bite of his hands on her thighs, his hiss of pleasure when her sheath sucked him deep, and then his weight sagging, his sigh, the satiny brush of his lips when he settled against her, cuddling, nuzzling. Tingles of warmth spread through her limbs, a numbing lassitude. She knew she couldn't have stood to save her life.

'Oh, darlin',' he said, his cheek hot and wet against hers. 'A man could get used to this.'

The words slapped her back to sanity. She lay beneath him as if a hurricane had blown her over. What the hell was wrong with her? She'd behaved like a sub with a fetish for constraint. Her breath panted in and out, as much from shock as fatigue. No, it was just a fluke. It had to be. But it was over now. All done. She shoved at Zach's weight and squirmed free. He mumbled but didn't rise, no doubt too exhausted to move.

She stumbled when she stood, her knees barely strong enough to hold her. Jesus, he'd done her in. She looked down at him, at his big, beautiful naked body. Her chest tightened. She'd left scratches on his back – long bloody rakes. Not on purpose, either. She hadn't even realised she'd done it until she saw them. The marks disturbed her more than any deliberate injury ever had.

She'd lost control. She'd given up control. Worst of all, she'd enjoyed it.

With an effort, she shook herself and turned away. Accept it and move on, she thought. But she had a feeling it wasn't going to be that easy.

Zach lifted his muzzy head. Julia was gone.

'Fuck,' he said. He sat up and scrubbed at his hair, willing his wits back into his brain. He couldn't have dozed off for more than a minute. A renewed pounding at his groin told him he was hard again. 'Fuck.'

Obviously he'd done something wrong, but damned if he knew what. She'd been fire in his arms. When she came, she'd clutched him so tightly he'd thought she'd yank it off. At that moment, she would have been welcome to. He'd have handed her his cock on a platter and said: It's all yours, sweetheart. Keep it as long as you want. God Almighty, he'd never felt anything so right as fucking her. Maybe he'd gone a little overboard in the enthusiasm department, but she'd liked it. A man would have to be deaf, blind and numb to think otherwise. She'd wailed like a calf getting branded. Her cream was still wet on his cock!

He dug the heels of his hands into his eyes. If he had to go through another song and dance to get between her legs again, he'd –

Oh, you'll what? He cut himself off. You'll do whatever it takes and you know it. That gal got under your skin. One or two or, for all you know, a hundred rolls in the hay won't cure you. He sighed and reached for his clothes. This heartsick puppy business was a pain in his hind parts. Come to think of it, Gracie had more dignity than he did. She didn't whine when Julia patted her head and went on her way.

Muttering to himself, he carried the blankets to the tack room. He found Carolyn waiting there, the last person on earth he wanted to see right then. Like a lost waif, she sat hunched on his decrepit office chair. Her nose and eyes were red and she'd clasped her thin little hands between her knees. She didn't look up as he entered, just twisted back and forth on that creaky chair.

He didn't need to be told she'd heard them making love.

161

He opened his mouth, but his mind chose that moment to seize up. He couldn't think of a solitary thing to say, not even a stupid thing. They'd never had the ghost of a tie between them, unless you counted pity. Surely even she'd scorn that. Maybe not, though. She'd posed herself before him just as pitifully as she could.

He set his mouth on a different kind of silence and walked past her with the blankets. Damned if he'd apologise for making love to the woman he should have waited for in the first place. He'd explained how it was last night when Carolyn tried to squirm into his room. If she chose to shadow him around in spite of that, that was her problem.

Unfortunately, when push came to shove, he couldn't quite walk out cold. He stopped beside the old chair and laid his hand on her shoulder, letting her feel its simple, human warmth.

She sniffed hard. 'I heard you,' she said. The words wobbled like a newborn foal, despite the accusation in them.

'Carolyn.' He touched her short, feathery hair. 'Don't do this to yourself.'

'You love her, don't you?' Her eyes were hard. 'You love that fat bitch.'

He pulled his hand back. He might have said a lot of things to that, but it wasn't his way to kick a woman when she was down. 'You're getting yourself into a taking for nothing. You know there never was anything between you and me.'

'There could have been,' she said, high and wild. 'You never gave me a chance.'

He spoke gently. 'I'm not a stranger to my feelings, Carolyn. I know when there's a chance and when there isn't.'

She covered her face and began to sob. He didn't comfort her a second time.

Marty sat on the edge of Julia's bed, dressed except for his socks, which he was sleepily pulling on. In her current state of mind, Julia had no desire to face him. Pride, however, was sufficient to keep her from turning back at the door.

'Good morning,' she said.

He grunted, then got down on his hands and knees to fish his shoes out from under the bed. Julia had to turn away. His position was too suggestive. Her palm tingled like a drunk's mouth watering at a whiff of bourbon. The shift from worrying about unsuspected submissive tendencies to fearing she might never escape being a dom made her dizzy. She stared at her open trunk of toys. Yes, the sight of the leather still made her pussy quiver. But so did the memory of Zach pinning her on those rough wool blankets. Her buttocks were hot. She suspected her skin was abraded from the vigour of his thrusts. The sensation shouldn't have made her want him again, but it did. Damn him. Why did he have to be the one to call this urge to grovel from her? She wanted to wrap herself around him, kiss him, lick him, fuck him until they both were raw.

No. She slammed the lid of the trunk down, then jumped when Marty's hands began kneading her neck.

'You up for a rematch tonight, Mueller?'

Julia rolled her head and tried to enjoy his ministrations. 'We might not have enough time to do a good job. The snow is slowing down. They'll dig us out soon enough.'

Before Marty could respond, Carolyn burst through the door. Her cheeks were mottled, her nose red, but the look in her eyes was steely. 'I'm ready,' she said, not sparing Marty a glance. 'Whatever you want to teach me, I'm ready to learn. If I'm going to be a doormat, I'm going to be the best damn doormat around: the toughest, the hardest. No one's going to break my heart again.'

'You know,' Marty said, 'you might knock.'

'Fuck you,' she snarled. Julia began to think she might have a little top in her, after all. She had no intention of saying so, however, or explaining that sensitivity was more prized in a bottom than toughness.

'Carolyn,' she said in a cool, clear voice. 'Apologise to your fellow trainee.'

Carolyn set her jaw and narrowed her eyes. 'I'm sorry,' she said with very ill grace.

Julia pointed at the floor. 'On your knees and kiss his feet.' Carolyn gaped. Marty laughed. Julia snapped her fingers in his face, close enough to make him flinch. 'Either you accept this gesture with dignity and respect or I'll have *you* kiss *her* feet.'

Marty's jaw tightened at that, but he nodded. He stood unmoving, unsmiling while Carolyn performed the obeisance. Arousal was not yet part of their reactions. That would come later. Just thinking about it, anticipation thickened the tender folds of her sex. Julia hadn't trained two at once since her rangers. The challenge would be heady – just the distraction she needed.

Carolyn rose to her feet and awaited further orders. Her expression was sullen, her cheeks pink. Marty rubbed his bushy eyebrow.

'That is all,' Julia said to both of them. 'If you wish to continue your training, return to my room after dinner.'

'Together?' Marty sounded reluctant.

Julia tossed her head. 'Together or not at all.'

When they were gone, she tapped her lips and smiled. She might not be thinking clearly right now, but, wise or not, she was going to enjoy this.

Chapter Nine

Nothing could put Marty off his feed, but Carolyn picked at her dinner, despite Zach having served a lean roast chicken for once, instead of the eternal beef. Though Julia understood the woman's nervousness, she could not allow this behaviour to stand. If Carolyn did not begin showing more respect for her body, she would make a very poor slave indeed. At the very least, undernourishment put a deplorable strain on the hormones. No one wanted a bottom whose libido might give out at any moment.

She handed Carolyn a plate as soon as she entered her room. She pointed to the bed.

'Sit,' she said, 'and eat.' Carolyn began to argue but Julia silenced her with a sharply raised hand. 'You claim you want to be strong. You can start by cleaning that plate.'

The dish contained chicken and steamed vegetables, a modest portion of each. There was, after all, no point

166

in asking more of Carolyn than she could give. Once Julia saw she was eating – somewhat mechanically, but eating – she turned to Marty.

He smiled, a combination of mischief and approval. 'Are you going to give us safe words now?'

'No,' she said so coolly his smile faltered. 'I don't use them. I require my trainees to place their complete trust in me. If you do not feel that level of trust, I advise you in the strongest possible terms to leave immediately.'

'No, no,' he said, palms outward. 'I trust you.'

'Good. Now remove your clothes and don't speak again unless I address you directly.'

Carolyn's head came up at the coldly worded order. Marty looked at her, then at Julia. A flush crept over his stubbled cheeks. His hands moved to the collar of his pale-yellow shirt. He pushed the first button through its hole, then the next. He had a barrel chest, not fat, but bear-like. A thick mat of hair led down his belly, circling his navel and diving into his casual trousers. His nipples were larger than most men's. They pouted now through his dark curls, beginning to erect in earnest. Carolyn's mouth fell open as she stared.

'You may watch,' Julia said to her, 'so long as you continue to eat.'

While Marty disrobed for his wide-eyed audience, Julia opened her chest of toys. She removed a spanking paddle, the cock-and-ball harness that had fascinated Marty the night before, and a purple bustier. The lingerie was for Carolyn. During this session, Julia would remain in her oversized sweatshirt and leggings. She preferred not to dress up when breaking in new trainees. If topping them required too many props, she had no business trying. The force of her personality must sway them on its own.

The clank of a belt buckle hitting the floor signalled Marty's progress. Julia turned and found him naked. His cock was half-hard and rising. She saw that Carolyn had finished her meal. The plate sat unheeded on her lap while she gaped at Marty's steadily engorging prick. Her cheeks were pink, her breathing shallow.

Julia was pleased. Carolyn's unwilling attraction to Marty would make her job easier. She retrieved the empty plate and set it aside. Carolyn was too busy checking out Marty to notice. Suppressing a smile, Julia pulled the room's single chair away from the window. All the guest rooms had these royal-blue armchairs. Their backs were fan-shaped with curving arcs of stuffing: old-fashioned comfort furniture. Julia would have laid money on Zach's grandmother having chosen them. In any case, they were appropriately throne-like.

Julia sat and crossed her legs, their firmness revealed by the skin-tight cotton of her leggings. Both Marty and Carolyn eyed her calves. Good. She had their attention. She nodded at Carolyn. 'You. Remove your clothes. Slowly, if you please, and with a bit of flair. By the time you finish I want Marty's cock hard enough to pound nails.'

As she'd expected, Carolyn balked. 'Fuck that,' she said.

Like a cobra striking a mouse, Julia reached out, grabbed Carolyn and turned her over her lap. The VP didn't even have time to shriek before the paddle fell with a resounding smack, striking her bottom cheeks in quick succession.

'Ow,' she protested. Julia covered her mouth and spanked her again, spreading the blows until the beating's heat radiated through her expensive cashmere trousers. Carolyn hiccupped her shock into Julia's palm, close to crying but not yet there. Julia laid down the paddle, her arm buzzing pleasantly from the brief exertion. She slid her hand over Carolyn's bottom and between her legs, then pressed the soft ivory cloth between the lips of her vulva. Carolyn moaned. She was very wet, wetter even than Julia had hoped. Her humiliation had to be intense. Not only had Julia subjected her to the ignominy of a spanking, but she'd aroused her with it. Far from besting Julia in a battle of the cunts, now her cunt belonged to Julia. Revenge was indeed sweet.

She pushed Carolyn's trouser seam into her dainty, cream-drenched folds. Her mons didn't have much flesh but it was nicely arched. Julia's hand was large enough to swallow it whole. The disparity in their sizes seemed to strike Carolyn at the same time. A wash of pink crept up her cheek. She trembled.

'You see,' Julia said, 'you can't fight your nature.' She worked her cloth-draped finger closer to Carolyn's clit, teasing the accretion of nerves. Carolyn squirmed, but not precisely away. 'You like being disciplined. You need it.'

Marty choked on a sound, drawing both the women's attention. Apparently, he'd enjoyed watching the spanking as much as Carolyn had enjoyed receiving it. He was fully hard now, his skin as stretched and red as a prime New York salami.

'Hm, it looks as if you've got a head start on your goal.' Julia helped a shaky Carolyn to her feet. 'But that doesn't mean you can skimp on the show. I want to see how a good slave strips off.'

This time, Carolyn's technique improved. Marty pressed his hand to his heart as, piece by piece, she slithered out of her clothes. When the last scrap of silk had fallen, she crossed her arms over her stomach and shivered. She was thin, painfully so, but even that could not obscure her fundamental loveliness. Her skin was translucently pink, her breasts delicate and high. A ballerina would not have scorned such graceful limbs. Twenty pounds more, Julia thought, and men would fall to their knees before her. As it was, her beauty tugged at the heart. A breath of wind might blow it away.

Julia stepped up to her, her eyes stinging against her will. It hurt her that any woman would do this to herself, and out of what: some perverse sense of what was fashionable? Carolyn would not look at her or Marty, only at her slender bare feet.

'Very pretty,' Julia said, more gently than was her wont. 'Now uncross your arms. I have something for you to wear.'

Carolyn's tension increased, then eased as Julia wrapped her in the mulberry-coloured basque. She kept her motions slow and soothing, her caresses maternal. She doubted if Carolyn had taken female lovers, but she did not flinch when Julia cupped her breasts to settle them into the lacy cups. In fact, their soft, apricot peaks budded under her palms. Promising, Julia thought, a tingle warming the tips of her own breasts. Carolyn sighed as she tightened the laces. It was a happy sigh, perhaps the sign of a latent bondage fetish. Julia filed the knowledge away for possible future use.

She stood back to study the results. The shiny satin basque stopped at the swell of Carolyn's hips and bared her narrow mound. The effect was a fraction short of tartish, an effective transformation. Gone was the successful businesswoman with million-dollar portfolios in her care; this Carolyn was a creature made for pleasure – seductive, soft and pliant. Julia circled her new possession. Apparently, she maintained the grooming habits of her youth. Her trimmed brown hair covered her pubis like smoke, the strands no more than a quarter-inch long. The peak of her clitoris peeped between her nearly nude labia. Its hood was peachy pink and glistened with fluid.

'Very pretty,' Julia repeated, giving the tiny erection a flick with her finger.

Carolyn squeaked and went up on her toes, but Julia had already moved on. She took Carolyn's shoulders and turned her to face the other way. Now Marty could watch Carolyn's bottom receive its share of caresses. Its flesh was too soft for the sort of discipline Julia liked to administer, but it did have a lovely high curve. Moreover, the pink glow that the spanking had left improved it considerably. Julia slipped her fingers down its deep, curving cleft. She reached a gathering of down, then the crisper hairs that circled her anus. Carolyn bit her lower lip and clenched her hands, seemingly determined not to react again.

Her determination would not serve. Julia knew she'd invaded a territory even more private than Carolyn's sex. Gently, she stroked the tight circle of folds. From the way they twitched at the tickling caress, it seemed no hand had ventured here before. The omission did not surprise her. Carolyn would not have chosen her many lovers for their imagination. Now, shocked by Julia's boldness, but probably too proud to complain, she could not restrain a tremor of excitement, or stop a tiny drop of cream from rolling down her inner thigh.

'This is a very nice bottom,' Julia said, careful to hide her knowledge of Carolyn's distress. 'Especially now

171

that it's pink and warm. By far your best feature. Wouldn't you agree, Marty?'

Marty coughed. 'Uh, yes.' His voice was so thick it sounded strangled. Did he suspect the depth of Carolyn's inexperience? Julia thought he might. Carolyn's woman-of-the-world pose was flimsy to everyone but Carolyn.

She leant closer to her ear. 'Do you hear his voice?' she murmured. 'Everything I do to you excites him. Your helplessness excites him. Your passivity. Your embarrassment. You can see I spoke truly when I said a slave wields power.'

Carolyn shuddered but did not answer. Her control was too steady. Obviously, it was time to challenge her again.

'Turn around,' Julia said. 'I want you to dress your fellow slave.'

She handed her the cock-and-ball ring. The change in tactics startled Carolyn. She squinted at the intricate leather contraption, then at Marty. The harness was designed to fit snugly around the base of his shaft and to lift and separate each testicle, creating – so Julia had heard – a pleasant stretching sensation. When tightened, it would restrict the flow of blood from Marty's penis. He would be harder and bigger for longer; a useful effect, since the last thing Julia wanted was a premature end to this game. Carolyn fiddled with the fasteners, then nodded her head. Julia had been prepared to instruct her, but apparently the VP's intelligence included a certain amount of mechanical savvy. Her only problem seemed to be how to put the harness on without touching Marty's prick. If it hadn't been a breach of authority, Julia would have laughed. Marty wasn't making things easier for Carolyn. Each time her fingers brushed him, his cock wriggled like an anxious puppy.

Finally Carolyn muttered something under her breath, grabbed the base of his shaft with one hand and stuffed him into the harness with the other. Annoyance drove her to cinch the strap tight. Marty swallowed back a whimper, then looked down at himself and flushed with pride. Julia didn't wonder at that. He was gorgeous: a short, hairy gladiator with a cock of steel. The shaft stood out thick and proud, its veins gnarled and strong, its head immense. She was sure he'd never seen himself look quite so imposing.

But there was no way Miss Priss was going to lick those hairy balls. Julia knew that as well as she knew her own name. She pulled a small jar from a hidden corner of the trunk, her private stash of custom-made depilatory. Only her best slaves received this treatment, but this was a special occasion. With an evil grin, she spread the cream over Marty's uplifted testicles. His eyes began to tear almost immediately. To his credit, he didn't utter a word.

Julia pressed her lips to his ear. 'Burns a bit, doesn't it?' He nodded and jigged on his feet. 'I had the cosmetologist put a dash of pepper in it. Otherwise it's very mild. It will leave you as smooth as a baby. I think Carolyn will enjoy that, don't you?'

His gaze snapped to hers, sharp with interest. Obviously, he liked the idea of Carolyn's attentions on his balls. Julia told him no more, merely wiped off the fast-acting cream with a soft, damp cloth. Once she'd removed the last speck of depilatory, his scrotum was as smooth as she had promised. Its surface was inflamed by the pepper, now the colour of a sweetheart rose. He would find the skin sensitive, deliciously so.

Despite her satisfaction, Julia pretended to tut at the

fit of the harness. 'This looks a bit snug.' She touched the uppermost strap and revelled in Marty's squirm. In truth, the fit was perfect. Julia had spent three months apprenticed to a Japanese bondage expert, and six picking the brains of one of New York's finest paramedics. No student would be injured on her watch. She'd learnt in the past, however, that her powers of persuasion were strong. She straightened and looked Marty in the eye. 'I think it's going to be very difficult for you to come while you're wearing this. Perhaps impossible.' Marty winced. Julia smiled. 'Ah, well, I suppose we'll have to hope for the best.'

She snapped for Carolyn to kneel before him. 'Start with the balls, slave.' Carolyn jerked at being called this for the first time, but she did grab his knees and bend forward. She gave his clean pink testicles a tiny lap, a kitten testing a titbit she wasn't sure of. Marty shivered. Carolyn lapped harder, using the full flat of her tongue and dragging it from the bottom of the constricted sphere to the top.

'That's it,' Julia praised. 'Give him a good washing. He's going to need a distraction from the pain.'

The pain was her province. She retrieved the paddle and shook her arm muscles loose. She drew back and swung. Marty hissed through his teeth as the first blow hit the meat of his buttock. Julia wasn't worried. She knew what he could take. His skin was thicker than Carolyn's, less likely to bruise. She basted his right cheek, then his left. Marty grunted, but Carolyn's whimpers were louder than his. She quivered with excitement at each slap. Her pelvis humped the air. Inflamed, Marty shoved his balls at her mouth. Her tongue lapped more energetically. All was as Julia wished. The mingling of pain and pleasure would be very close. Soon they wouldn't know the difference.

Her veins thrummed with energy. These two were her puppets, her creatures. She made their pleasure possible; she polished it; she sharpened it. Without her, they would never glimpse this knife-edge ecstasy. Her senses sharpened. She felt goddess-tall, goddess-strong. She knew she could not make a wrong move. She had found the smooth, slick groove of power, where instinct and intuition hold hands.

'Suck his dick,' she ordered, and Carolyn immediately obeyed. Marty cursed with pleasure. 'Silence, slave. And put your arms behind your back. You are not to touch her. Ever.'

Both Marty and Carolyn moaned.

Her arm was tireless, her aim sure. But there was a boundary here, one she must not cross. A minute later, she halted the spanking. The sudden silence was filled with the harsh, excited breathing of her two new slaves. Carolyn still sucked Marty's dick but Marty hadn't come. Julia knew he would have by now if she hadn't planted the suggestion that he couldn't. Now his subconscious would keep him from it, even though Carolyn was focusing her efforts almost entirely on the head of his cock: Marty's personal ultra-hot spot. His skin shivered as twinges of feeling flashed through his nerves; not just the skin of his groin, but his shoulders, his calves, even the muscles of his cheeks flickered with overstimulation. His face was swarthy and tight, a mask of tortured lust. He was in for a treat, she thought. When she finally released him, he was going to blast off like the space shuttle.

She betrayed none of this knowledge as she knelt down behind his fellator. Her greater height dwarfed the smaller woman. Carolyn stiffened, but did not stop what she was doing.

'Hm,' Julia said, so close her breath ruffled the thick

175

black hair at Marty's groin. 'You have not made as much progress as I'd hoped. Perhaps you need instruction in the fine art of oral sex.'

'Like hell I do,' Carolyn gasped.

Julia punished her with a slow, mocking smile. She knew they were both thinking of Zach, and of Zach's ultimate choice in partners. Carolyn subsided with a sullen grimace. 'Good. Now if you're ready to listen, I will instruct you. First of all, you need to use more force. Marty here isn't made of glass. Second, if you can't get all of him in your mouth, there's no law that says you can't use your hands.' By way of demonstration, she lifted Carolyn's right hand and wrapped it around the base of his cock. She cupped the left around his balls and gave it a light squeeze. 'Here you can be gentle.' She nudged both her thumb and Carolyn's over the rosy swollen curve. Marty's skin twitched. 'See how sensitive he is here? You want to pay close attention to his reactions, and adjust your technique accordingly.'

She dropped her hands so that Carolyn could try again. 'Yes, that's the idea, but get him wetter. Spit is a crucial component of a good blow job.'

Carolyn shuddered. Julia took her jaw in her hand and pulled her free. 'Does my suggestion disgust you?'

'No,' said Carolyn, but she didn't sound sure.

'Oral sex is not a coin you offer to get something in return.' She pinned Carolyn's eyes, refusing to let her look away. 'There's no substitute for loving this, for loving a man's silk-covered heat in your mouth, his textures and smells, his taste. You will have few opportunities to give a man more pleasure, or to have him more completely in your power. Whatever prejudice is standing in your way, I advise you to get rid of it.

Technique will never be more important than enthusiasm.'

She stroked Carolyn's cheek, her voice deceptively gentle. 'You said it was love at first touch between you and a man's cock. Here's your chance to enjoy.'

'*My* chance to enjoy!' Carolyn burst out. 'Try his.'

Julia drew her forefinger across Carolyn's trembling lower lip. 'Do you begrudge him his enjoyment? Do you begrudge all men their enjoyment?'

'If they don't return the favour, I do.'

Julia smiled for her honesty and kissed her, a gentle moulding together of closed lips. It was not a sexual kiss, but not quite a platonic one, either. It seemed to shock Carolyn more than the spanking had. Her body jerked as if electrified, but her mouth remained soft and accepting. When Julia released her, her eyes did not immediately refocus.

'If you want to do this well,' Julia said, 'you need to give freely and expect nothing in return. Let the act be its own reward. Your gift, Carolyn, is to take pleasure in giving pleasure. When you fight your nature or choose partners who do not appreciate it, that gift is wasted.'

Carolyn's gaze turned to Marty. Julia could feel her weighing his potential for appreciation. The line between giving freely and acting the fool was fine, but Julia knew it existed. For the moment Carolyn would have to take it on faith.

'I understand,' Carolyn said more staunchly.

'Good,' said Julia. 'Now stop swallowing and get the man wet.'

Carolyn's squeamishness was still in evidence as she slathered Marty up and down, but he obviously appreciated the change. His heightened responses soon struck sparks in his partner. Her rhythm steadied. Her sucking grew louder. Her body moved as if they were making love. Now, Julia thought. Time for the *coup de grâce*.

Still kneeling behind Carolyn, she began to stroke her, her fingertips trailing from knee to hipbone. The touch was intended to be pleasant, but not obviously sexual. Only gradually did she shift to the more sensitive skin of her inner thighs. Carolyn seemed oblivious to the change. Marty's rather galvanic reaction to her new technique had distracted her. Instead, Julia's actions crept subtly, insidiously into her awareness. First they relaxed her, then aroused her, and then – when her arousal became too strong to ignore – they unnerved her. But it was too late to deny her pleasure. By the time Julia's hands closed, one over her breast and one over her delicate mound, Carolyn had been roused too well to turn the touch away. Julia took her earlobe between her teeth, slid one finger between her labia and massaged the weeping furrow.

Carolyn's breath hissed inward. She slapped her hand over Julia's. For a second it seemed she would try to pull it away. In the end she pressed it tighter.

'Oh, God,' said Marty, quivering at the sight.

Firmly, mercilessly, Julia returned Carolyn's hand to Marty's shaft. She slipped her own under the lacy cup of Carolyn's basque and pinched the pointy nipple she found within. Carolyn cried out. Julia pinched her again and a gush of cream dampened the palm that wrapped her sex. 'Don't presume to instruct your teacher,' she said in a low, velvety tone. 'Ms Mueller knows what pleases you. More importantly, she knows what you deserve. In the future your hands will remain where I place them.'

She resumed her slow exploration of Carolyn's cunt, spreading her juices through its twists and turns, pinching her clit, dipping briefly, teasingly into the squirming heat of her sheath. Carolyn began to groan around Marty's cock. Her hips rocked back and forth under Julia's hand. She was close to coming, very close.

'Now,' Julia purred, taking her clitoral hood between finger and thumb. Too lightly to make her climax, she used the soft skin to massage the slippery pearl inside. Her own heart pounded. Her own cunt swam. This was the moment when all was won or lost, when she pushed her slave past what the slave believed she would ever do. 'Answer me a question, slave.' Carolyn whimpered as she strained for the orgasm Julia held just out of reach. 'Tell me who is the boss here?'

Marty's cock slipped from her mouth with a rude popping noise. 'Fuck,' she said, fighting this final surrender.

Julia slid her last two fingers into Carolyn's sheath and tapped them, gently, but firmly, against Carolyn's G-spot, just hard enough to tease her with the promise of release. 'Tell me, slave, and I'll let you come. Who is the boss?'

'Oh, fuck. Shit. You are, damn it. You are.'

'I am what, slave?'

Carolyn groaned. Her forehead sank to Marty's hip and rolled from side to side. 'You're the boss, Ms Mueller. You're the boss of me.'

Immediately Julia brought her to a hard, jerking climax. The ripples clutched her pumping fingers, drenching them in warm, musky fluid.

'Ah,' Carolyn cried as Julia drew the spasm out. 'Ah, ah, ah.'

She collapsed back against her when it ended. Julia held her for a moment, stroking her damp hair, then lifted her off and propped her on the bed. She was pleased with Carolyn's surrender, but more objectives remained to win.

She rose to face her second slave. Marty took an instinctive step back. His gaze slid to her fingers, shiny now with Carolyn's juice. How delightful he was, how predictable. Smiling, she wiped them on his bushy chest hair. His pectoral muscles jumped, but he did not break form. His arms remained clasped behind his back, his sturdy legs spread.

'What do you think, slave? Wasn't that the sort of show any red-blooded male would enjoy: two lusty women taking pleasure in each other?' She stuck her pinky in her mouth and sucked it clean. Marty blinked sweat from his eyes. 'You may speak, slave. I wish to know what you think.'

'I think –' His voice was so gravelly he had to clear his throat. 'I think I'd appreciate your taking off this fucking harness so I could come . . . Ms Mueller.'

'But it looks so pretty,' Julia said. She drew one finger up his raphe. The ridge was hard as bone. His veins pulsed madly under the light touch. 'I really think I could make it come. It just needs extra –' she swiped her thumb over the bulging head '– special treatment.'

'Please.' An edge of panic entered his voice. 'I really can't stand any more. Please, take it off.'

She kissed his rough cheek. 'Don't you trust your teacher? Don't you know how good a hard come is?'

He couldn't answer. He moaned behind tightly clenched teeth. He seemed to have forgotten his hands were free. He could have loosened the harness himself, if he chose. This was enough of a surrender for Julia. She slid her hands down the sides of his body as she knelt, caressing the slight love handles at his waist, the heavy muscles of his thighs and calves. Behind her,

Carolyn gasped in surprise. The lesson hadn't sunk in yet. But she would learn that no act was inherently subservient. The server could rule and the ruler could serve. Julia licked her lips. Marty's cock vibrated with excitement as her mouth approached. She rubbed her cheek up its side and kissed its dripping crest.

'Tell me, slave. Is the other slave watching us?'

In a low, trembling voice, Marty verified that Carolyn was.

'Good. Tell her to touch herself.'

'What?'

'Tell her to touch herself.' Julia kneaded the inside of his thighs and rubbed her face down the other side of his shaft. 'You have my permission. I want you to give her explicit instructions.'

She continued stroking Marty's thighs while he told Carolyn to touch her breasts, to pull her nipples out and let them snap back, to stroke her belly and comb her fingers through her thatch, to part her thighs and expose herself to him. His instructions were half-panted, half-groaned. Julia did not need to turn to know Carolyn obeyed. Pre-ejaculate ran down his shaft in oily streams. Stretched taut by the harness, his skin was a hot, angry red. Even his balls seemed to stand erect. When he told Carolyn to part her labia and stroke her clit, Julia swallowed his cock-head.

His knees wobbled and for one disobedient instant his hand cupped the back of her head. Ignoring the infraction, Julia began a steady push and pull on his shaft.

'Oh, yeah,' he said, recovering. 'Yeah, pull back the skin so I can see your clit. Now use your other hand and put your – oh, God – put your finger in your –' He huffed to speechlessness as Julia fluttered her tongue beneath his glans. 'Put your finger in your pussy and get it wet. Yeah, that's good. Now two fingers. That's right. Push them in and out. Faster. That's it. Jesus. I'm dying, Julia. I can't stand it.' His knees jerked back and forth. 'Oh, God. I need to come. I can't fucking come.'

'Shh,' she soothed against the head of his cock. 'You're almost there.'

'No. The harness is too tight. I can't fucking come. I can't.'

'You can.' She pressed her thumbs behind his lifted balls, pushing their pads into the firm swell of his perineum, where the root of his cock extended inside his body. Such a sweet, neglected erogenous zone. She worked her thumbs in slow circles, digging them in and then vibrating them quickly in opposite directions so that ripples of feeling could pass deep, deep into his flesh, through his cock and into his swollen prostate.

Marty gasped something unintelligible. His hands jerked forward, then snapped back to their designated position.

'It's all right,' she said, and swirled her tongue around the flare. 'I want you to hold my head. I want you to fuck my mouth. It's the only way you'll come.'

'Yes, teacher,' he said, his tone dazed and reverent. He pressed her ears between an iron grip. Thus braced, his hips rolled strongly forward. His cock was just long enough to breach her throat, but she was ready. When he saw she could take him, he went wild. He jerked in and out, his thrusts frantic, out of control. He moaned each time she tightened the suction of her lips. 'Yes,' he cried. 'Yes.' His thigh muscles knotted. He gulped for air. 'Please. God.' He thrust. His cock quivered in her mouth and swelled, and shot hot bursts of come. He growled with the spasms, his hip marking time as if he were hammering tacks. The pulses slowed. He sighed. His hands relaxed and stroked her hair. He thrust slowly, drawing fully in and out, milking the sweetness until finally he slipped from her mouth, wet and sleepy-limp.

Julia wiped her face on the back of her sleeve and smiled at him.

He shook his head as if he couldn't believe what she'd done. Then he dropped to his knees and kissed her, deep and sloppy, rocking her from side to side in a rib-creaking hug.

'Enough,' she said, laughing as she wrestled free. 'Your teacher needs to breathe.' She used his sweaty shoulder to push herself to her feet. Carolyn was lying flat on the bed, her legs still splayed, her hands curled over her thighs. Her eyes were closed. Julia suspected she'd brought herself to as spectacular a finish as Marty. Satisfied that all was well, she headed for the door. 'I'll leave you two to pull yourselves together.'

'Wait,' said Marty. 'What about you?'

Julia winked at him over her shoulder. 'Trust me, Marty. I had my reward.'

She had, too. He'd reminded her how much fun domination could be. Her body sang with arousal, but her climax would keep. She assured herself she wasn't saving it for anyone special. That would have been foolish. Besides, she had other uses for that energy.

A soft sound caught her attention as she advanced down the hall, a sound like footsteps moving quickly away. When she reached the great room, however, no one was about. She wondered if someone had been watching them from Carolyn's room. She'd drawn the blind down on her side of the wall, but there could have been a crack. Her brows pinched together. Zach might have an interest in what she was doing, but she couldn't imagine him with his nose to the window and his ear to the wall, even if he were curious. No, the noise was probably nothing. Maybe Gracie the cow-dog had snuck into the house and didn't want to get caught.

Nonetheless, she couldn't quite shake her unease as she headed down the stairs to the gym.

Sublimation could be productive, she decided as she turned under the hot, pounding spray. Between her lingering arousal and Zach's free weights, she'd worked up a good endorphin rush. She felt tired now, but utterly relaxed. The lack of interruptions had been nice: just her muscles, the weights, and pumping towards the burn. Life definitely had its moments.

She braced her hands on the acrylic-sealed brick and let the shower pummel the muscles at the back of her neck. The ranch had been designed to support the needs of at least a dozen guests. Zach had incredible hot-water pressure. Julia sighed with pleasure. A woman could get used to this.

The sound of the door creaking open brought her head around. A halogen lamp with a conical shade hung from the room's central arch. The illumination it provided was bright, but Julia's marathon shower had filled the room with steam, great rolling clouds of it. Whoever had opened the door was only a tall, dark shadow. She turned to face it, interested but not alarmed. From what she could tell, the shadow was naked. It touched the control panel by the door and four more shower heads sprang to life, roaring like Niagara Falls. Whatever the intruder intended, no one would hear it but her.

She didn't ask who it was. That would have given the shadow too much advantage. She stood, calmly, and waited for it to come to her.

Halfway across the room, the shape resolved itself

as Ben Isaacs. So. He'd grown impatient. He stalked her cautiously through the steam, as if he expected her to run. He looked angry. When he finally grabbed her hands and slammed them into the wall on either side of her head, he felt angry, too. Julia knew then that he'd been the eavesdropper in Carolyn's room. The cock he pressed into the curve of her belly was hot and long and wrapped in filmy latex. He felt good naked. His satiny skin draped lean, hard muscle. He tightened his hold on her wrists. Unlike Zach's display of aggression, however, Ben's did nothing for her.

Well, she thought, half-disgusted, half-relieved. At least that narrowed the problem down. She didn't bother to fight his hold or the press of his body which, admittedly, was not unpleasant. She knew he'd state his business soon enough.

He brought his face close to hers, his nostrils flaring, his toast-brown skin glittering with spray. When he spoke, his voice was as hard as his cock. 'Tell me, Julia. Why is it you'll screw everyone on this ranch but me? Marty and the cowboy I could understand, but Carolyn?' He snorted. 'She's hardly worth your time.'

'Ben.' She searched for words that would not hurt him. 'Forgive me if I'm wrong, but you can't really want to pretend you're my slave.'

This took him aback. His grip on her wrists loosened. 'That's all you're about? Playing those sick little games?' He shook water from his eyes. 'I don't believe it. There's more to you than that.'

Julia opened her mouth to explain. Sick wasn't a particular act; sick was an attitude. Sick was a lack of respect for yourself or your partner. But what was the point? To Ben, what she'd done with Marty and Carolyn was sick. Why try to convince him otherwise? What good could it do him? She didn't think he'd enjoy S&M, even if she could convince him to try it.

'It's what I like,' she said instead. 'It's what I'm good at.'

The smudged charcoal arch of his brows drew together. 'Maybe you've never had the right lover.'

Julia laughed softly at his naïveté. 'I've had more lovers than you can count. I enjoy vanilla sex, but that's all it is to me: vanilla. And I'm a caramel ripple, choco-chunk kind of woman. That's what I like.'

'I don't believe it.' He kissed her for the first time, a hard press of lips against her cheekbone, a wilful kiss, a denying kiss. 'You've got a big heart, Julia. I've seen it.'

She sighed and wrapped her arms around his back, more as comfort than embrace. 'I think you've got a saviour complex, Isaacs. Or maybe you think you need an excuse to fuck another white woman.'

'Don't.' He turned his mouth over hers. 'Don't be ugly. This isn't like that.'

He kissed her. Julia did not stop him. He was a beautiful, potent creature. She had neither the energy to reject him nor the will. With lazy pleasure, she caressed his strong back. They had left the centre of the spray. Its edges prickled like Perrier over her arms. She remembered the story he'd told by the fire. Was he watching his dark hands explore her water-dappled paleness? Was he ashamed of himself for being aroused by the contrast? Did all his fantasies have to be routed into tracks he could approve of?

She smiled. If she'd let that stop her, she'd never have had sex in the first place.

Ben felt the smile but not the thoughts behind it. He drew her closer. He must have believed she was giving him a chance to prove his point. His hands slid over her buttocks, gently moulding and parting. His height matched hers precisely. The blunt crown of his cock probed her lips, sliding through water and cream, through curls and flesh. He broke the kiss and she knew, despite his guilt, that he couldn't resist watching it go in. Julia looked down herself. His cock was darker than the rest of him, like newly turned earth. Her curls gleamed gold against its brown, a provocative sight, even for her. He began to tremble as he pushed, slowly, slowly, prolonging the entry. His cock had a lovely upward curve, as if it had been designed to fit a woman's body. He would press her G-spot as he thrust, without even trying. Julia shivered. She stroked the tight, wet curls of his skull, the bowed arch of his neck. He was still no more than halfway in.

He panted against her upper chest but didn't say a word. Perhaps he didn't dare. So many forbidden thoughts must be racing through his mind. She curled her hands behind his shoulders and hiked her legs off the floor. She wrapped them around his waist, her heels digging into the high round muscles of his buttocks. With that for encouragement, he pushed her into the wall and hilted. He made a low, tortured sound. His erection throbbed strongly inside her, as if he'd gone a long time without coming. Perhaps he didn't approve of jerking off. Julia melted at the thought. That would certainly explain why he'd charged in here tonight. If he'd been watching people pair up all weekend, while taking no relief for himself, he must be quite frustrated.

He shifted his hips and pressed a fraction deeper. 'There,' he said.

Julia wasn't sure what to make of the satisfaction in his voice. She stared at him. He seemed untroubled by her watchfulness. He stroked her hair back from her face. He licked a drop of heated water from the corner of her mouth. Both were tender gestures, both sweet. A devil whispered in her ear. Instinct told her to heed it.

'Are you going to save me now?' she teased.

'Damn you,' he said, but his cock remained insistent.

She let her amusement show. 'Don't fuck the woman you want me to be. Fuck the woman I am.'

She thought he'd pull out then, but after a moment of stunned silence, he gripped her tight and started pounding.

'You're more,' he said, underscoring the claim with a heavy, ploughing thrust. 'You're not just a dominatrix. You're more.'

He spread his feet wider, their soles slapping the wet tile. His balance sure now, he pushed harder, grunting with pleasure when she crossed her heels a little higher on his back. His energy was impressive. She'd have been more impressed, though, if he hadn't come so quickly. Three minutes passed at most before he screwed his eyes shut and spasmed. She was sure he hadn't meant to. His groan of dismay spoke eloquently enough, even if he hadn't immediately gone to his knees to mouth her to her finish. He was skilled enough at that. She couldn't help wondering, though, as he drew her closer to climax, whether he liked her pretty blonde thatch as much as Marty had. He wove his fingers through it as he worked, combing through the wet strands. Though his fascination intrigued her, she had no desire to draw this out. She came almost as swiftly as he had.

It was a perfectly ordinary orgasm, physically satisfying, emotionally neutral. It meant no more to her than a swallow of water when her mouth was dry.

When it was over, Ben rose and touched her face.

Before he could make another argument in defence of vanilla sex, she covered his mouth with her fingers. She felt dangerously close to tears and suspected he'd respond to them in a way she didn't want. He'd taught her something today, though probably not what he'd hoped. She knew now that her sexuality wasn't as flexible as her encounters with Zach had led her to believe. She also knew she wasn't as ashamed of being a dom as she'd led herself to believe.

She didn't want to be saved, certainly not by Ben and maybe not by anybody. Redemption was too big a responsibility to put in anyone's hands but her own.

Which still begged the important question: who did Julia Mueller want to be?

Chapter Ten

Sunday night

*A*fter her shower, Julia wrapped herself in a thick terry-cloth robe with TAYLOR RANCH embroidered on the back. It seemed silly to wear any more when everyone in the place had seen her naked.

Ben, of course, remained in the cellar to dress. She didn't wait for him. Their encounter had left her more restless than satisfied. She wandered into the kitchen and realised she was starving. A peek in the big refrigerator revealed, among other goodies, a bowl of leftover scalloped potatoes and half a bunch of seedless red grapes. The promise of a solid dose of carbo-hydrates had her mouth watering. She zapped the potatoes in the microwave and set them on a tray with the grapes to take to her room.

The sound of Marty comforting someone stopped her outside the great room. She assumed it was Caro-lyn and that she was struggling to assimilate what had happened during their first training session. Julia didn't want to interrupt this slave–slave bonding, or be drawn into participating. Unfortunately, there was no way to reach her room without passing through this one.

When she entered, though, she saw only Marty. He was hunched over one of the phones in the adjoining office alcove. The receiver was wedged between his shoulder and ear and he was squeezing his temples. 'No, sweetheart,' he was saying. 'You don't want to do that.'

He waved Julia over as soon as he saw her. The smell of food must have caught his attention because he grabbed the bowl of potatoes and dug in. Standing next to him, she could hear a plaintive female on the other end of the line. If Marty had looked any less worried, she'd have abandoned him and her late-night snack. Instead, she sat on the arm of his chair and rubbed the broad expanse of his back. He slipped his arm around her waist.

'Didi,' he said into a brief pause, his voice patient and firm. 'Didi, call your sponsor. Call Harriet. No, I can't wire you any money.' He winced at another burst of sound. 'Whether I have it or not isn't the point. You know you can't go to Atlantic City. I don't care if the Long Island ladies are only going to see the shows, you can't afford to go near a casino. It's only been six months since your last slip. Do you want to have to start from the beginning again?'

A fusillade of promises shot through the line. Marty closed his eyes. 'Didn't you promise the last time, too? Don't you always promise? And don't you remember how bad you felt when you couldn't keep your promise? Please, Didi, call Harriet. You can go to a meeting together. It'll be – no, don't ask Miriam Rafferty to float you a loan. Didi? Fuck.' He let the phone slip from between his ear and shoulder. 'She hung up.' He stared at the receiver, then gathered himself. 'I'm not supposed to do this, but to hell with it.'

He punched in a number that was obviously familiar. 'Hi, Harriet? It's Marty Fine. Look, I know Didi is supposed to call, not me, but I'm out of town and she's having a little crisis. She wants to go to Atlantic City to see a show. Yeah. Tom Fucking Jones, only he just happens to have lemons for eyes and a long silver arm. Do you think you could go over there and talk to her? I know. No promises. But you're supposed to be better at telling her she's full of shit than the near and dear.' He laughed at something Harriet said, a rough, strained sound. 'I'll take that as a compliment. God bless you, Harriet. I'll send you a mink for Christmas. Oh, right, you'd only hock it and blow the money on lottery tickets. Bye then, sweetie. You know I won't blame you if it doesn't work.'

He hung up with a sigh and sagged back into the calfskin chair. His arm still hugged Julia's waist. He pulled her into his side. 'That was Didi's sponsor at Gamblers Anonymous. Great lady. They assign veteran members to look out for the "newly recovering". They reckon the old dogs have tried every trick themselves and won't be taken in.' He rubbed his hand over his face, pulling its tired lines towards his jowls. 'Didi gets like this when I leave town. Says it makes her nervous. But I can't stand guard over her all the time, and I can't let her make me responsible if she fucks up.'

'No, you can't,' Julia said.

The eyes Marty turned to her glistened with tears. 'So why do I feel like such a skunk?'

Julia didn't hesitate. She slid into his lap and held him. He buried his face in her neck, his tears spilling on to the collar of her robe. 'Oh, God,' he said with a snorting laugh. 'I am a skunk, a philandering skunk who doesn't deserve anyone's pity, much less yours.'

'I'm no saint,' Julia said.

He snuffled, calming, but still holding tight. 'I'll bet you never lied to a lover.'

'Does Didi always tell the truth?'

'Ha. We lie to each other. It's our strongest bond.' He sighed, a little-boy sigh from a big, boisterous man. 'Letting go today was good, Mueller. Letting someone else be responsible; it was really great.'

She rested her cheek against his curly hair. 'I suspect you wouldn't want to do it all the time.'

'Nah. Probably not.' He sat back from her and wiped his face. He grinned. 'I got a maternal streak you wouldn't believe. I always gotta be taking care of somebody.'

'Then you and Didi are a match made in heaven.'

He rolled his eyes. 'That, or someplace warmer.'

Despite Julia's fatigue, sleep eluded her. Pictures turned through her head: Starlight in the paddock, Zach in the loft, Marty and Carolyn, Ben. She seemed no closer to answering the questions that plagued her, except for one: the identity of Durbin's traitor. With a compulsive gambler for a wife, Marty certainly had financial cause to sell out DMI.

But would he? Whatever his faults as a husband, Marty was obviously supporting Didi through thick and thin. Was that the behaviour of a traitor? But if not Marty, then who? Ben was too much the straight arrow and she was beginning to doubt Carolyn had the nerve, unless jealousy had driven her to it. She had resented Marty's promotion.

Julia turned on to her stomach and punched her pillow. She wished she'd never agreed to spy for

Durbin. This was one mystery she doubted she wanted to solve.

Zach should have been asleep. Days started early out here. Unfortunately, memories of Julia slipping away after they had made love in the loft kept him wired. For the hundredth time, he relived the moment when he woke and found her gone. How did a man like him get through to a woman like her, especially when he had so little time? He knew once she returned to New York, she'd forget him. She'd force herself to. For whatever reason, he made her too skittish to respond any other way. He reached overhead and flicked on the wall lamp, wishing he could banish his inner gloom as easily. She'd barely said 'boo' during dinner, and afterwards all his guests had disappeared. It was enough to make any man toss and turn.

He needed time to court her, to understand her. He hadn't finished making sense of the story she'd told by the fire yet, or the feelings it stirred. Julia was a dominatrix. She whipped her lovers for pleasure, theirs and hers, and she'd been doing it since she was a teenager. Zach didn't doubt there were one or two like-minded females in Montana, but the fact was he'd never met them; had never even watched those talk shows where they trotted such people out like two-headed calves.

Why did people do these things and what did it say about him that he wasn't horrified, that he was, truth be told, halfway down the road to titillated? Was Julia a dangerous character? He couldn't imagine it. She seemed a paragon of responsibility. But was she sick? For that matter, was he? Most of all, where in hell was he going to get the information he needed to reason this through?

Then he remembered his grandmother's secret library. She'd shared this suite of rooms with his grandfather. There was a length of panelling, near the head of the bed, that slid aside to reveal a hidden stack of shelves. It held Grandpa's favourite issues of *Playboy*, dirty books various guests had left, and a few educational tomes that Zach suspected Grandma had bought for herself. She'd always had a curious mind. Grandpa liked to say she'd read anything that wasn't nailed down. Consequently, Zach was pleased, but not surprised, to discover a volume on dominance and submission.

Its presence eased some of the tightness from his shoulders. If Grandma thought the topic worth studying, how bad could it be? He opened the cover and began to read. To his surprise the essays inside were not by psychiatrists, but by people who actually practised 'the lifestyle', as they put it. The frankness of the accounts fascinated him. Many shocked him more than Julia's had, but some he could sort of understand. Taming a submissive wasn't so different from taming a horse. The point wasn't to break their spirits, but to form a partnership that offered each more pleasure than they could find alone. To Zach's way of thinking, any trainer who didn't want a happy horse wasn't worthy of the name.

Still, he couldn't deny some of this stuff sounded silly. A chapter on erotic enemas had him wrinkling his nose. Could that really be pleasant? A tap on the door jerked him upright. His face sizzling with embarrassment, he slammed the book shut and shoved it under the bed.

'Zach,' said the voice at the door to the sitting room. 'It's Julia.'

He moved so fast his socks skidded across the floorboards. She looked startled when he opened the door, and a bit shy, as if she wasn't sure of her welcome. Her gaze drifted down his bare chest to the front of his thermal underwear. Zach's crotch felt heavy from speculating on the things in that book, but he didn't think he was hard.

Of course, he might get that way quick if she kept staring at him.

'Come in,' he said, and stepped aside to let her.

She smoothed the front of her grey velvet robe. 'I don't want to intrude.'

'Nothing to intrude on,' he said, disinclined to tell her what he'd been doing.

She turned in a circle, taking in the sitting room: his computer and desk tucked in the corner, the wingback chairs and fussy mahogany tables left over from his grandmother's day. The bookshelves held volumes on every topic under the sun, most of them hers, but some of them his. Julia's expression was calm as she scanned the titles, but he knew thoughts ticked like calculator keys inside that elegant head. He tried not to hold his breath.

She opened the lid of a carved cedar box and found his boyhood collection of river rocks. Though she couldn't have known which was his favourite, she lifted the palm-sized, butter-smooth rose quartz and rubbed it absently over her lips. His cock thickened at the unconsciously sensual gesture. She was nicely oral, his Julia, nicely tactile. The trait inspired all sorts of depraved ideas.

'This is a nice room,' she said, still tapping the clear rock against her lip. 'Very cosy.'

The stubborn part of him dared her to disapprove. 'It's pretty much the way Grandma left it. I wanted to keep that last bit of her around. We were close.'

196

'I got that impression,' she said, her grey-green eyes warming with amusement.

She looked different when she smiled, less perfect, but more appealing. The smile was crooked, a little wry, but there was understanding in it. She might laugh, but she wouldn't judge. He realised how lonely he'd been for that since Grandma passed away. His heart turned over with a funny lurch, then beat so hard he felt the pulse in his throat. Lord, he thought, I am in love with her.

The question spilt out before he could stop it. 'Did I do something wrong this afternoon?'

She didn't pretend not to understand. She stepped closer and twined her hands behind his neck. That one point of contact sent a shiver of heat down his spine. Her smile was gone, but her face remained soft. 'You made me nervous,' she said.

Nervous, he repeated silently. That didn't sound good. He forced himself to breathe. 'I didn't mean to come on so strong.'

Her fingers stroked his nape. 'I didn't say I didn't enjoy it. I said it made me nervous. I thought –' A faint flush crept up her sculpted cheeks. 'I thought we might try again, so I could see if I'd imagined how good it was.'

He blinked. The hair on the back of his neck stood up. She wanted to try again? She thought she might have imagined how good it was? He knew she wasn't telling the whole story, but at that moment he didn't care. She was inviting him to do what he longed for most in all the world. Not needing to be asked twice, he untied the belt of her robe and slipped his arms inside, circling her naked waist. He loved how tall she was. When he pulled her closer, her breasts nestled against his chest and her hips snugged his groin. He hadn't known such comfort existed short of heaven.

'I'll be gentle this time,' he promised, stroking the long, warm curve of her back. 'You'll have no cause for nervousness tonight.'

Julia didn't know how to tell him her nerves were exactly what she wanted him to test. She needed to know whether her response to his roughness had been a fluke, as her lacklustre experience with Ben might suggest. If the effect was repeatable, she'd know more about her future options. On the other hand, what he was doing now felt very pleasant.

He nibbled his way down the side of her neck, tender, teasing kisses that left soft bursts of warmth in their wake. He parted the lapels of her robe, smoothing it back over her breasts and shoulders until it dropped to the floor. She almost tripped over it when he nudged her backward, but he caught her before she could fall and lifted her off her feet. Warnings of hernias sprung to her lips, but he kissed her into silence, kissed her with lips and tongue and teeth, with an intensity of attention that robbed her of breath, let alone words.

She couldn't get over how good he tasted. The effect wasn't toothpaste or mouthwash: it was him. Her head tipped back under the invasion, a hum of pleasure warming her vulnerable throat. He answered it, delved deeper, then broke free.

'I've got a bed right back there,' he said, moving towards it. 'A nice wide bed with a prickle-free mattress.'

She tucked her head into his shoulder and clung to him. For one singular moment, she knew what it meant to be small and delicate, to be a woman that a man could sweep off her feet. It wasn't bad, not when Zach was doing the sweeping. He laid her gently across the bed and stood back, his eyes admiring her curves, while his thumbs slid in a restless arc beneath the waistband of his thermal underwear. Such a plain, homely garment. Hard to believe what that loose, porridge-coloured knit did for him, and for her. There was something so old-fashioned about it. It inspired fantasies of seducing old-fashioned men, overcoming old-fashioned inhibitions. She pressed her fingers to the pulsing hollow at the base of her throat. Oh, what his erection did to that stretchy front placket! She could see a slice of its arch between the two flaps, a hint of blood-bronzed skin and gorgeous branching vein.

'Shall I take them off?' he asked, demonstrating a surprising awareness of her fascination.

She nodded and he pushed the undergarment down his legs. Creases marked his lean stomach as he bent. When he straightened, his cock rose in a thick, smooth arrow from the dark cloud of hair at his groin.

Once again, she marvelled at its beauty. Someone should make a mould of him, she thought, and put him in a temple, twenty feet tall and wrapped in beaten gold. The village maidens would kiss him for luck on their wedding nights, and the village men would quail before his strength.

'What are you grinning at?' he said, climbing on to the mattress and hanging over her. His bed was big and heavy and simple. A soft rumpled blanket covered it, stereotypically masculine in bold red and black checks. His rodeo buckles glinted above the crackling fireplace, the cowboy version of counting coup on vanquished enemies: vanquished bulls, in this case. Zach might be gentle; he might leave his beloved grandmother's furnishings intact, but here in this bedroom she could see he was all man. Her grin broadened.

'What?' he said. 'Tell me what's so funny.'

She smoothed her hand up the centre of his chest. 'Just a fantasy.'

'I like fantasies. Want to share?'

'Actually, I'd rather you told me yours.'

Her words caught him halfway towards suckling her nipple. He backed up. 'Don't know that I have any.'

'You must. Everybody does.' She ringed the base of his cock between her finger and thumb. Zach's pupils dilated. Pleased, she pulled lightly until the head slipped free of her hold, then repeated the caress with her second hand. 'There must be some image that goes through your head when you get yourself off. Something you always wanted to do but never got the chance.'

Zach wriggled under her third teasing stroke. She knew he had something in mind from the way his eyes evaded hers. 'Maybe there is something,' he said. 'But I don't know that it qualifies as a fantasy.'

'Tell me.' She reached for him again.

He caught her hand and carried it to his lips. One by one he kissed the tips of her fingers. She shivered at the brush of his moustache.

'Well,' he drawled. 'Seems I never get to make love as slow as I'd like. Just once, I want to take my time without the woman wondering whether there's something wrong with me.'

'I see,' she said. This was not what she had expected. Given what she'd seen of him, as slow as he'd like could be very slow indeed. 'You wouldn't want the woman to wait to come until you did, would you?'

'Of course not,' he said, but a sheepish wince gave him away.

She laughed and shoved his shoulders. 'You would!'

He hung his head. 'Well, in my fantasy she waits, though I can see that might be inconsiderate in real life.'

'No, no, Zach. You've put me on my mettle now. I feel obliged to put my self-control to the test.'

Test it, he did. He began with a leisurely kissing tour of her body, one that searched out all her tender spots and culminated between her legs.

'I think this is cheating,' she gasped as his fingers slid over her plumping folds.

He kissed the cushion of her mound. 'No such thing. A woman needs to be wet for the sort of ride I have in mind. Anyway, you won't be able to come from what I intend to do to you.'

That promise did not reassure her. He opened her slowly, petal by petal, lick by lick. Rather than trying to fuck her with his tongue, he rimmed the entrance of her sheath, staying where the nerves were thickest, never penetrating more than an inch. His moustache grew as slick as his mouth. Then he turned his head to suck either side of her gate between his lips and tongue, deepening the feeling. Through all this, he did not touch her clitoris. Nothing distracted her from the subtle ebb and flow of pleasurable sensation. Her body alternated between relaxing and tensing, between wanting it to end and wanting it to go on for ever. All her strength of will was required to refrain from pulling him closer.

'Now.' He shifted up her body in a smooth, brushing glide. 'I think these trains are ready to couple.'

'I don't get to tease you?' Her voice was gaspingly weak.

He shook his head with laughing eyes. 'This is my fantasy and in my fantasy –' he reached between them to align his cock with her body '– I'm the only tease around.'

She had agreed to this, if only by implication. She could not back out now. Indeed, she forgot she wanted to the moment he entered her, a slow gliding pressure that didn't stop until his pubis nestled flush to hers. The heat of him warmed her from the inside. She counted pulse beats. Hers? His? His head lowered. He rubbed their cheeks together, then their lips, dry silk rasping.

'You feel like home,' he whispered, shy and serious.

A strange, tingling rush moved through her at his declaration. She found she could not hold his gaze. This man is brave, she thought. Braver than I am.

He fucked her slowly, dreamily. He spread her hair across his pillow. He kissed her. He stroked her. The way his body rocked hers reminded her of a lazy massage, one that was supposed to arouse, one she could moan at as loudly as she wished. His cock slid to and fro inside her cunt, mesmerising, memorising probes, as if he were reading her through his thinnest, most sensitive skin. Though she'd expected him to try to make her come before him, he did not. The pleasure he inspired was diffuse, like molten toffee spreading out across a pan. Like toffee, its level rose millimetre by millimetre until it seemed a breath would make her come.

She stretched beneath him, hands and legs roving his work-hard limbs, revelling in the deepening tension, needing to throw it off.

'Almost there,' he whispered, his eyelids heavy, his mouth soft.

She closed her eyes and stopped thrusting, just feeling the soft in-and-out glide, the damp warmth of his skin, the gentleness of his callused hands. She had to breathe deeply to keep her climax off. The pulsations of his cock within her sheath, and of her sheath around his cock, were almost enough to push her over. She could not control the twitching of her inner walls. Her sex had taken on a life of its own.

'Look at me,' he said.

She looked at him. Her face tingled, and her hands, and the front of her body, as if warm, liquid electricity were running over her skin. The tingle reached her pussy. He shivered.

'Do you feel that?' he said. 'Your cunt is magic.'

But it wasn't her. It was him, the soft, blue heat in his eyes, the animal knowing in his hands. An ache began to gather deep inside her. 'I can't stop it,' she said. 'I'm going to come.'

He smiled, eyes crinkling, moustache lifting. 'Count to three, darlin'.' He drew back even more slowly than before, then pushed. Her muscles tightened around his re-entry, naturally, without strain or effort. One, she thought, and sighed when he withdrew. She slid her hand down his spine and around his buttocks, cradling his sac from behind as he pressed forward again. His balls were tight and hard inside. She compressed them gently. His hips juddered in reaction. Two, she thought, thrilled by the tiny quake. As he pulled back one last time, she felt him thicken and heat. Her orgasm teetered on its edge.

'Three,' she said, and came with his push. Her contractions were slow and deep, an intense but dreamy climax. He joined her before the second wave of sensation faded. Swimming in his own pleasure, he moaned, a rich, drawn-out baritone. Her body softened at the sound, melting even as it throbbed. When they'd both gone limp, he withdrew and sank to her side.

'Nice,' he said, hugging her loosely. 'That was real nice.'

Without warning, tears stung her eyes. She pressed her palm to the centre of her forehead, trying to force them back. Lord, what a leaky tap she'd been lately. She couldn't help it, though. He could have mastered her again, easily; could have forced her to come twenty times before he'd finished. Instead, he'd shown her the sweetest, most egalitarian lovemaking she'd ever known. It wasn't 'nice'. It was earth-shattering.

She hadn't thought once of the general or his belt. In fact, she hadn't visited that fantasy with Marty and Carolyn, or with Ben. Her hand fell to her side. She hadn't thought of the general since Zach made love to her in the loft. By that single act, he seemed to have exorcised a lifelong obsession.

But how could that be? How could any of this be? And what if Zach were the only man who had this effect on her?

As if he sensed her worries, he shifted closer and nuzzled the hollow between her neck and shoulder. 'Don't let me sleep all night,' he said. 'Now that I've got you in my bed, I don't want to waste a minute.'

A chill gripped Julia's heart. She remembered his nickname, and the reason for it. Oh, God, she thought. Two down and five to go.

Twice more that night he made love to her. The first was hard and fast. He woke her with stinging kisses and drove his cock inside before she was ready. Her dryness shocked him.

'Oh, darlin'.' He clasped her face and closed her eyes with penitent kisses. 'I'm sorry. I'm sorry.'

But it didn't matter. His very roughness had woken her sex; had drawn the smooth, rich fluid from its scarlet walls. Too sleepy to worry about her reaction and too aroused to deny it, she wrapped her heels behind his neck and drew him deep, deep inside. He coughed, no doubt surprised to find her so flexible. She laughed. 'Fuck me like you mean it, cowboy.'

'Oh, I mean it,' he assured her, beginning to pump. 'Christ, do I mean it.'

His broncs couldn't have bucked harder than she did. She wanted it rougher; wanted everything he had. He gritted his teeth and gave her his all. The box-spring squealed. The headboard thumped against the wall. Every breath he took had a sound: a gasp, a grunt, a tortured groan. He worked one arm under her hips to steady her.

'Easy,' he said. 'Easy.' But neither of them could slow. Their bodies collided within a clinch of arms and legs, drawing back just far enough to gather momentum for another thump, another pump, another bone-bruising grind. He gripped her hair hard and pulled her head back, his mouth clamping on the exposed skin.

He'd mark her again, but she didn't care. She dug her nails into his buttocks, thrilling to his flinch, then drove her longest finger into his anus with as little preparation as he'd driven his cock into her cunt. He froze. He released her throat and panted in her ear. 'What . . . are you doing?'

Had no one touched him here before? Such a childish thrill, that she should be the first. She could not shake it off; could not resist it. She'd always enjoyed breaking virgin ground. She pushed her finger in an inch, enough for a neophyte. His sphincter twitched; tightened in protest. She stroked the sensitive flesh just inside his entrance. His cock jumped.

'I guess –' he began, his voice frayed. His hips

wagged, intensifying the pressure her finger exerted. 'I guess there is something to be said for playing around back there.'

The laugh burbled out of her. She licked his crimsoned earlobe. 'Yes, there is, and it's just as much fun when you're the one doing the playing.'

His eyes widened. He made a leap she didn't expect. 'You'd let me do that? You'd let me take you the way Marty took that pool-boy?'

'That way and plenty more.'

His pupils glittered, as if all the ways he might take her were flashing through his mind. Then the reins snapped. He drove his cock downward into her sheath, deep and quick, pumping the head and ridge tight to the back wall. It was a selfish stroke, one that ignored the placement of her most sensitive nerves, one she doubted he indulged in very often. She loved it. She loved that she'd made him forget himself. She loved that he was out of control, that he was racing towards climax in a way he never had before. She let herself come before she normally would because she didn't want to miss a second of his crash and burn.

'Yes,' she hissed, gyrating her finger inside his rim. 'Come, Zach, come.'

He thrust so hard the back of her skull hit the headboard. 'Fuck,' he said. 'Julia!'

He came with the low, kick-in-the gut bellow she'd heard Carolyn draw from him that first night. Her sense of victory was as sweet as it was unexpected. She hadn't known she wanted that proof until she heard it. He sank on to her with a groan of contrition.

'Julia.' He rubbed the bump on the back of her head. 'Julia. My God.'

A second later he was dead to the world. She held him as he slept, rubbing his back with his cock spent but nestled inside her. Unlike Marty, he did snore – softly, but he did. Julia didn't care. The way his moustache fluttered against her neck made her smile.

He hardened before he woke. She lay there, laughing to herself, waiting for him to register his own condition. She had more than enough time to reach in his bedside table for an assortment of condoms. Three decorated her cleavage by the time his brain caught up to his cock. 'Mph,' he said, choosing one with bleary eyes and fumbling fingers. She put the others aside, but she didn't help. She loved watching him handle himself, especially since he wasn't all business. He seemed to enjoy touching himself as he smoothed the latex down, as he circled the crest with one lazy finger, as he squeezed the base with his fist.

Still half-asleep, he turned her on to her belly. Immediately, Julia knew what was coming. She'd given him permission and now he couldn't wait to play. He kissed her bottom and pushed her thighs gently outward. He parted her cheeks. He dipped into her sheath with his cock, swirling it around a few times before shifting back to that other, darker mouth. She'd grown wet as he slept inside her, and adding this to the condom's lubrication allowed his cock to slide easily past her sphincter.

'Oh,' he said in revelation at the warm, satiny passage. Then all she heard was the concentrated rhythm of his breathing as he worked deeper and deeper and finally began to thrust. He curled his hand under her mons, supporting her for his strokes. The broad flare of his glans was heaven against her outer reaches. He seem to know it, for he drew fully in and out each time.

'Shh,' he said when she tried to move. He seemed to require nothing beyond acquiescence. She could have gone back to sleep if she'd wanted, but she didn't. This was too lovely, too luxurious, feeling his slow rise towards orgasm, his hums, his sighs. Her very own intrepid explorer. He came before she did, then palmed her to climax, remaining inside her to the end. Her own finish was a gentle burst of pleasure, a knot of tension falling open. When it was over, Zach turned her to face him and cuddled her close as if she were a much smaller woman.

'I've been curious about something,' he said, the words slurred by satiation. Lulled, Julia hummed her willingness to talk. 'Is your mother still alive?'

She lifted her head. Of all the questions he might have asked, she hadn't seen this one coming. Her hands pressed the hard curve of his upper chest, opening an inch of space between them. 'Why do you ask?'

He shrugged. 'Just wondered. You seem kind of detached from the usual ties.'

Was that what an orphan was: detached? Or was that what Julia had been since the day she was born?

'She died when I was eighteen,' she said. 'A drunk driver hit her on her way to my high-school graduation.' She blew the air out of her lungs; blew away Zach's murmur of sympathy. 'I didn't want to go. I barely knew my classmates. But Mother assumed we would, even acted – in her stiff Swiss way – as if she was looking forward to it. She'd bought a new camera. When the paramedics cut her from the wreckage, it lay on the seat next to her. Didn't have a scratch on it.'

Julia shook her head, remembering the discovery. Her mother never took pictures of anything, but she'd wanted to take pictures of Julia's graduation. Her mother had loved her more than she'd realised. She'd just never known how to show it.

'And after that you were alone,' Zach said.

Julia closed her eyes. She hadn't been alone, not entirely. 'After that, I went straight to secretarial school. I wanted to be out in the world supporting myself.'

'You didn't want to work for the army?'

'No.' Her neck was stiff. Zach's hands crept under her hair and kneaded the cramped muscles. Apparently, he read her body as easily as he read his horses'.

'I don't suppose the general had anything to do with your wanting to leave.'

Julia could not deny his guess. The general had everything to do with her hasty departure from the base. He'd been crazed with despair; too crazed not to turn to the one person who knew his secret, who had it within her means to offer the only kind of comfort he craved.

'I almost stayed,' she said, not sure why she was answering. 'Part of me wanted to.'

'I see,' he said. 'I guess you needed to stretch your own wings, not your mother's.'

'Yes.' His tone was so tolerant she thought he must not understand what she'd meant. Her chest hurt. He begged me to whip him, she wanted to say. He cried and clung to my knees. I wanted to do it. I almost did. Even now, she wasn't sure what stopped her.

'He was a father to you,' he said, his perception uncanny, at once terrifying and welcome. 'He should have treated you like a daughter.'

'Yes,' she said. She could admit that hurt now, that betrayal. She hadn't always viewed him as a daughter should, but at that time, fair or not, she'd wanted him to offer a father's unconditional, undemanding support. Instead, he'd tried to make her over in her

209

mother's image. Her hand curled into a fist over Zach's heart.

He lifted it and kissed its knuckles, one by one. 'I'm glad you're here,' he said.

Her throat tightened. Why did this man's kindness mean so much to her? Why did his presence comfort her when they couldn't have been more different?

'I'm glad I'm here, too,' she said. Her voice shook. He had lightened the pain and it frightened her. Did he guess that, too? She looked at him. His gaze mild, he kissed her brow.

'Sleep,' he said, and she did.

He woke her at sunrise. This time, he rolled her on top of him, letting her take him at her own pace.

'Won't the horses be hungry?' she asked.

He smiled and smoothed her tousled hair down the rise of her breasts. She tried to remember the last time anyone had seen her so mussed. 'The horses will wait this once,' he said. 'You look beautiful like this. I wish we could stay in bed all day.'

So did she, but she knew it couldn't be.

Chapter Eleven

Monday morning

Julia entered the dining room just as Zach set one last steaming platter on the table. His smile was warm but cautious. She should have known he would not flaunt his conquest. He was a private man himself, a private man with private limits. Her answering smile felt like a grimace. She took the seat that had become hers, opposite Marty and Ben.

Marty said something that made Ben laugh. Julia didn't have the faintest idea what. She spread a film of butter across a slice of chewy home-made bread. Her skin prickled. Without looking, she knew Zach was staring at her. This had happened now and then with a new submissive. A bond formed, almost preternatural. She would know when she had their complete attention; could guess what they wanted before they did.

What did Zach want? She turned and their eyes connected. He smiled over the rim of his coffee mug.

She remembered how his moustache tickled when he put his mouth on her sex. Her pulse quickened. Her concentration slipped. It was hopeless. She could not interpret the thoughts behind his grin. Zach was too guarded for her, too patient. Too alien, she added, though for all she knew he'd been visiting the same memory. Vaguely irritated, she turned back to the rest of the table.

Carolyn, she noticed, was quiet this morning. His maternal streak showing, Marty filled her plate and made sure she ate what was on it. Her head was down, her slender neck bowed. But it wouldn't have mattered if she'd lifted it; her gaze was turned inward today.

Julia had seen this before. Carolyn was absorbing her first submissive experience, examining it, savouring it. She stroked her silverware as if the world had, overnight, become a more sensual place. Julia knew the VP was feeling more alive than she ever had. She could not, however, decide what she felt about Carolyn's transformation. Triumph? Satisfaction? Unease? She could admit to all three. But her emotions had no focus. They were muddled and shifting.

She sipped her orange juice, the cool liquid slipping down her throat. She could not ground herself. She felt disjointed. She knew Zach was the reason why.

'Where the hell are you?' Durbin demanded, his voice bullish. 'It's nearly noon. We've got that client lunch today.'

Julia swivelled her chair to face the windows. She sat in the office alcove next to the great room. Outside, snow drifted like drunken feathers to the ground, little more than a flurry. Beautiful as it was, the dwindling fall depressed her. 'Haven't you heard?' she said. 'We're snowed in.'

'Snowed in? As in no planes taking off?'

'That's right.'

'Oh.' She heard his blunt fingers drum the desktop, thwarted anger searching for a target. 'Well, when do you think you'll get back?'

'I'm not a weatherman.' Her answer was purposefully cold. His breathing shifted and she knew she'd inadvertently aroused him. He inhaled as if to say something, but she cut him off. 'Take Jody Lundeen with you to lunch. The union men like her and she knows those tax-free municipals inside out.'

'I thought I'd take Charlie. He's been golfing with them.'

'You can't take Charlie if they're serving alcohol. He gets too loud. Anyway, Jody knows their portfolio better.'

Durbin sighed. 'I hate it when you're right. I also hate it when you're gone.' His chair creaked. She pictured him bending closer to the phone. 'You have no idea how much I look forward to Monday. All weekend I dream about you sailing into the office in those snug grey suits. I love hearing you snap out orders to the rest of the staff. I always think maybe that night or the next, you'll be snapping out orders to me.' The words came from low in his chest, gravelled with lust. The evidence of her power over him made her pussy swell. Peeved with herself, she uncrossed her legs and straightened her spine.

'I told you,' she said. 'I'm ending our relationship.'

'Never,' he growled. 'You know you're lying. What we've got is too hot to give up. Shit, we've been on the line two minutes and I'm hard as a rock. I've got my hand in my pocket, Jules. I'm rubbing my big, hot prick. I'm almost coming from knowing you're listening on the other end; from knowing you're sitting there, creaming those French silk panties you like. I'll have to pull my zip down pretty soon or I'll leave a big wet spot on my fly. You know I'm not wearing underwear. You know I wouldn't dare disobey you. But maybe you want me to make a mess. Maybe you want to order me to do it.'

He was breathing roughly, probably as close to coming as he'd threatened. Was he crazy enough to shoot off inside his trousers minutes before a client meeting? Julia didn't know the answer any more. She didn't want to play along, but she didn't know how else to stop him from making a fool of himself.

'I didn't give you permission to touch yourself,' she said in her sharpest, most domineering voice. He moaned and she knew she had seconds to act. 'Open your zip. Now!' She heard the rasp of the metal teeth; heard his whimper of pre-orgasmic panic. 'Roll your chair under your desk. Grab a tissue.'

Wheels squeaked. Something fell to the floor. Durbin cursed, then groaned. She knew it was too late. She knew he was coming. She waited.

'My hand,' he gasped when he could speak again. 'I couldn't get the tissue in time, Ms Mueller. It's dripping all over my hand.'

No doubt he expected her to punish him for that. Julia closed her eyes and prayed for patience. 'Fine,' she said. 'Just tidy up and put your cock away.'

'All right,' he said. Obviously disappointed, he didn't forget his manners entirely. 'Thanks, Jules. That was great.'

Julia didn't tell him he was welcome. 'Is there anything else?'

'What? Oh, yeah. Have you made any progress finding our leak?'

'No,' she said, more emphatic than truthful.

'No?' He made a throat-clearing noise. She knew this was not the answer he'd expected. 'Well, keep at it. I'm sure you'll dig up something.'

'Right.' She pinched the bridge of her nose. 'Do you have any more questions?'

'No-o,' he said unsurely. She wasn't usually so brusque when discussing business. 'Just get back here as soon as you can and, you know, call me. I miss you.'

'I'll see if I have time.' She hung up before he could complain. 'Fuck,' she said to the silent phone. Durbin was in worse shape than she'd known. Maybe she should have told him she'd slept with Marty. Frankly, though, she wasn't sure the knowledge that she'd seduced his entire management team would be enough to disenchant him. He'd think she'd done it for him, to torture him. He thought everything centred on him.

She twisted the chair away from the window and found Zach standing in the middle of the great room, her long leather coat draped over his arm. A flush darkened his rugged face. His brow puckered with what could have been worry or disapproval.

He must have heard her conversation with Durbin. An unwelcome heat suffused her cheeks. Part of her, a disturbingly large part, wished she could have hidden the exchange from him. Hearing a story about her sexual practices was hardly the same as seeing them in action. But screw that, she thought. She had nothing to be ashamed of. Her relationship with Durbin was consensual and intended to give pleasure on both sides. The problem lay not in what they did, but in Durbin's inability to keep it in perspective, a problem she fully intended to address. None of which was any of Zach's business.

'I, uh –' He lifted her coat in silent explanation. 'I

wondered if you wanted to help me with the horses today.'

Julia folded her hands in her lap and tried to forget this was the man who'd made love to her all night long. Six times now. Six times he'd turned her inside out and showed her she didn't know herself at all. 'I have plans,' she said.

His flush deepened at the chill in her voice and, damn it, so did hers. For a second she thought he'd leave, but he dropped her coat and walked towards her. He cupped her face, his eyes wrinkling with concern, his thumb stroking soft as goose-down over her cheek. 'Are you all right?'

Meeting his laser-blue gaze required an effort of will. 'Don't imagine I'm a victim here. My boss hasn't forced me into anything. Our relationship is entirely consensual and it continues only so long as I want it to.'

He nodded and swallowed, then turned his face to the frost-rimed window. 'It's none of my business.'

'Exactly,' she agreed, though she wasn't sure either of them meant it.

His eyes returned to hers. His hand fell from her cheek. Immediately, she missed its rough warmth.

'Do you really have plans today?'

She nodded. Again, it seemed as if he'd leave but at the last moment he turned back and kissed her. His tongue played at the seam of her lips before pressing gently inward. She gripped the arms of her chair, wishing she could fight even as she opened to him, even as her spine sagged with pleasure. The motions of his tongue were as delicate as butterfly wings. Where had this big man learnt such tenderness, and why did he offer it to her? She lifted one arm and cupped the back of his silky head. His breath sighed against her cheek. He changed the slant of his mouth.

The kiss gentled even more, a lullaby of lips and tongue. When he finally drew away, her body was as loose and warm as if she'd been lying in the sun.

He trailed one finger down the side of her face. 'Save some time for me, darlin'. Life is short and feelings like this don't come along every day.'

Then he did leave. She almost called him back. What feelings was he talking about? Did he love her? Could he? In spite of everything he knew?

She slammed her hands on the arms of her chair. 'Could he love me?' Her lips made a silent simper of the words. She was behaving like a schoolgirl, the sort she'd never been and never hoped to be. One more fuck, she told herself. One more and it was over for her and 'Sev'.

She ignored the way this made her stomach clench. She rose to prepare for her slaves.

This time she dressed: full regalia, her blood simmering with a defiance she hadn't felt since her mother died. She knew her behaviour was childish. She couldn't reclaim her shaken identity by playing dressing-up.

But she could remind herself how good it felt to don the trappings of power.

She pulled the black deerskin boots up her legs and nodded with satisfaction. Criss-crossed laces extended from their steel-tipped toes to their thigh-high hem. She snugged them, loop by loop, and tied them at the top. The tall heels tightened her buttocks and calves, the tilt making her aware of her height, her power, her femininity.

A leather corset, also black, topped the boots. This leather was thick and brutal. She cinched it just tight enough to enhance the natural curve of her waist, but not tight enough to restrict her breathing. The corset's

217

bra was a warrior queen's breastplate. Two brass nipples studded each circular cup. Inside their hollowed centres, her own nipples lay, tightened by cold and arousal. A pair of black opera-length gloves completed the ensemble, their fingers cut out so as not to hamper the administration of discipline.

Her slaves entered at precisely the appointed time. They wore the white cotton robes she'd given them earlier. Carolyn resembled a tiny karate student in hers, Marty a jolly monk. When Carolyn caught sight of Julia in full gear, her lower lip quivered.

'Ms Mueller,' she whispered, and dropped to her knees to kiss Julia's boots.

Marty's eyes widened as if to say: I hope you don't expect me to do that. Julia shook her head and eased back from Carolyn.

'I will tell you when I wish you to perform obeisance,' she said.

Carolyn bowed her head, her body vibrating with excitement. 'Yes, Ms Mueller.'

The intensity of her response disturbed Julia. A slave needed a certain amount of resistance, both to protect herself and to give her master something to work against. Carolyn seemed to be surrendering all after a single session.

'Take off your robe,' she said, setting her qualms aside for the moment.

Carolyn obeyed without hesitation, then resumed her kneeling position. Julia circled her, thinking, planning. With the snow melting, she might not get another chance to discover the truth. She needed to break the VP now, today. Carolyn dried her palms on her naked thighs. Her pink-tipped breasts trembled with the beating of her heart. She shifted on her heels, her knees easing further apart. Julia spied a sheen of moisture on her mouse-brown curls. Her sex gave a little jump, the old pleasure twining round her core like a soft black cat. Whatever the drawbacks, a wholehearted surrender had its charms.

When she judged Carolyn's tension had reached a sufficient pitch, she lifted a willow-ware bowl from her bedside table and handed it to Marty. 'Open the window,' she said, 'and fill it with snow.'

Carolyn shivered. Obviously, she had some idea of what was coming. When Marty returned with the heaped dish of snow, Julia toed Carolyn's lily-white thighs apart and ordered her to lace her hands behind her neck. The position lifted her delicate breasts, which shimmied with agitation, their nipples drawn into hard pink buds.

Marty stood at Julia's shoulder in the pose of an obedient acolyte, eyes lowered, both hands holding the bowl before his chest. His erection pushed his robe out before him, the tip nudging through the flaps. Good. She had his attention, too.

'We're going to play a game,' she said, scooping up a handful of snow. 'It's called "Truth is its Own Reward".' She trailed the snow up the underside of Carolyn's raised arm. Carolyn bit her lip but did not make a sound. Julia smiled to herself. Just wait, she thought. Just wait. She watched a trickle of ice-water roll down Carolyn's ribs before continuing. 'In this game, I ask a question and if you tell me the truth, you get a reward. Are you ready?'

'Yes, Ms Mueller.'

'Very well. Here is the first question. Do you think DMI pays you what you deserve?'

Carolyn's head snapped up. Obviously this topic caught her by surprise. Her mouth gaped for a moment before any sound came out. 'No,' she said with a hint of her old spirit. 'I think I deserve to be paid more.'

'Very good,' said Julia. 'And here is your reward.' She bent over Carolyn from behind. The position offered Marty a fine view of her corset-plumped breasts. She didn't want him wondering why she'd chosen this line of inquiry. Happily, his eyes homed in on her cleavage, then followed the approach of her snow-filled glove to Carolyn's breast.

Carolyn's breath hissed between her teeth as the snow touched her nipple. Its distension immediately increased and its colour deepened to a fine, plummy red. Julia circled the areola, then cupped it, trapping the snow between Carolyn's breast and her palm. Carolyn struggled not to jerk away.

'Cold, isn't it?' Julia said. 'It excites even as it numbs. Makes you feel all warm and tingly inside.' Carolyn's tongue crept out to moisten her upper lip. 'I'd bet you'd like me to do the other nipple, too, wouldn't you?'

'Yes,' Carolyn whispered. She moaned when Julia drew her hand away.

'For shame,' she said. 'You can't have a reward until you've earnt it. Here's your second question: does Marty Fine turn you on?'

'God, no,' Carolyn said, then flinched at Julia's mocking laugh.

'Liar. I guess I'll have to give Marty your reward.'

'No!' Carolyn cried, but Julia refused to respond. Instead, she pushed Marty's robe open, grabbed another handful of snow and cupped it over his balls.

Marty yelped, almost dropping the bowl in shock. His erection sagged over Julia's hand.

'Poor thing.' Julia tutted in crocodile dismay. She went to her knees and drew his waning shaft into the hot wet comfort of her mouth. At once it rallied, despite her continuing to press snow over his shrinking sac. He widened his stance to keep his balance, which gave her more access. As she sucked, she rubbed the melting snow over his perineum and on to the tight wrinkled star of his anus. Marty went up on his toes. His cock swelled in her mouth, harder than it had been before she shocked it. She let go and backed away.

Marty panted once and set his jaw against whatever protest he'd wanted to make.

'Now.' Julia dipped into the bowl and turned to Carolyn. The woman's hands were fisted on her thighs. 'Let's try this again.' She held her icy handful above Carolyn's breast and let it drip. 'Are you jealous of Marty Fine?'

Carolyn's gaze darted towards Marty but did not rise. 'Yes.'

Julia shifted the snow so that it dripped directly on to her nipple. 'Were you annoyed when he was promoted and you weren't?'

'Yes,' she gasped, straining upward towards the taunting hand.

'I bet you'd have done a great deal to get even.'

'Yes,' she said. 'Yes!' Her face was red, her breathing quick and light. Julia lowered her dripping hand. Carolyn twisted, trying to reach it without leaving the position she'd been ordered to assume. She was Julia's creature now. She'd answer any question, admit to any crime, even a crime whose exposure could end her career. All Julia had to do was ask: did you betray DMI to Santorini?

Without warning, Julia's stomach turned over. She felt queasy, her enjoyment gone. For a moment, she could not imagine why this should be so. But then she knew. It was not her awareness of Carolyn's fragility

221

that had ruined the game, or her niggling fear that Zach would discover what she'd done and disapprove. No. The problem was that *she* disapproved. She had broken her own rule, and the most sacred at that: that this should always be done with the intent to heighten pleasure. Not to steal a secret. Not to find a traitor for a man who, Julia knew, had done little to earn anyone's loyalty.

This was a travesty of all she believed in. It must stop.

Her arm fell to her side. Her fingers opened. The snow splashed to the toe of her boot. She didn't care. She didn't care.

'No,' Carolyn wailed, clutching her knees. 'I'll be good. I'll answer anything you want. You're the boss of me, please. You're the boss of me.'

Julia closed her eyes. She had put those words in Carolyn's mouth; she and no one else. What had she done to this vulnerable young woman? She prayed she could undo it. Gathering her strength, she clasped Carolyn's face and lifted it, one glove warm, one glove cold. 'I lied to you,' she said, putting all her persuasion into her gaze. 'I'm not the boss of you. You are. You always were. You always will be. Any power I had over you, you gave me.'

'No.' Carolyn was sobbing in earnest now, hiding her face between Julia's knees. 'You can't leave me like this. You can't take me this far and leave me.'

'Julia.' The voice was Marty's. She looked at him, feeling as lost as Carolyn sounded. His expression was strange. Did he know what she'd been trying to get Carolyn to admit? Did he know because he was guilty? She shook her head, throwing off the question. To hell with that. It didn't matter.

'Julia,' Marty said again. He opened his arms. 'Give

her to me. I'll take care of her.' Carolyn clung and cried but he managed to prise her free. Then she clung to him. He stroked her bony back. The sharpness of her shoulder blades made Julia's breath catch. 'It's all right,' Marty said to both of them. 'I'll take care of her. Just go.'

But Julia couldn't just go. She met his eyes, taking his measure. Did he realise Carolyn wasn't the responsibility of a night or a week; that she was perhaps a responsibility he could not handle without professional help – and not Julia's sort of professional help? He already had his wife to take care of. Did he really want to add Carolyn to the mix?

'I can handle it,' he said.

'And if you can't?'

'Then I'll find someone who can.'

She saw that he meant it; that the challenge had energised him. He had the potential to be an excellent switch, dominant or submissive as the situation required. Perhaps that was what Carolyn needed: someone who could feed her submissive tendencies while also inspiring her aggressive ones. Perhaps together they would find a happy balance.

Grabbing the first clothes that came to hand, she nodded at Marty and withdrew. The last thing she heard as she headed to the bathroom to change was the sound of a brisk spanking. For the space of a heartbeat, she wondered who was administering it.

She went to the stables; searching for Zach, she admitted, though the horses were a lure as well. If they rejected her, she would know she'd slipped beyond redemption. If they accepted her, she didn't know what she'd do. Hope, she supposed. But for what, and from whom?

The question turned out to be moot. The horses were absent and so was Zach. She wandered into the tack room feeling wobbly and strange. A broken bridle lay across his desk, the same one she'd seen there before. They'd been keeping him busy, or perhaps his chores were always more than he could keep up with. She knew he wasn't lazy. His work ethic was one characteristic they shared. A melancholy sigh escaped her iron grip. When had the stupid cowboy become a man she admired?

Pushing the question away, she sat in his beat-up desk chair. The impression of his buttocks had shaped the seat. The hollows clasped her, taunted her. She ran her hands along the edge of the tan metal desk. Her fingertips took inventory of the scratches and dents, the coffee stains and sticky spots. Which had Zach made, and which his grandfather? The number for the vet was taped to the bottom of an old rotary phone. Oh, how awful if the horses got sick, she thought. How lost Zach would be. She touched the receiver. Scores of fingerprints dulled its black plastic shine. No one had cleaned this for a long, long time.

The multi-generational mess should have horrified her. Instead, for no reason she could fathom, she burst into tears.

Once they started, they fell in torrents, as if every hurt she'd refrained from crying about must be cried about now. She cried for her father and her mother, married but not in love. She cried for the general and the dog she hadn't been allowed to buy. She cried for Carolyn and Marty, and for Marty's poor compulsive gambling wife. Mostly, though, she cried for herself. What was the matter with her? How had she become this ridiculous drippy mess? If this was what it meant to have a heart, the vanilla world could keep it.

'Hey, what's wrong?' said a soft, masculine voice. A hand settled between her shoulder blades. It wasn't Zach's. It was Ben's. She grabbed a dusty rag. It looked like an old T-shirt. The cotton smelled of Zach, in other words: wonderful. She cried harder.

'Hey.' Ben crouched down beside her and pulled her close. 'Tell me what's wrong. I'm sure it's not as bad as you think.'

She blew her nose into the rag and blinked at him through blurry eyes. What a confessor he would make: sure to disapprove, unlikely to understand. But maybe she needed someone to agree with her own estimation of her sins. Maybe that would snap her out of this idiocy.

'Are you sure you want to know?' she said. 'It isn't a pretty story.'

He shook his head and smiled. 'If I can help, I want to know.'

She didn't tell him about Zach. She didn't share her crisis over being a dom. She did tell him about training Marty and Carolyn. As she'd expected, that was enough to shock him. When she explained what she'd almost forced Carolyn to admit, however, she saw something she'd never expected to see in his handsome face: she saw guilt.

'Julia.' He rubbed his smooth lean jaw, his eyes looking everywhere but into hers. 'There's something I need to tell you.'

No, she thought. 'No,' she said. She rolled the battered chair back from him, but retreat was useless. The pieces fell together against her will. She remembered his description of the first white woman he'd slept with, the woman he'd said he met at an office party. The whispery voice, the big doe-like eyes. They could only belong to one person: Sheila Fassbinder, the wife

225

of Go-Tech's chairman, the company whose account had been stolen from DMI. She didn't understand the connection between that and Ben's betrayal, but she knew there was one. 'You?' she said. 'You leaked our proposal to Santorini?'

He seemed relieved not to have to initiate the confession. Still crouched on the balls of his feet, he picked at the peeling arm of her chair. 'You know the woman I told the story about? She was Nate Fassbinder's wife. I slept with her a few times. She liked to talk about her husband after we, you know. She told me he was using Go-Tech's accounts to launder drug money. She didn't have proof, but I didn't want DMI to win their business and end up getting tarred with the same brush.'

'And you couldn't tell Durbin not to bid without telling him where you'd heard the rumour.'

Ben spread his hands, his eyes begging her to understand. 'I couldn't betray Sheila's trust. She didn't want to leave her husband. I feel bad enough that I sent an anonymous tip to the Securities and Exchange Commission. I don't know what will happen if they investigate.'

'Oh, Ben.' Julia covered her face. She didn't want to be hearing this, not when she'd finally decided the traitor's identity didn't matter.

'I'll tell Durbin everything,' he said, 'as soon as we get back.'

'But he'll ruin you.' She took his hands and squeezed them. 'He won't care that you were trying to protect him. He'll make sure you never work on Wall Street again.'

Ben's expression assumed a stubborn cast. 'I can't keep it a secret now I know he's suspecting the others. It wouldn't be fair.'

'Fuck fair,' Julia said. His eyebrows rose. She pushed

herself to her feet and paced the tiny room. 'I know there's a way out of this. I just need to think.' A spark of an idea shimmered through her mind. She stopped. She pressed her hands over her mouth and smiled. Oh, it was too delicious.

'What?' asked Ben.

She faced him. He was standing now, his long frame propped back on the cluttered desk. 'I've thought of a huge favour you can do me.'

'Name it.'

Her glee rose. She tossed her head and laughed. 'You can tell Durbin I'm the traitor. I know just how to prove it, too.'

'I can't do that,' he said.

'Oh, yes, you can,' she answered. 'Because it's the only way I'll get clear of him.'

He took some convincing, but she talked him round in the end. At last, she'd found a sin Durbin would not forgive: a threat to his bottom line. When he heard about this, he'd demand she never see him again. Even Ben could see the value of that.

'But what if he tries to get even?' he said.

'That's the beauty of me taking the fall. Durbin wouldn't dare expose me because I'd expose him. Believe me, I've got the evidence to do it.'

Ben waved his hands in front of his face. 'I don't want to know.'

That's when she knew she had him. Otherwise, plausible deniability would have been irrelevant.

Considering the morning that preceded it, lunch was not pleasant. Carolyn was subdued, Ben jittery and Zach as stone-faced as the carvings on Mount Rushmore. Asking people if they wanted seconds appeared to require a major effort. Was he angry at her for refusing his invitation to help with the horses? Or at himself for suggesting he wanted her to? Whatever the reason, he was making up for his earlier openness. Of the five of them, only Marty seemed calm, and he was too caught up in his thoughts to contribute his usual witty repartee.

As soon as they'd cleared the dishes, Julia headed for the well-appointed office Zach kept for his guests. She refused to waste time smoothing ruffled feathers. She had work to do and futures to safeguard, her own included.

She used Zach's modem to connect to the network in New York. After that, planting the evidence of her 'crime' was simple. Julia knew DMI's system intimately, having been involved in testing it prior to purchase. She inserted a few incriminating files into her personal computer, pre-dated them, then deleted them, but not so completely they wouldn't leave a trace. Then she hacked into the main server, a task made easy by possession of access codes usually reserved for designers. Once in the main server, she copied the incriminating files to the company's back-up system which, unbeknownst to most employees, recorded their every keystroke. Luckily, the back-up wasn't due to be removed for off-site storage for another week. Finally, she terminated the connection and hacked into the network. Careful to leave a mess behind her, she faked an attempt to delete the back-up files she'd just introduced. Now it looked as though Julia had modemed the Go-Tech proposal to Santorini, become afraid she'd got caught, then tried – unsuccessfully – to delete the evidence. DMI's overworked computer geeks might take a while to notice the break-in, but once Ben returned with his tale of treachery, they'd be certain to look for confirmation.

Satisfied they'd find it, she leant back in the swivel chair and stretched her arms. It had taken three hours to dot her 'i's and cross her 't's, but she was reasonably certain her deception would stand up under scrutiny. Durbin wouldn't want to believe she'd sold him out, but he'd be forced to when he saw this.

Her gaze swept the woods outside the house. The snow had ceased. She'd burnt her last bridge. A tension that was part excitement, part dread tightened in her chest. From this day forward, her old life was history.

She was rehearsing how she'd coach Ben to deliver the revelation, when Marty strolled in and pulled up a second chair. He patted her hand. 'You done working for the day?'

'Yes.'

'Good. I've been meaning to talk to you. You looked a bit red-eyed at lunch. I wanted to make sure you were OK.'

Her hand flew to her face. Her weeping fit came rushing back. She cried so seldom she'd forgotten what it did to a person's looks. Had Zach noticed? But, no, he wouldn't have been so ill-tempered if he had. 'I'm fine,' she said to Marty. 'I was upset but I'm over it.'

'She's all right, you know. Carolyn likes to be dramatic. Always gives a hundred and ten per cent to everything, including misery. But she'll bounce back.' He wagged his bushy brows. 'She might even decide she doesn't need my masterful help.'

Julia rolled her eyes. 'That might be the best thing. Carolyn could turn out to be a handful.'

'Nonsense.' He winked. 'I enjoy a new project. It makes me feel needed.'

She did not ignore the opening. 'If you really want to feel needed . . .'

'Yes?' he said.

'You could keep an eye out for Ben when you get back.'

He frowned. 'For Ben?'

'He might find himself in over his head.'

'In what over his head?'

'Trust me. You're better off not knowing.'

Marty's frown deepened, but after a brief stare he shrugged. 'All right. Keep your secrets. I'll look out for him. To tell you the truth –' he bumped chair wheels with her '– I've been thinking of starting my own operation. Investment advice for individual investors, preferably rich ones. I was hoping I could lure Ben with me. Those blue-haired biddies love that man's manners.'

'That might be a good idea.'

He scratched his stubbled cheek. 'Actually, I was hoping I could lure you away from Durbin, too.'

The prospect did not appeal as much as it might have. Marty would never give her as much responsibility as Durbin had. He wouldn't need to. Marty was capable of staying on top of things himself. She smoothed her skirt over her knees. 'It's kind of you to think of me.'

'Yeah, well, too bad the Big Apple won't be seeing you for a while.'

She stared at him. 'I never said I wasn't going back to New York, just not to DMI.'

'No?' He brushed a piece of lint from his shoulder. 'I must have been mistaken.'

'You were.'

Was that a smirk he was hiding? If it was, when he looked up it was gone. 'Maybe I'll give you a call then, when I'm set up.'

'Fine,' she said, still annoyed and hardly aware what she was agreeing to. How ludicrous. Why wouldn't she return to New York? Surely he couldn't imagine there was anything to hold her here.

Zach couldn't keep to his rooms. His bed was too empty and the sound of icicles dripping from the eaves was driving him nuts. The wind had changed. A thaw was setting in. The time that remained to break down Julia's wall was getting shorter by the minute.

He found her in the great room, sitting in the dark staring at the fire. Shadows leapt around the room, bathing the andirons, the ceiling beams, her regal silhouette.

'Are you all right?' he asked.

She started in surprise. A smile curled her lips. 'I'm fine,' she said. 'I took steps towards leaving my employer today.'

'Oh.' He rubbed his moustache. 'That's good.'

'Yes,' she said. 'It is.'

He wondered what, if anything, he ought to make of this. Would she be taking up with Marty now? Something was going on between those two, though he couldn't figure out what. Too distracted to consider whether his company was welcome, he plunked down beside her on the couch, half a cushion stretching like a gulf between them.

They sat in silence. Julia stared at the rodeo picture above the fire, the one his grandma had dusted clean every Sunday morning, last thing before she went to church. Its glass was a shifting river of gold and black. Zach wished he could think of something – anything – entertaining to say. After five of the longest minutes of his life, she turned towards him with a soft, crunching squeak of leather. Her knee brushed his thigh and a wash of heat flooded his groin. Unfortunately, she wasn't making a pass. 'When did your grandmother die?' she asked.

It was the first personal question he could recall her asking. She'd gone to the heart of him with it, as if she'd read his mind. He pressed his palms into his thighs, willing his arousal to recede, willing his brain to work. 'Last year. Right around this time.'

'You miss her.' It wasn't a question.

He nodded. 'I loved Grandpa, but she was my best friend in the world. The guests adored her. She always knew how to make people feel at home. I sure as hell wish I did.'

Julia touched his cheek with the back of her fingers. His heart literally skipped a beat. 'You do all right.'

The touch broke his patience. He faced her. 'Hell, Julia. We made love and it was really special. It kills me that I don't know what to say to you that won't scare you off.'

Not that, apparently. Her hand withdrew, leaving a patch of cold behind. 'You don't mean that. You don't even know me.'

'Then tell me what I don't know!' His voice cracked in frustration. 'I'll listen to all of it. Every heartbeat. Every hope. You name it, Julia, I'll open my ears and try to understand.'

She jumped off the couch, her eyes huge in the firelight, her hands clutched together before her breastbone. She looked wilder than he'd ever seen her, panicked. 'It's only a weekend,' she said, backing away. 'You don't even know me.'

I know enough, he thought as her footsteps receded towards her room. He knew his heart was set on her and nothing would shock him out of it, more fool he. He rose to damp the fire. The thought of what he was willing to do to keep her happy didn't scare him half as much as the thought of losing her.

Chapter Twelve

Monday night

*O*nce inside her room, Julia smacked her thighs with her fists. She was a fool, a rabbit bolting for her hole. What was she thinking, telling him he didn't know her? In one weekend, he'd learnt more than most people who'd known her for years. The stories she'd told weren't the only reason, either. The cowboy had instincts. He knew things about her he probably didn't know he knew. Why he hadn't run screaming she couldn't say, but she knew why she was scared. Because it *was* only a weekend. As Carolyn's experience proved, those ladies in Taylorsville didn't call him 'Sev' for nothing.

She stripped off her clothes and threw them into a corner, pausing only when a plane rumbled overhead. She stared at the pine-panelled ceiling. A plane. That meant the airport was open. As soon as they cleared a path down this mountain they could leave. Fine, she thought. The sooner the better. But she balled up her panties and tossed them angrily away. Pulling on her favourite silk chemise, she crawled into bed and curled up around the pillow. She gritted her teeth against an urge to cry. Once a day was plenty.

The knock took her by surprise. Heart pounding, she sat up. Zach entered without waiting for a response, his tall frame backlit by the light from the hall. He wore the long underwear that had given her such a creaming fit the night before, except this pair was red. The sudden hum in her groin told her she was developing a new fetish. The red cotton hung from the solid points of his hipbones, draping the hefty basket that dangled between his legs. Immune to the cautions of her brain, Julia's body softened in welcome. Zach elbowed the door shut and pulled a chair to the side of her bed.

'I can't let things go on like this,' he said.

She almost asked what he meant, but she hadn't grown as dishonest as that. Instead, she smoothed the covers over her waist. Zach heaved a weary sigh. Every cell in her body yearned to soothe him. Was this love, this helpless tenderness? Had she found what she'd been seeking even as she ran from it? Flo from the Coffee Stop had misled her. This was the man those women wanted to marry; not the indefatigable love machine, but this shy, earnest hunk. God help her. Julia wasn't any more sensible than they were.

When he took her hand in his, his palm was cold. 'Do you want to hear about my first lover, the story I wouldn't share that night by the fire?'

She couldn't make out his expression, but his eyes glittered in the dark. She knew this offer meant something to him; it had set his pulse racing. 'Yes,' she said, without letting herself wonder why he wanted to tell her, without letting herself hope. He shifted in the old-fashioned chair.

'Her name was Constance,' he began. 'She was my father's lover.'

Her spine straightened in surprise. She knew other people's families weren't perfect, but she hadn't expected Zach's to engage in adultery. 'Your father's?' she said.

He shrugged, a hint of defensiveness in it. 'He wasn't a womaniser. Constance was his only affair. If my mother knew, she pretended not to. Too old-school, I guess. Anyway, Constance and my father were habitually on-again, off-again. The way they fought you'd have thought they were married. My brother and I knew about her, but not my sisters. Tom and I made sure of that.'

Zach turned her hand and smoothed the cup of her palm. Julia couldn't take her eyes from his shadowed profile. She assumed Tom was his brother. He'd mentioned sisters, plural. Were there more than two? Her brain shifted, trying to fit this into her picture of him. The rodeo was there already, and the lovesick women of Taylorsville. The man who'd fucked her into submission in the loft was part of it, and the one who'd loved her to exhaustion in his bed. And who could forget the hedonist who'd let Carolyn blow him in broad daylight, or the saint who'd taught her to pet a skittish horse? Now to all this she could add a family: one with a philandering father and at least a pair of sheltered sisters. She bet Zach was the eldest. Were you? she wanted to ask, but she was afraid to break his storyteller's nerve.

His thumb traced the soft pads of flesh at the base of her fingers. 'My father and I didn't get on. We had different ideas about how stock should be treated and

235

my rapport with the horses made him nervous. Dad believed in breaking horses, in whipping them into submission. Whenever I showed him that my way worked and, what's more, worked better than his, he'd act as if I'd slapped him. So we never did get on and Constance knew it.

'On my seventeenth birthday, he and Constance had a big fight. Like most ranchers, my dad is careful with money, sometimes too careful. As I recall, he wouldn't lend her a couple of hundred to repair her car. They were hollering about it in front of the feed shop. I thought someone would hear and get word back to Mom, so I offered to loan Constance what she needed. I had some rodeo prizes stashed and nothing in particular I wanted to spend them on. I wasn't trying to make Dad look bad. I was just trying to shut Constance up. But he was so angry he got in to the car and drove off without me. He stranded me twenty miles from home in the dead of winter.

'Constance couldn't drive me since her car was shot, so she told me I could stay with her. I guess I was pretty naïve because I didn't think anything of it. She was a lot younger than my dad but, to me, I was a kid and she was a grown-up. I learnt differently when she crawled into my bed that night. I'm not sure I can describe what her hands did to me. Up till then, I'd never had a girl do more than kiss me. Now, this voluptuous older woman was touching me in places that had never felt any hand but mine, plus a few that hadn't felt that. She'd come to me naked. Her breasts were softer than anything I'd known. I hardly dared touch them, but her hands were all over me, waking my nerves like firecrackers, and suddenly I realised I was supposed to touch her. That was what was fair.' Zach's moustache slanted with his smile. 'I nearly fainted when I felt her nipples bud up under my palms. I couldn't have been more stunned if I'd woken one morning knowing how to pluck rabbits out of hats. My skin was on fire; my cock so hard it stung. I was so excited I could hardly breathe.

'Lord, I was a mess. Constance had to pull me on top of her or I would have spent all night going over her like a blind man. I jumped halfway to the ceiling when she wrapped her fingers around my cock. Then she put me inside her.

'I thought I'd died and gone to heaven. She was warm and slippery and her sex moved around me like a cat on heat. I was shaking worse than a newborn calf. I knew I was supposed to move, but I couldn't figure out how to balance and thrust at the same time. Finally, she rolled me under her and straddled me. She was a beautiful woman and, boy, did she love to rock and roll. I remember watching her come and thinking this must be how people who found Jesus felt. Sex was that amazing to me: a revelation.

'As things progressed, though, I started to wonder if something was wrong with me. Everything felt incredible, but I hadn't come yet. My friends who'd done it said it only took a few minutes, a few seconds the first time.

'When I apologised for taking so long, Constance laughed. "You take as long as you want, Little Zach." I could tell she was enjoying herself, so I relaxed and let her explain a few things about the female body that my buddies had never mentioned. "What a dear!" she said when I did what she'd showed me to her clit. I did it some more and pretty soon she came again, even harder than the first time. When she caught her breath, she told me I'd earnt a reward. By then, I was ready for one. I thought I'd bust if I didn't come. Constance pulled off me and took my cock into her mouth. Then I really thought I'd gone to heaven. I blasted off in about two seconds. The orgasm was better than anything I'd ever done for myself, deeper and harder. I thought for sure she'd wrung me dry, but a minute later, I was raring to go again. Just thinking about what we'd done got me all steamed up. We went at it until we were both too tired to move. Constance could be a bitch, but she was pure fun between the sheets. I was enjoying myself so much, I never stopped to wonder how my father would feel about being kicked out of his mistress's bed by his own son. Or how I'd feel if he didn't forgive me. I was too damn randy to use my brain.

'That first night led to a second, then to a week, then two. Constance called in sick at work and we screwed morning, noon and night. In the end, Grandpa came down from the mountain to give me a talking to.'

Zach's laugh was a rush of air. 'Grandpa never raised his voice, but he had a knack for making a person see the error of his ways. Before long I felt lower than a snake's belly. I said goodbye to Constance, thanked her for being such a good teacher and dragged myself back home. Unfortunately, my dad wouldn't let me in the house. My grandpa had come with me, expecting there'd be trouble, but even he couldn't convince my dad to forgive me. Grandpa took me home with him and, apart from holidays and birthdays, I've spent every night since under this roof.'

'You and your dad still don't talk?'

'We say "howdy" and shake hands, but we never talked much to start with. We disagree about most everything. It's easier for everybody if we keep our distance.' He patted her hand as if to comfort her. His was shaking, a token of how seldom he bared his soul.

She squeezed his fingers. 'Why did you tell me this?'

'I want you to know me,' he said.

It was a simple answer: no promises, no declarations, just 'I want you to know me'.

Julia stared at their joined hands. She supposed she'd wanted a declaration of love. But maybe this was better. He wanted her to know him. Even if the knowing didn't outlive another dawn, for a private man like Zach that offer was rare. Didn't she have the courage to accept it, regardless of the cost to her heart? She fought a sigh. She couldn't deny any longer that her heart was at risk. Whatever love was, this turmoil he stirred in her must be a cousin to it. But she'd taken too long to respond.

'Julia?' he said. She lifted her head, glad of the darkness that hid her brimming eyes. He carried her hand to his chest and pressed her palm over his heart. When he spoke, his voice was hushed. 'Tell me what you want from me. Do I need to bend to you? Do you want to use your belt on me?'

'No,' she said, shaken by his offer.

'I'm not sure I'd mind. I suspect I'd find you irresistible even if you painted me blue and chained me to the bedpost.'

'No.' Her free hand reached for his face. 'That's not what I want from you.'

'Then what do you want?'

She stroked his cheek from temple to jaw. 'I want to make love again. I want to show you how tender I can be.'

His smile brought a crease to his beard-shaded cheek. 'I'd like that very much.'

She tugged him on to the bed and pushed him gently down, knowing it was the last time but feeling as if it were the first. Her hands tingled with awareness. A small brass reading lamp extended from the wall above the bed. She flicked it on. Zach lay quietly, watching as she stripped off her rose-pink chemise and draped it over the shade. The light dimmed and warmed. Zach shifted his hips. His erection formed a thick arch behind the red cotton drawers, but he did not reach for her. Slowly, giving herself time to enjoy the unveiling, she peeled the long underwear down his legs. When she reached his feet, she bent to kiss his toes. He had crooked, battered toes, but they were as sensitive as the rest of him. They curled strongly at the touch of her tongue. Sucking one into her mouth, she scratched his soles with her nails. His knees wavered up and down. He truly was a pleasure to tease. She would miss that most of all.

'Come here,' he growled, but he lay as passively as if she'd bound him.

He probably thought he was being a gentleman, letting a lady take the lead. To a woman of her bent, however, any subservience carried a special cachet. A peculiar thrill quivered up her spine, peculiar because it felt so fresh, as if she had never mastered anyone before. She knew her control over Zach was fragile. He might overturn it at any moment. That was thrilling, too, perhaps because she knew she'd let him.

She crawled up his body and straddled his hips. He clasped her waist but presumed no further. She sat back until her bottom rested on warm, hairy thighs. His hands slid up her ribs. She caught them before he could fondle her breasts.

'Let me,' she said, her voice unrecognisably soft. 'Let me pleasure you. Let me go as slowly as I want.'

Surrender and anticipation mingled in his sigh. He nodded.

With a sigh of her own, she traced his receding

hairline with her fingertips, lingering on the smooth, sensitive skin at his temples. His golden-brown hair was clipped so short it bristled like a Marine's. His quadriceps tightened when she tickled the rims of his ears. He closed his eyes when she scratched back over his skull.

'I'm going to touch your forgotten places,' she said, stroking her thumbs together towards his chin. 'I'm going to love them all.'

'Julia,' he whispered.

She caressed the winter-chapped fullness of his lower lip. She smoothed his eyebrows, then his nose, then the silky brush of his moustache. With his eyes shut, she could study him as she wished. She loved the seams that Montana's weather had left in his skin. More than laugh lines; these were character lines. They spoke of hard work and sunshine and strength. They spoke of patience and pain and a big capacity for love. His face would age well, she thought. Sadness spread through her chest in a hot, heavy wave. She would never see him age. She would never find another man who called so strongly to the different sides of her soul. She would never fall in love.

Unless she had already.

But what if she had? What use was denying it, or crying over it? The world was full of people who'd lived through broken hearts. She would, too. She was Julia Mueller, the terror of DMI. She wouldn't let love make a coward of her. With a wistful smile, she bent forward to lick the corded tendons of his neck. His cock lurched under her belly. His hands tightened on her waist.

'Shh,' she said, and his grip loosened. She bent to suckle his tiny, sharp nipples. His fingers spread over her bottom.

'Julia,' he said, stroking her curves. 'That feels so good.'

She kissed his nipples until his back arched with pleasure. Then she coaxed him on to his belly. He relaxed into the full-body rubdown as ecstatically as his horse. She smiled to herself, half expecting to see his ears flop down. Maybe he'd had the right idea about how to tame a lover. She licked the salty crease between his buttocks and legs, then spread his cheeks. Lubrication was as close as the warm, weeping slit of her sex. When she pressed her slippery fingers to his tightly pinched anus, his head came around on the pillow, alert but not alarmed. Despite all he knew of her, he trusted her. Her gratification was immense. This man, neither slave nor submissive, trusted her. Excitement gushed from the heart of her sex. Tonight she'd take him all the way.

'I'm going to go further this time,' she said. 'Tell me if anything hurts. Because it shouldn't. It should only feel good.'

To her relief, he relaxed instinctively. Her two longest fingers slid easily into the flickering passage. As she progressed, he hummed like a man considering a new wine. The hum deepened abruptly when she found the small, hard swell of his prostate. She stroked gently, relishing his twists and squirms, the expressions of pleasure that twitched the muscles of his face. Then she pressed.

'Ah,' he said, jerking. 'Do that again.'

She did it again, and again, and bent to knead his buttocks with her other hand. She bit their muscled curves: lover's bites, a tender mingling of pain and pleasure. He thrust at her, fucking himself on her fingers. The mattress creaked. The sheets rustled. A fevered glow washed over her at the sight of the sweat that bathed his muscled back. Her juices trickled down her inner thighs. Unable to bear the wait, she rubbed herself against the bulge of his calf. She licked the skin next to her working fingers. He moaned, low and anguished in his throat. He didn't come, though. For long, panting minutes he took what would have sent most men over the edge twice over. His tension wound tighter. His moans grew louder.

'Enough,' he gasped. 'It's too good. I can't take any more.'

She pulled free and wiped her hand. He turned over between her legs. The skin of his cock bore sheet marks from being pressed so tightly to the bed. She saw veins she'd never noticed before, bulging blue and thick around the shaft. Sweat matted the hair at the base. She combed it outward with her fingers, then ran her hands up his chest.

'Fuck me,' he said, his blue eyes burning, his ribs moving quickly in and out. 'Fuck me hard.'

'Soft,' she said, with a teasing smile. 'Soft and slow.'

He moaned when she positioned him for entry, parting her lips with the hot red silk of his glans. They sighed together as she sank on to him. It was good to be filled, good to have something to work that deep, wet ache against.

'Julia,' he crooned.

'Zach,' she responded, a laugh in it.

She kissed him and he clasped her face. Their mouths tangled, and their desires. His cock pulsed inside her. He pushed deeper. They broke free from the kiss to drag air into their lungs.

'Now,' he said, smiling, flushed. 'Please.'

She pushed back on her arms and began to rock, as slowly as she'd threatened. He did not oppose her. He followed her pace and force, and nothing in him seemed to resent it. He held her gaze with his and every so often he'd grin and say her name, as if pleasure were bubbling up inside him and that was the only way to release it. Julia slowed her breathing. Without being told, he matched that, too, until their ribs expanded in unison. An eerie energy sprung up between them, flowing between and around their bodies. It felt like water, or a light breeze. She'd experienced something like it that night in his room, but this was even stronger. The current had a slow rhythmic beat. Julia knew it must be her heart and yet it seemed as if it were the mountain's heart, as if the earth beneath them had joined their play. She had never felt so close to another human being. She wanted to ask Zach if he felt it, too, but she was afraid to hear he did. What did it mean? Her throat hurt. Her pussy tightened. When she came, she came alone.

Zach nursed the spasms with his thumbs. 'That was real nice,' he said, once she'd settled. 'I felt that down to my toes.'

Julia shook off her melancholy and grinned. 'I'll show you nice.'

She eased off his rigid cock and took it in her mouth.

'Oh, God,' he said, hips arching. 'Julia.'

She sucked him deep, well aware that she was fulfilling his seventeen-year-old definition of heaven. His penis was smooth and hot and tasted of her and him. With her tongue she learnt its swells and folds, its sweet spots, its ticklish patches. He was every bit as responsive as she'd hoped and, for the first time since she'd met him, she sensed him trying to hold back orgasm, rather than strive for it. He didn't want to go over. He wanted to savour this.

She slowed her rise and fall; gentled her suction. He sighed with heartfelt gratitude and spread her hair across his groin, petting it in a rhythm she was wise enough to follow.

'Julia,' he murmured. 'Darlin'. Sweet. Heart.'

She held his hips to steady him, to quiet his compulsive thrusts. His hands fisted in her hair. He groaned. She rose to his glans, swirled her tongue around the flare, then plucked the rosy plum with a soft, smacking kiss. She released him and watched his flesh shudder. The slit at the tip of his cock fluttered, pushing out a thick drop of pre-ejaculate.

'I'm going to finish you now,' she whispered, the words a breeze across that lust-tautened skin. 'I want you to breathe deeply and bear down.'

With her palm she gathered his scrotum, plump now and high with arousal. The tips of her fingers rubbed his perineum. Its ridge shifted as he bore down internally. She swallowed his shaft. His body tightened: thighs, arms, belly. For a moment he forgot to breathe and then she heard him remember, first with a short, hitching breath and then a deep one. She rubbed and squeezed and sucked to the pattern of his inhalation. A groan rattled in his chest. He clutched her head. He thrust. Then he let go. His shaft stiffening, he pulsed hard against the verge of her throat. Every throb was sweet, every gasp.

She released him with reluctance and kissed him goodbye.

After that, she lacked the will to move. He bent over her and pulled her up the length of his body. Before she realised what he intended, he'd positioned her leg over his hip and worked his softening penis into her sex. He curled his hands over her buttocks and snugged her safely close. The feel of his soft, wet length was strangely comforting. She tightened her calf behind his thighs.

'Now this,' he said, 'is heaven.'

Julia's head fell to his shoulder as if it had been meant to fit there. It was over. She'd expected to fight tears, but she was drained of emotion. She told herself she had nothing to regret. She'd done what she'd meant to do. She'd proven that when her heart was engaged, the softest lovemaking could be as rewarding as the hardest. Now all she had to do was find a man who called to her as Zach did, a man who set no numerical limit on his relations.

Bitterness escaped by way of a muffled snort. That shouldn't take more than a lifetime.

Zach stroked her hair, the motion languid. 'What's wrong?'

She kissed his jaw. 'Nothing.'

'Would that be an "I don't want to tell you" nothing or a "please keep asking until I do"?'

Julia couldn't think of a single snappy answer. She hugged him tighter.

Zach yawned. 'If you give me half an hour, I might get a second wind.'

'Mm,' said Julia, then realised what he'd said. She pushed back from his chest. Zach grabbed her waist before she could de-couple them. 'What about your limit?' she demanded.

'My what?'

'Your seven-fuck limit, the one you set to keep the women round these parts from dragging you to the altar.'

He blushed to the arch of his hairline. 'Oh, that limit. Shit. Who told you about that?'

'The kindly waitress at the Coffee Stop.'

He scratched the back of his head. 'I didn't mean for you to know. Anyway, I wasn't keeping count.'

'Well, I was and that was seven.'

He rolled her beneath him before she could escape, his weight pinning her to the mattress. His cock hardened with a swiftness that shocked her. Apparently, anger was an aphrodisiac for him. 'I don't want to count with you. I want to keep going.'

But Julia wasn't putting herself through this again. She'd prepared herself for seven fucks. She'd made her peace with it. She pushed his shoulders. He didn't budge. 'Come on, Zach. What if I'm like those other women? What if I decide I want to marry you?'

His jaw ticked with anger. His cock stretched. He shoved it deeper. 'I guess I'd thank my lucky stars.'

That shut her up. At least for a moment. 'No.' She shook her head. 'You don't mean that.'

His expression softened, though it didn't grow any less stubborn. 'I know this isn't the way to tell a woman you want her to stick around, but the airport's open and I don't exactly have time to be romantic.'

'You want me to stick around,' she said, deciding she must have misheard him before. 'Stick around' made sense. 'Marry me' was crazy.

Zach stroked the side of her face and took a deep breath. 'I've been thinking I could use someone like you to manage my properties while I get my horse-training business started. I need someone who can stand up to those smarmy Californians who want to turn this state into a theme park for rich people. It strikes me you know a lot about finance, and you did say you and your boss are parting ways.'

She narrowed her eyes. 'Let me get this straight. You want me to work for you.'

'Not just that.' He pinched his moustache and let the words out in a rush. 'Shoot, Julia. I fell in love with you pretty much the first time I heard your voice. I know it's crazy, but I can't help that. Nothing I've

247

learnt about you since has made me feel any differently. If anything, I'm twice as hooked as I was before. I never met a woman who turned me inside out the way you do. I feel as if I never knew myself. I want things I never knew I could want. Not necessarily to get down on my knees and kiss your boots, but I guess –' his brow furrowed '– I guess if you really wanted that I'd give it a try.'

'I don't want that,' she said. ' Not from you.' She touched his cheek, needing to reassure herself she wasn't dreaming. Hearing him echo her own thoughts, that she made him feel as if he never knew himself, brought a threat of tears. She blinked them back and asked the one question that couldn't wait. 'You fell in love with me?'

He shifted on his elbows. 'I couldn't help it. Look, I know you don't love me, but it seems to me there's a chance you might some day. We get on pretty good when we put our minds to it. I'm not the sort of man to hobble a creature he loves and shut it in a box. I'd give you plenty of running room. All I ask is a chance for us to get to know each other, to build something that will last.'

'Oh!' she said, the word a cry just short of tears. It was a pathetic sound: a girlish sound. Julia didn't give a damn. She pressed her hands together in front of her trembling lips, then flung her arms around his back and hugged him with all her might.

Zach grunted, half-startled, half-pleased. His cock gave a funny leap inside her, as if it were wriggling with happiness. His mind caught up a second later. 'Does this mean you don't mind my being in love with you?'

'No,' she said, finally spilling over. 'I don't mind at all.'

* * *

248

She tried to break the news to Marty early the next morning, while Zach did his chores. Marty had chores of his own, however. She found the senior VP occupied with Carolyn's continuing education. While Carolyn was obviously annoyed by the interruption, she seemed to have put her misery behind her. Julia smiled to herself and shut the door on their bare-bottomed tableau. She'd talk to Marty later.

Ben turned up at the kitchen table, hunched over his first cup of coffee. He sighed when she told him she'd be staying on with Zach. 'Well, he is an improvement over Durbin.'

'It's not a reflection on you.'

He rubbed his handsome, sleepy face. 'Of course it is. But so what? I should have known I couldn't handle you.'

She squeezed his hand and felt a wisp of the old attraction. He was a lovely man. Nonetheless, she was more relieved than sorry to be parting.

'You'll be happy,' he said. 'He's a good man. And it will be easier to serve you up as the sacrificial lamb knowing someone is taking care of you here.'

'I've asked Marty to look out for you if you get into trouble with Durbin.'

Ben rolled his eyes. 'God help me if I need Marty's help.'

'Don't make a face. When it comes down to it, Marty is stronger than Durbin. Not more powerful, not yet, but more reliable. You won't go wrong if you stick with him.'

Ben leant across the table and kissed her on the lips. 'I'll remember,' he said, 'and thank you for worrying.'

Marty caught up to her as she typed their last notes into one of Zach's computers. Durbin might or might not end up reading this report, but if he did he'd find no fault with his three portfolio managers' work.

Marty pulled a second chair next to hers. His curls were wet from a recent shower. 'Did you hear the snow plough go by?'

She nodded. He sighed.

'Ben tells me you're staying with Zach. Please tell me you're not giving up being a dominatrix. You can't. You're Michael-fucking-Angelo. A real artist. And what if I need more training? Mastering Carolyn won't be easy.'

Julia pinched his doleful cheek. 'Mastering Carolyn might be impossible. In fact, if both of you are going to be happy, you might have to learn to switch hit.'

'All the more reason to continue my training.' He bent over his knees and clasped his hands together. 'Can't I come and visit now and then? Get a refresher course?'

The idea intrigued her, but she wasn't sure how Zach would respond. How odd that was: taking someone else's moral preference into account. But it wasn't altogether unpleasant. If their positions were reversed, she'd want Zach to consider hers. 'Maybe,' she said. 'And in the meantime, you can certainly call for advice.'

'You'll miss New York,' he predicted.

Julia shrugged. 'Zach has an adventurous streak. He might enjoy the occasional trip to Sodom and Gomorrah.'

Marty surrendered with a grin. He hugged her. 'Be happy, Mueller.'

'I suspect I will,' she said.

Later, but not much, she stood alone on the back veranda. The portfolio managers were packing. Zach was shovelling the driveway. Perhaps she would go and help soon, but it was good to have a moment to herself, to let her decision sink in. Patches of blue had appeared between the clouds. Water dripped from the icicles with a cheery plinkety-plink, melting as surely as her heart. The Ice Queen was dead. Long live Julia Mueller.

She stared through the curtain of drops at the next mountain over, and the next and the next, until the range faded into an iron-grey mist. The breeze was warm; a chinook, Zach called it. He'd promised to take her out Going-to-the-Sun Road once the thaw was sure. He wanted to show her Glacier National Park. 'The best Montana,' he'd said, button-bursting proud. 'The dazzling Montana.' She'd been dazzled from the start, but she supposed her heart could take it. 'And skiing,' he said. 'You'll love Big Mountain.' He was so pleased to discover she liked to ski, she might have given him the Nobel Prize. Her cowboy certainly was cute. She hugged the corner post and grinned, even though their plans scared her witless.

They'd made a deal, a one-year agreement to cohabit and work together. After the year, they'd reassess. 'Not that I'll need to,' Zach said with a confidence she could barely comprehend. His sureness made her fear for him. She didn't want to hurt him, and she couldn't guarantee she wouldn't.

That's life, she reminded herself. That's what it means to live by your heart. Despite which, her grin didn't fade. This love business was pristine territory for her, a new adventure, perhaps her biggest adventure yet.

She leant back from the post and swung like a truant schoolgirl. Maybe she would miss her whips; and maybe she and Zach would find a way to play that pleased them both. He certainly hadn't ruled it out and, with or without whips, there would be games. When men and women came together, there always were. One of the things she liked best about being a dominatrix was bringing those games into the open.

Still ... She watched a hawk ride an up-draught towards a stony outcropping. It wasn't uninteresting to let the struggle for power slip underground; to play the game without props or calculation. Nor was it uninteresting to explore the precarious edge where top and bottom met, where no one was in charge. Zach offered her the opportunity to walk both these roads. Maybe someday she would tire of them but, at the moment, she couldn't imagine when.

Zach watched her from the kitchen. She was swinging on the rail in her sloppy sweatshirt and leggings. She seemed achingly young, even innocent in her joy. He was looking forward to coaxing her into a pair of well-worn jeans, maybe with one of his old flannel shirts to top it off. You might as well brand her, he teased himself, but his pride in even partial possession was irrepressible. How had this gorgeous blonde Amazonian princess ended up in love with him? She hadn't said it yet, but he knew she was, same as he knew Starlight loved him. It was in the eyes; in the way she leant into his touch and sighed his name. She loved him and some day, by God, she'd tell him so.

He grinned. Grandma must have put a good word in with the angels. Stubborn as Julia was, he couldn't believe he'd convinced her to stay a year. He'd have been grateful for another week, not that he'd tell her that.

Her head turned as soon as the screen door creaked open before him. He handed her the steaming mug of coffee that was his excuse for interrupting her reverie. She took a sip, hummed at the real cream and sugar, then handed it back to share. They leant shoulder to shoulder over the railing. Zach thought he'd never been so happy.

'Second thoughts?' he said for the pleasure of hearing her deny it.

She didn't disappoint him. 'No. I think I've never been so happy.'

His grin threatened to crack his face. Grandma and Grandpa used to share words that way. God willing, he and Julia would be together as long as they had. 'Did you tell the others you'll be staying on?'

Julia slanted a look of amusement from under her brows. 'Yes. Ben was relieved. He thinks you're going to save me from my wicked ways. Marty says *mazel tov*, and Carolyn was too busy moaning "harder, Marty, harder" to say much of anything.'

'Ah,' Zach said, surprised by this last bit of news. But who was he to say it wouldn't work out? Cats and dogs had been known to do more than fight. Then it occurred to him that 'harder' might not mean what he'd assumed. He'd heard some odd sounds as he'd been walking through the house earlier. 'Julia, was he spanking her?'

She bumped his shoulder and winked. 'Can't pull any wool over your eyes.'

Obviously, some people could. He turned sideways to face her. 'Was that what you were doing when you disappeared the other day: playing dom for them?'

Her eyes twinkled, but her gaze was sharp. 'Shocked?'

'No,' he said slowly, and he wasn't. Interest heated his groin, the blood pooling and pulsing so strongly each beat drummed fire through his cock and balls.

Julia eyed his crotch, marking his erection's speedy rise. Her beautiful lips curled in a smile. She reached out and cupped him from beneath. Her fingers rippled over his sac, sending a spine-tingling wave of sensation through his groin. He had to swallow a moan.

'Want me to tell you about it?' she offered, Scheherazade's timeless lure.

'Maybe later,' he said, and pushed himself into her hand.

Epilogue

Julia stood naked before the bedroom window, her hair spilling cool and long down her back. She gazed into the darkness towards the barn where three new mares and a two-year-old colt had joined Starlight and Buck. A heady bouquet of smells wafted around her: alpine flowers, spring grass, hay, horses and, best of all, the soapy-musky scent that her lover left tangled among the sheets.

Seven months had passed since they'd formulated their agreement. Overseeing Zach's business interests didn't take much time once she established a routine. Consequently, she'd been helping him with his little herd. Zach was teaching her to work the new horses on the lunge line. The going was slow; she'd had to learn a whole new language of control. Amazingly, Gracie the cow-dog was her biggest help. She'd nip those horses' heels if she thought they weren't showing 'her' Julia enough respect. Bit by bit, though, she and the horses were developing a rapport.

She loved every minute of the work, even the hard

minutes, and she had calluses to prove it. Zach teased her about acting like a teenage girl, more horse-crazy than boy-crazy. He claimed she'd rather spend the night in the stable than with him.

That, at least, wasn't true.

She looked back at the king-sized bed they shared, admiring the sturdy pine frame Zach had built and finished himself. Julia hadn't wanted him to change his granny's old rooms, so they'd knocked together four of the former guest rooms to make one large bedroom that was all their own. She'd never seen a man work so hard, or so enjoyed soothing his aches and pains. Sometimes she hardly recognised the woman she'd become.

Except this morning, in honour of her birthday, he'd given her a pair of handcuffs. 'For your use or mine,' he'd said. 'Whichever you prefer. Whenever you're ready.'

His gift lay now on the bolster of the turned-down bed, gleaming in the light of a dozen beeswax candles. She'd already decided she'd let him lock her up.

Smiling, she swept one hand down the slope of her breast until her palm covered the softly erected peak. There she let it rest, feeling the hardness increase. The prospect of turning herself over to him inspired a tremulous pulse of excitement, one coloured neither by fear nor regret. Time and again he had proven himself worthy of her trust. She was far more hesitant about exerting mastery over him.

She had a feeling, however, that Zach was going to put an end to her hesitance soon. He'd been goading her lately, wrestling with her until she couldn't resist wrestling back, or assuming subtly submissive postures during lovemaking. He knew his behaviour aroused her, and she knew he wouldn't let her abandon half her nature.

Or half his own, she thought with a delicious shiver.

As if on cue, his reflection appeared in the window pane, tall and smiling, wrapped in a rumpled flannel bathrobe. How her cowboy made such homely apparel seem sexy she'd never know.

She turned and beamed at him.

'I have a surprise for you,' he said, his grin creasing his face. He undid the tie and dropped the robe.

Julia covered her mouth with her hands. He wore his old fringed rodeo chaps . . . and not a stitch more. He pirouetted slowly, like a runway model, showing off the wide, floppy leather. She supposed the chaps were designed to protect his inner thighs, because they didn't cover much else. His hard, muscular butt was bare, and most of his outer legs, and all of his family jewels. His cock thrust thick and high towards the belt that secured the chaps at his waist. The crown looked terribly pert, as if it were sniffing around for something good. The laugh she'd been holding back bubbled free.

'Oh,' she gasped, both arms wrapped over her belly. 'Oh, I'm sorry. It's just –' She dissolved again. 'It's just that outfit doesn't hide any good parts, does it?'

Zach crossed to her and hugged her close. He chuckled into her hair. 'I thought this would get you.'

She tilted her head to look at him. 'You wanted me to laugh?'

'Well,' he said, his drawl as comical as his get-up. 'At first I wanted to you to laugh. Then I reckoned you'd realise how handy this outfit is and we'd get down to business. These chaps are leather, you know.'

Julia sighed and wiped her eyes. 'I've had men make fools of themselves for me, but never just to hear me laugh.'

257

'Your laugh is my favourite music,' he said.

Her eyes filled again, and not with laughter.

'I love you,' she said.

'I know,' he said, his moustache twitching with mischief.

They smiled at each other, supremely pleased with themselves, their lives precisely as they desired.

BLACK LACE NEW BOOKS

Published in September

DEVIL'S FIRE
Melissa MacNeal
£5.99

Destitute but beautiful Mary visits handsome but lecherous mortician
Hyde Fortune, in the hope he can help her out of her impoverished
predicament. It isn't long before they're consummating their lust for
each other and involving Fortune's exotic housekeeper and his young
assistant Sebastian. When Mary gets a live-in position at the local
abbey, she becomes an active participant in the curious erotic rites
practised by the not-so-very pious monks. This marvellously entertaining story is set in 19th century America.

ISBN 0 352 33527 0

THE NAKED FLAME
Crystalle Valentino
£5.99

Venetia Halliday's a go-getting girl who is determined her Camden
Town restaurant is going to win the prestigious Blue Ribbon award.
Her new chef is the cheeky over-confident East End wide boy Mickey
Quinn, who knows just what it takes to break down her cool exterior.
He's hot, he's horny, and he's got his eyes on the prize – in her bed
and her restaurant. Will Venetia pull herself together, or will her 'bit
of rough' ride roughshod over everything?

ISBN 0 352 33528 9

CRASH COURSE
Juliet Hastings
£5.99

Kate is a successful management consultant. When she's asked to run a training course at an exclusive hotel at short notice, she thinks the stress will be too much. But three of the participants are young, attractive, powerful men, and Kate cannot resist the temptation to get to know them sexually as well as professionally. Her problem is that one of the women on the course is feeling left out. Jealousy and passion simmer beneath the surface as Kate tries to get the best performance out of all her clients. *Crash Course* is a Black Lace special reprint.

ISBN 0 352 33018 X

Published in October

LURED BY LUST
Tania Picarda
£5.99

Clara Fox works at an exclusive art gallery. One day she gets an email from someone calling himself Mr X, and very soon she's exploring the dark side of her sexuality with this enigmatic stranger. The attraction of bondage, fetish clothes and SM is becoming stronger with each communication, and Clara is encouraged to act out adventurous sex games. But can she juggle her secret involvement with Mr X along with her other, increasingly intense, relationships?

ISBN 0 352 33533 5

ON THE EDGE
Laura Hamilton
£5.99

Julie Gibson lands a job as a crime reporter for a newspaper. The English seaside town to which she's been assigned has seen better days, but she finds plenty of action hanging out with the macho cops at the local police station. She starts dating a detective inspector, but cannot resist the rough charms of biker Johnny Drew when she's asked to investigate the murder of his friend. Trying to juggle hot sex action with two very different but dominant men means things get wild and dangerous.

ISBN 0 352 33534 3

To be published in November

LEARNING TO LOVE IT
Alison Tyler
£5.99

Art historian Lissa and doctor Colin meet at the Frankfurt Book Fair, where they are both promoting their latest books. At the fair, and then through Europe, the two lovers embark on an exploration of their sexual fantasies, playing dirty games of bondage and dressing up. Lissa loves humiliation, and Colin is just the man to provide her with the pleasure she craves. Unbeknown to Lissa, their meeting was not accidental, but planned ahead by a mysterious patron of the erotic arts.

ISBN 0 352 33535 1

THE HOTTEST PLACE
Tabitha Flyte
£5.99

Abigail is having a great time relaxing on a hot and steamy tropical island in Thailand. She tries to stay faithful to her boyfriend back in England, but it isn't easy when a variety of attractive, fun-loving young people want to get into her pants. When Abby's boyfriend, Roger, finds out what's going on, he's on the first plane over there, determined to dish out some punishment.

And that's when the fun really starts hotting up.

ISBN 0 352 33536 X

If you would like a complete list of plot summaries of Black Lace titles, or would like to receive information on other publications available, please send a stamped addressed envelope to:

Black Lace, Thames Wharf Studios,
Rainville Road, London W6 9HA

BLACK LACE BOOKLIST

Information is correct at time of printing. To check availability go to www.blacklace-books.co.uk

All books are priced £5.99 unless another price is given.

Black Lace books with a contemporary setting

THE NAME OF AN ANGEL £6.99	Laura Thornton ISBN 0 352 33205 0	☐
FEMININE WILES £7.99	Karina Moore ISBN 0 352 33235 2	☐
DARK OBSESSION £7.99	Fredrica Alleyn ISBN 0 352 33281 6	☐
THE TOP OF HER GAME	Emma Holly ISBN 0 352 33337 5	☐
LIKE MOTHER, LIKE DAUGHTER	Georgina Brown ISBN 0 352 33422 3	☐
THE TIES THAT BIND	Tesni Morgan ISBN 0 352 33438 X	☐
VELVET GLOVE	Emma Holly ISBN 0 352 33448 7	☐
DOCTOR'S ORDERS	Deanna Ashford ISBN 0 352 33453 3	☐
SHAMELESS	Stella Black ISBN 0 352 33485 1	☐
TONGUE IN CHEEK	Tabitha Flyte ISBN 0 352 33484 3	☐
FIRE AND ICE	Laura Hamilton ISBN 0 352 33486 X	☐
SAUCE FOR THE GOOSE	Mary Rose Maxwell ISBN 0 352 33492 4	☐
HARD CORPS	Claire Thompson ISBN 0 352 33491 6	☐
INTENSE BLUE	Lyn Wood ISBN 0 352 33496 7	☐
THE NAKED TRUTH	Natasha Rostova ISBN 0 352 33497 5	☐
A SPORTING CHANCE	Susie Raymond ISBN 0 352 33501 7	☐

---------✂--------------------------

Please send me the books I have ticked above.

Name   ....

Address   ....

....

....

.... Post Code ....

Send to: **Cash Sales, Black Lace Books, Thames Wharf Studios, Rainville Road, London W6 9HA.**

US customers: for prices and details of how to order books for delivery by mail, call 1-800-805-1083.

Please enclose a cheque or postal order, made payable to **Virgin Publishing Ltd**, to the value of the books you have ordered plus postage and packing costs as follows:

UK and BFPO – £1.00 for the first book, 50p for each subsequent book.

Overseas (including Republic of Ireland) – £2.00 for the first book, £1.00 for each subsequent book.

If you would prefer to pay by VISA, ACCESS/MASTER-CARD, DINERS CLUB, AMEX or SWITCH, please write your card number and expiry date here:

....

Please allow up to 28 days for delivery.

Signature   ....

---------✂--------------------------